Karma may be a bitch, but sometimes she knows what she's doing.

When author Lexi Marshall's perfectly fabulous life of designer clothes, nights on the town with her sexy boyfriend, and a successful writing career literally go up in flames, she must take on Karma and fight to gain control over her life.

Lexi believes her cliché-filled novels are the reason for Karma's wrath and after a high calorie pity party, she's determined to rebuild her life to what it once was...that is, until her gynecologist utters a phrase she never expected or wanted to hear: she's pregnant. Unfortunately, the father is her fresh out-of-the-closet best friend and not the new man in her life..

I0665192

A Bitch Named Karma

By Stephanie Haefner

KENSINGTON BOOKS
Kensington Publishing Corp.
www.kensingtonbooks.com

LYRICAL PRESS
An imprint of Kensington Publishing Corp.

Lyrical Press books are published by
Kensington Publishing Corp. 119 West 40th Street New York, NY 10018

All Kensington titles, imprints, and distributed lines are available at special quantity discounts for bulk purchases for sales promotion, premiums, fund- raising, and educational or institutional use.

Special book excerpts or customized printings can also be created to fit specific needs. For details, write or phone the office of the Kensington Special Sales Manager: Kensington Publishing Corp., 119 West 40th Street, New York, NY 10018. Attn. Special Sales Department. Phone: 1-800-221-2647.

First Electronic Edition: June 2010
eISBN-13: 978-1-61650-233-1
eISBN-10: 1-61650-233-9

First Print Edition: June 2010
ISBN-13: 978-1-61650-725-1
ISBN-10: 1-61650-725-X

Printed in the United States of America

Chapter 1

"Finito!" I screamed, not caring if the entire building heard me.

I'd just typed The End on my latest manuscript and that meant another Lexi Marshall masterpiece was ready for the printers. Val would be ecstatic. As friend, confidante and editor extraordinaire, her job title usually included "nag" as well. But for once, I was two weeks ahead of my deadline.

Dressed in satin pajamas, I sprawled across my purple velvet duvet, marabou-covered slippers on my feet. My chocolaty rich curls were twisted on top of my head, held in place by a jewel-adorned clip. I stretched my arms above my head and pointed my toes, feeling a tingle throughout my body. The deep stretch loosened everything. Man, that felt great!

My laptop lay in front of me, glowing with accomplishment. She was my faithful friend who stuck by me through writer's block and bad metaphors. Even when I'd threatened to pick her up and throw her across the room, she never gave me even a moment of spiteful malfunction. This was just as much her success as it was mine.

I clicked Save and copied the file to disc. This first installment, Marisol Takes Manhattan, was the beginning of a three book series. Book two would follow my heroine as she searched for Mr. Right. Of course it wouldn't be easy. I'd throw all kinds of bumps in her road. And the final book, the piece de resistance, would be my first ever wedding-themed novel, a journey down the aisle complete with bridesmaids from hell and one wedding disaster after another. I'd been waiting forever for a three-book deal!

I closed the computer and hopped off the bed, pressing Play on my favorite 80's CD. I did a happy dance around the room, belting out the lyrics at the top of my lungs. Not only was I delirious with joy, but the feeling of accomplishment put me in a horny mood. My boyfriend, Zak, and I had spent most of the previous month buried in our own workloads, rarely having the energy for a quick missionary, let alone any fun kinky stuff.

Finishing this book gave me a sense of uninhibited freedom and a delicious thought crossed my mind. I could dress in my black hooker boots—as Zak affectionately named them—and trench coat, absolutely nothing underneath. A little nookie in his office would be quite a surprising way to spend the afternoon. It sounded completely insane but also quite fun. I just had to do it.

The sexy office tryst had to wait a bit, though. I shimmied into a black lace thong, classy pinstriped pants and said hooker boots, then finished the rest of my primping. Cha Cha, my Chihuahua, scurried after me as I headed toward the door. I gave her a little kiss on the nose before dashing out.

I found Val hidden behind a pile of manuscripts. She took one look at me and sighed.

"Please don't tell me you need some coddling today. I'm drowning in alien love stories and super-spy dramas. And if I have to read one more teen vampire knock-off, I might just roll up the pages and fashion them into a noose!"

"Val, I know you thrive on drama, but isn't this a little much?"

"If you had to read through as many of these as I did, you wouldn't think so."

"Well, I have great news! Marisol Takes Manhattan is finished."

"You're kidding. Please don't joke with me, not today." A pencil sat behind each ear and in her hand, another half-chewed one.

"No joke. Here she is."

I handed her the disc, her eyes suddenly widening.

"I'll leave you to your, uh, noose," I said with a smile then turned to leave.

"Did I tell you I love you?"

"Not today!"

I headed to Accounting to pick up my latest royalty check. After being handed a perfectly plain number ten envelope—something I had become quite infatuated with over the years—I carefully placed it in my purse. As much as I wanted to tear it open and kiss its beautiful figures, I had other needs to attend to.

Inside the bathroom at Smith & Roland Publishing, I shed my pinstripe pants and silk cami. After stuffing them into my silver metallic Fendi bag, I wrapped my sleek black trench around me tightly. Every button had been slipped through its corresponding hole while the belt sat in a secure knot at my waist. My lips were painted with a shade of M.A.C. lipstick appropriately named Eager. The twenty-dollar pout screamed "kiss me now." My body emanated Zak's favorite perfume, its sweet yet sensual mix of aniseed, violets, vanilla and musk. The day we'd bought it, a tester bottle in a Martinique gift shop led to hours of love-making in a tropical paradise.

I walked the five blocks to Zak's office, the satin lining of my coat rubbing on my thighs. Riding the elevator to the tenth floor among businessmen in suits and secretaries in conservative blouses and skirts, I felt quite naughty. If they only knew what lay under my simple black coat—barely a square foot of transparent fabric covering only my most intimate body parts.

Thoughts of what I could do when I walked into Zak's office swirled through my brain and brought a goofy smirk to my face. Just thinking of my finished manuscript made me a little wet. If I thought of all the Kama Sutra positions we could do in his desk chair, I'd be dripping by the time I actually made it to his office.

Zak's secretary Ruth sat manning her post outside his office picking at an over micro-waved lasagna in a cardboard tray. Her graying hair and decades-old wardrobe made her a prime candidate for a makeover show, one where the victim is ambushed at work, their friends and family waiting in the wings.

After wiping a spot of sauce from the corner of her mouth, Ruth buzzed Zak on the intercom and alerted him of my presence.

"Well, um, go ahead and send her in," he said over the speakerphone. Even with a McDonald's drive-through quality, the sound of his voice had added to my arousal.

"Tough day, baby?" I asked in my most seductive manner as I strutted into his office.

"Oh, yeah...crazy," he said without looking up, his fingers fast at work on the computer's keyboard. I watched them peck at the keys with precision, yearning for them to be on me instead. Looking back to his face, I saw a bead of sweat roll down his forehead and noticed his tie was loosened too.

"Ooh, it's hot in here, isn't it?" I untied my belt and unbuttoned my coat, then inched it down my shoulders and onto the floor, a seductive move I'd learned during a strip-tease class. Zak looked up from the computer as I leaned on the desk, cleavage pouring from my tiny transparent bra. His bottom jaw fell to the keyboard.

I felt something scratchy under my hand and looked down to find an emery board.

"What's this for?" I asked, stepping out of my starring roll in this office porno flick.

"Uh, nothing. I guess Ruth left it there when she came in earlier."

Not really caring about the answer, I flung the nail file aside and got back into character. I walked around Zak's desk and straddled myself around my man, grinding on his already hard protrusion. Just the sight of my half naked body excited him and I loved that. My hands yanked the tie from his neck and began opening his shirt. I pressed my lips to his, forcing them apart as I pushed my tongue deep inside. He tasted like cinnamon Binaca, his breath refresher of choice.

"We can't do this! What if someone walks in?" he asked in a semi-panicked tone.

"Zaky, you know no one comes in here without Ruth buzzing you first. Come on, let Georgie Boy come out and play!" I unhooked my bra.

Zak's eyes fixated on my erect cotton candy colored nipples—he was always a breast man.

My lips traced a path to his ear and whispered my most favorite dirty line, "Georgie Porgie, put it in my pie!"

* * * *

Once I'd gotten what I wanted from Zak, I kissed him one last time and told him I'd see him at home. His labored breathing continued even as I walked out the door.

The sun shone over the city on a beautiful Indian summer day and the warmth penetrated my dark long-sleeve coat. I wished I could take it off and soak in some Vitamin D but as adventurous as I was, I wouldn't dare walk down the street in lingerie.

My mind replayed the fantastic orgasm I'd experienced, bringing a goofy smirk to my face and a flutter throughout my body. It reminded me of the euphoria I'd felt after finishing my manuscript a couple hours earlier. And the royalty check that had been shoved to the bottom of my Fendi bag when I topped it with my discarded pants and shirt. It stood next in line for my love and devotion and maybe even a hot kiss or two. I caressed its body first, then like a giddy kid in a candy store, ripped open the envelope. Staring back at me was a check for a quarter of the amount I normally received.

A glitch in the system most likely. There had to be a zero or something missing. I got on my cell and called Val, but was sent directly to her voicemail.

"Val, babe. I just opened my check and there must have been a problem in Accounting. I think someone needs to be fired!" I said in my silly diva tone. "But anyway, call me after you straighten it out and I can stop by for the rest of my money. Ciao!"

* * * *

After a shower and wardrobe change I made my way to my favorite shoe boutique, regardless of the figures on my check. A computer glitch didn't scare me one bit. I wouldn't let it keep me from a well-deserved treat.

Tristan greeted me as I walked in, and air-kissed both my cheeks.

"Daaahling! Where on earth have you been?"

"Oh, busy with the latest masterpiece. You know how that goes!"

"Can't wait to read it!" He grinned at me. "Have a seat and I'll be right with you. Some new little peaches just arrived and I know you'll love them!"

Tristan returned a few minutes later with eight boxes of shoes, each one in my dainty size six and a half. Each pair he unveiled became my favorite. Making the decision on which to adopt would be excruciating. Each adorable twosome stared up at me with puppy dog eyes and pleaded, "Pick me! Choose me! Love me!"

Buying a pair of shoes is much more than strapping some pieces of leather to your feet and taking home the first ones that fit right. It is a commitment, a long lasting relationship—usually longer than most boyfriends. These shoes had to be sturdy, dependable and able to support me through anything. They'd show me off and make me look spectacular. These amazing little ego boosts did so much more than protect my feet from the rigid Earth.

I narrowed my decision down to red kitten heel slides and a pair of cheetah print stilettos with an open toe. Decisions, decisions! After mulling it over and modeling them for Tristan one last time, I still couldn't make up my mind.

"You know, there's only one solution to this problem," he said to me with twinkling eyes. "Take them both!"

"I like the way you think!"

Pleased with my purchases, I turned to leave the boutique, spying something cute near the door.

"Oh my God, those aren't..." I turned back to Tristan.

"Yes, they are!"

Examining the minuscule hot pink doggie boots, I knew Cha Cha's wardrobe couldn't be complete without them. Leaving the shop with a couple treasures for myself and also something for my baby, I promised Tristan I'd visit again soon. I sent Zak a naughty text message, describing the newest additions to my shoe fetish collection and which sexual positions I'd be modeling them for him in.

Chapter 2

When the clock struck five on a Friday afternoon, it signaled the end of the hectic workweek and start of weekend bliss. I walked to Cosmos, where each week I met Marcus, Brenda and Rachel, for happy hour, and I swore I heard the entire city breathe a sigh of relief.

Outside the bar, a strange woman stood nearby wearing a long patchwork dress fusing together hideous mismatched fabrics, one appearing to be burlap or something else equally coarse. Her long reddish-orange hair flowed past her behind and she ranted about something. I ignored her screeches as I walked by until her pale hand shoved a photocopied paper in front of my face.

"Change your destiny!" she screamed. "Karma will destroy your life if you don't change your ways!"

"Yeah, okay lady." I pushed the Karma Kronicle back at her.

"You'll be sorry…" I faintly heard as I continued on.

Whatever. I had much more important things to deal with than loonies on the street.

I entered Cosmos a little after five and Marcus waved me over to a table. Smiling at him, I snaked through the crowd.

"Hi!" I kissed his cheek and waved to our usual waitress, who winked and told me she'd be over in a second.

"Late, as usual?" I asked, referring to the two empty seats at our table reserved for Brenda and Rachel.

"Would it be normal if they were actually on time?"

I'd met Brenda a few years back when in desperate need of a dye job. In order to save a few bucks, I came up with the brilliant idea to do it myself at home. Wet hair, apply dye, let sit—it couldn't be that hard. I couldn't have been more wrong and somehow managed to turn half my head a bright crimson and the other half black. After tucking my disaster into a hat, I'd bolted to the nearest salon.

A rare cancellation put me in Brenda's chair that day. Her look scared me a bit but I'd figured my situation couldn't get any worse. As she'd surveyed the damage known as my hair, I wondered how someone covered head to toe in Goth could possibly know how to dye a normal person's hair. But even with her spiky hair-do in a bright blue shade—her chosen hue of the month—and patent leather bustier, she was my salvation and I felt indebted to her for the rest of my life. She became the only stylist allowed near my locks, including myself! We'd been the closest of friends ever since. There is a special bond between a woman and her hairdresser; in some ways it's more serious than a marriage.

Rachel and I met through Brenda. They'd been friends since their training bra days and couldn't be more opposite. Rachel embodied the sweet girl-next-door persona, with never a mean word to say about anyone. Her glistening all natural blond locks were set off by ocean blue eyes. She looked like a GAP or Abercrombie and Fitch model, but prettier. Brenda and I begged her for at least a year, though she would never even consider pursuing a career where people ogled her. Always filled with modesty, Rachel wore the simplest clothes to hide her perfect body and kept her hair plain and long. So many times Brenda wanted to drag her to the salon and strap her down, forcing her to get some foil highlights and a hip cut. But even with their numerous differences, they always remained close. I had my theory why. Rachel kept Brenda in line and sane.

Then there was Marcus. Our moms became best gal pals during their pregnancies, bonding over pickle cravings and stretch mark artwork. Marcus and I became attached at the hip while still in utero. We share quite a long and somewhat twisted history that started with shared naps in either my crib or his while our moms played cards and drank iced tea. It continued though playground fights and puberty and the four years of teenage drama known as High School. Marcus and I played doctor as kids and he gave me my first French kiss when we were pre-teens. We tried the boyfriend-girlfriend thing once at the beginning of high school. A gorgeous guy even at the awkward age of fourteen, he had dark dreamy eyes and a Beverly Hills 90210 hair cut. I reveled in being the envy of a majority of the female freshman population but everything changed when he tried to round second base with me. I envisioned my brother groping my 32AA's and it grossed me out. We called it quits but our friendship continued and I knew I could count on him for anything, anytime.

Marcus, Brenda, Rachel and I were often found working out together, doing lunch or having all-night margarita gab fests. They were great inspiration for my books, many of which stemmed from topics discussed during our drunken nights together. I always traveled with a notebook so I could jot down anything remotely interesting. The tough part was deciphering the intoxicated scribbles the next morning.

The girls finally arrived and completed our happy little foursome. We immediately flagged down the waitress and started our Friday celebration.

"So Brenda," I said after we received our drinks. Brenda and I had ordered the specialty of the house, a bright pink cosmopolitan. Marcus held a glass of merlot by the stem and breathed in its aroma while the ever conservative Rachel sipped a glass of diet cola through a straw. "I found a guy for you!"

"Lex, don't even think about setting me up!"

"Why? This one is perfect! He even has green hair!"

"Ewww!" Rachel squealed. "Green hair?"

"Wait, you're fine with Brenda having pink hair," Marcus chimed in, motioning toward Brenda's head. "But a guy with green hair is disgusting?"

"I never said I was fine with it!" Rachel giggled, pushing her own shimmering blond tresses from her face.

"So anyway, back to Slade!" I continued.

"Slade? That's the guy's name?" Brenda asked.

"Yes. I like it. It's unique. Who wants a Bob or a Dan? Snore! You need someone with a strong, sexy name. Slade is a tattoo artist, photographer and newly published author. His book is being released in a few weeks. It's called Tat- A Gallery of American Tattoo Art. You'll love it. I met him at my publisher's office and I think you two would be perfect for each other. As soon as I saw him, I just knew. I got his number and we should call him and invite him for drinks."

"No, thanks."

"Why? You haven't gone out with anyone in months!"

Rachel began hacking and grabbed for a napkin, covering her mouth. She cleared her throat as we all stared at her.

"Um, went down the wrong tube."

I shook off her inability to drink like a normal person and looked back at Brenda.

"So, I'm gonna call and invite Slade for Happy Hour next Friday."

"I'm not looking right now," she said and suddenly became engrossed with her cocktail napkin, folding it into some kind of origami creature. Brenda's nails, which were always done in some funky color with airbrushed designs, were a simple black with silver glittered tips. She'd recently began learning nail design and practiced on herself constantly.

"Come on! You have to meet him. At the very least, you'd get a couple good fucks out of him!"

"Lex, for the last time, no."

"Okay, fine. Keep having fun with your vibrator. Wear out a million batteries for all I care!"

* * * *

Val had set up an interview for me with one of the hottest radio morning show tag teams: Wild Will and Tina of WBLV's Rock Your Way to Work Show. She'd been trying to get me on-air with one of the Top 40 stations for some time, hoping to boost sales in a few new markets. I yawned as I walked into the station, still half asleep. Mornings were so not my thing.

The broadcast took place in a small room, much smaller than I had imagined in my glamorous Radio Day Dream. I'd envisioned walls plastered with autographed posters of the hottest singers of the day with gleaming microphones and the occasional star walking through the door to say a quick "whud up" to their disc jockey homies. What I walked into reminded me of the hall closet in my apartment—tiny and jammed with miscellaneous books, papers and a desk chair with ripped and faded upholstery.

They sat me down and gave me a pair of ancient looking headphones to wear that pinched at my ear and smooshed down my curls. I watched Wild Will make an announcement on air, his smooth voice rolling off his tongue. He winked at me and smiled as he told his listeners he and Tina would be talking with me after the break. The station went to commercial and a balding man in headphones gave me some last minute instructions.

"Good morning, rockers," Wild Will crooned after the commercial. "If you're just tuning in, we're here with multi-published author Lexi Marshall. She's written several chick lit books that are selling like boxes of condoms before prom night. So, Lexi," he said and turned to me with a sexy grin. "What exactly is chick lit?"

"Well, I define chick lit as a story about a woman, facing many of the obstacles the everyday woman faces. Career problems, family problems and of course problems with love. The women in my stories are confident and smart and embody female empowerment. Sometimes they are knocked down, but it's only temporary. They pick themselves up, dust off and rise above their problems, coming out new women in the end. They're inspiring stories, giving women the courage to stand up to the wrong doings in their lives."

"And of course, look fabulous while doing it!" Tina chimed in.

I laughed. "Yes, that too! Many of my characters are trendy and hip, wearing designer clothing and shoes."

"Yep, just like those cute Jimmy Choos I saw on your feet as you strolled in," Tina added.

"Hey, you can't write it if you don't live it!" I said, spouting off my life motto.

"Now Lexi, what do you think of these critics who call chick lit 'fluff'? They say it's not serious writing," Will commented.

"My answer to that is not appropriate for the airwaves!"

"O...kay!" Will then continued with the interview, taking a few calls.

* * * *

"Are you seriously making me go to dinner tonight with your friends?" Zak whined. "I can't stand being around Marcus. And those women are just plain annoying."

I watched him flip through a rack of button-down shirts, then flop onto the bed in only his boxer briefs. Zak's body rivaled even the buffest Greek god. His pecs were chiseled like a statue's and he had an eight pack. A freakin' eight pack! The two hours he spent at the gym each morning were certainly worth it.

He let out an irritated moan.

"Oh, stop! Marcus is my best friend. And what do you have against Brenda and Rachel?"

"Uh, let's see. One wears black lipstick, black nail polish and has black hair with red stripes."

"That was so two days ago. It's all pink now."

"Regardless. Her piercings disgust me. And the other one has a voice that makes nails on a chalkboard sound like a symphony."

"Come on, they're not that bad! I love those girls and Marcus. They've been my friends forever."

"I don't have to like them or sit with them and try to keep my dinner down."

"You have to come tonight. We're celebrating the radio interview."

I crawled on top of him wearing only a pair of red panties, and kissed a trail down his chest, stopping at the elastic of his briefs.

"Zak, come on. This is important to me. I want all my favorite people together for one night."

He stared down at me as I popped Mr. George out and began caressing him with my tongue, kissing his head in preparation of devouring him completely.

"Fine, I'll go." He pushed me off of him and sat up on the edge of the bed. "You'll owe me big time for this. And it's only dinner, right? No hanging around for dessert or drinks afterward."

"Oh, come on! You know how horny chocolate and martinis make me!" I pressed my body to him again, this time my tongue making circles on the back of his neck.

He stood and I almost fell on the ground. He walked to the closet, thumbing through his shirts again. "No distractions. I want to get there as soon as possible, so we can get it over with and leave."

"Fine, but you don't need to be an ass about it!"

Zak could be a real jerk sometimes, though I guiltily admit it turned me on.

"I want to be home and in bed early anyway. I have a meeting with Val tomorrow morning and at ten I have a massage appointment."

I walked over to my closet. The door opened and my clothes looked ready to burst out at me. One pull of the wrong hanger could lead to an eruption of silk and cashmere that would bury me alive. My mind began to wander, thinking I should call the interior designer Marcus used for his apartment. For my own safety, I needed a complete re-organization of my closet space.

"What are you doing tomorrow? A massage?" Zak asked as I flipped through my wardrobe. "What kind?"

"Should I wear this or this?" I asked holding up two entirely different wrap dresses.

"They look the same to me. Just pick one. What about this massage now?"

I continued flipping through my closet. "Oh, it's one of those hot rock massages. They're supposed to be completely relaxing. And I think my back's a little out of whack, so I could really use it. Remember that yoga class I told you about? That evil Naziwoman instructor who had us contorted all funny? I don't think the human body is meant to bend quite that way. It wasn't even a good sex pose!" I pulled out a royal blue tank dress with a plunging neckline. Loved the way it made my boobs look. "But anyway, I might have a facial and manicure while I'm there too."

"Sounds nice."

* * * *

Zak seemed to do a one-eighty, laughing at my stories and even making a few jokes of his own. He made conversation with Marcus, a rarity. The two had never really gotten along. I'd read about men being jealous of their girlfriends' male friends and even as cocky as Zak was, he surely felt envious of my friendship with Marcus.

After savoring our favorite dishes between bursts of laughter, Marcus raised his glass.

"To Lexi—may your success continue to flourish!"

"Hear, hear!"

As we drank, the waitress began clearing our plates. She brought the dessert menu and I looked to Zak. He seemed in no hurry to leave and nodded his approval. I ordered the triple chocolate mousse cake and a Godiva martini.

Four martinis later I crawled into bed, exhausted and glad Zak didn't ask for an ass massage, his not-so-subtle way of trying to get laid. I drifted off to sleep dreaming of my meeting with Val.

She gushed about my manuscript and the fabulousness of each and every word. I saw myself sitting in her office, reaching and grabbing the hearts as they flew out of her mouth like a silly video game. Each heart I touched made a Ding! and my points skyrocketed.

Still in my dream world, I left her office and proceeded to my favorite boutique, spying a hot ruby-colored frock sure to look fantastic on me. I saw the only size four in the hands of a wide-hipped woman with greasy black hair.

"That won't fit you," I said matter-of-factly and snatched the dress, flashing my stellar smile.

I slipped into the first dressing room I came to and admired my reflection. The clingy charmeuse fabric made my curves look even curvier and my skin seem brighter, not that I needed it much anyway. My hair looked shinier and even my breasts appeared plumper, like I'd already had the boob job I planned as a Christmas present to myself.

I turned and appreciated the reflection some more, marveling at the sleekness of my legs.

"Oh, I have to have this dress!" I stated aloud and began removing it from my body. As I shimmied it down, I heard the loud, unmistakable sound of ripping fabric. I jumped the rest of the way out of the dress and held it up. The entire left side gaped open and threads dangled from the jagged frayed fabric.

A wave of sadness rushed over me as I put the torn dress back on its padded hanger. I then caught my reflection in the mirror, smirking at me, still wearing the dress completely intact. It let out an ear piercing cackle, very Wicked Witch of the West.

I immediately looked down at my body, clothed in panties and a bra. The dress hung to my right from a hook on the dressing room wall. My first instinct told me to scream and run, but the draw of my reflection kept me silent and my bare feet planted.

"I look fabulous, don't I?" she said to me, flipping my, er, her chocolate hair. "Too bad you ripped the only one!"

"Who are you?" I whispered.

"Isn't it funny how things happen in life? You do something bad and something bad happens to you."

"Why are you here?"

"I'm always here with you. Every day. I watch you, I see everything."

"O…kay…"

"Ever hear of a little thing called karma?" she asked.

"Yeah, I guess. It's some stupid hippie voodoo thing, right?"

"It's not some thing. You should take it seriously."

"I don't believe in that crap."

"Oh, you will." She smiled at me and cackled again. The laughter faded as her body disappeared, leaving my reflection staring back at me in my pink satin and black lace lingerie.

My eyes jolted open. My dream, or more correctly, nightmare, had left me in a cold sweat. I pushed the covers from my body to cool it off. But then felt a bizarre feeling in the pit of my stomach—like someone was watching me. I yanked the covers back up to my chin, then over my head.

Chapter 3

Marcus and I met for breakfast the next morning before he headed to work and I headed to Val's office. He carried the plates with bagels and lox and I had both beverages. Maneuvering through the crowded café, a businessman in a suit two sizes too small bumped my hand with his laptop case. My caramel macchiato crashed to the floor and splattered on my shoes.

"Watch it, asshole!"

All I received in return was a dirty look. An employee appeared and cleaned the spill and my shoes and fetched me another drink.

"What do you think about karma?" I asked Marcus once I'd sat down at the table.

"I don't know. Never gave it much thought, I guess."

"I had a bizarre dream about it last night. Do you think it exists?"

"Could, I guess."

"Like my macchiato. Last week I bumped someone and she spilled coffee on her shirt. Do you think the scene this morning could be karma?"

"Like the universe is out to get you for a simple accident? I don't think so."

"Yeah, you're right. It's stupid. Forget I said it."

* * * *

Later that morning, the elevator door opened to the offices of Smith & Roland, people sprinting around, every one with armloads of papers and boxes. The place normally resembled the theater a few blocks down that only showed nature documentaries—quiet and boring with most of the audience half asleep. Something was definitely up.

Val's office looked like a battle had just taken place. I stepped around cardboard boxes as she popped up from behind her desk.

"What's going on?" I asked.

"Oh, Lexi. Everything is a mess! I don't even know how to tell you this. You better sit down." Her gravity-defying hair looked a bit more frizzed out than normal. "I'm not gonna be your editor anymore."

"That's ridiculous."

She sighed and sat in her chair. "It's true."

"I don't believe it."

"Here, look." Val brought up the email sent to her the afternoon before, from Mr. Smith's secretary no less. A short and simple "Please clear out your office within twenty-four hours and report to Human Resources for your new job assignment."

After reading the single line of text that so swiftly changed Val's career, I wanted to scream and cry and throw myself on the ground in a toddler-esque tantrum yelling, "No! No! No!"

"Your last royalty check—it wasn't a mistake," she said and looked to me with glossy eyes. "Your book sales have dropped. So have some of my other authors. They say it's all my fault."

She stood and began placing some things in a box as she told me about her replacement—an outsider. This supposed miracle-worker of an editor had been lured away from another publishing house. Mr. Smith and Mr. Roland needed to make some major changes for the good of the company and hoped the big bucks they threw at this new woman would save it.

"She's here already," Val said, stifling her tears. "You're meeting with her today in her temporary office. As soon as I'm cleared out, she'll be moving in here."

My relationship with Val far surpassed the editor-author marriage. We were also friends. She'd established my career and walked me through my first publishing experience. She'd given me my first big break and now she was my rock. How the hell would I do any of this without her?

As she reached to pull one of her photos off the wall, she broke down crying. I did the only thing I could think of.

"These assholes can't fuck you over like this! This is unacceptable! If they don't give you your job back, I'll walk!"

"Lexi, no. They mean business. For the sake of your career, you need to stay put."

Our eyes met. She was serious. I'd trusted Val on every aspect of my career in the past, no questions asked, and had no reason to doubt her advice now.

"Fine. I'll meet with her. But if I don't like her, she can go to hell. They all can."

I walked down the hall confident as my Manolo Blahniks click-clacked on the marble, ready to raise some hell. A handwritten sign had been plastered to the door: Sheila Brown— Editor. The scent of a black Sharpie wafted into my nostrils as I pounded on the door. I heard a screechy "Come in" and found a middle-aged woman sitting behind the desk.

She flipped through a manuscript and didn't look up when I strode through the door.

"Sit, Ms. Marshall."

"I didn't tell you who I am." I wanted to show off my tough side.

"I already know," she said and finally looked up at me. A fluorescent shade of pink lipstick decorated her lips, doing nothing to improve her ghastly pale skin and salt-and-pepper bob. "I've read all your books, including the latest."

"Oh, I see."

She was well prepared for only being on the job one day.

"Marisol Takes Manhattan, your newest and first in a series." She paused to push her glasses up on her nose, and I awaited her praise. "It absolutely sucks."

Feeling like a vacuum had sucked all the air out of my lungs, I struggled for oxygen. Everything around me went gray and the words "absolutely sucks" echoed in my brain over and over. I'd slaved over this book for the better part of six months, making every sentence perfect.

A shrill laugh blared into my ears. It sounded familiar. I couldn't place it, but knew it didn't come from Sheila. She sat emotionless.

"What do you mean? Are you sure you read the whole thing?"

"Yes, every boring, plotless, cliché-filled word."

The room started to spin and a tingle radiated throughout my legs. Fearful that I might black out, I moved a box of office supplies from a chair and sat down. I breathed slowly and deeply, staring at her, wondering if I'd heard her right. How could she possibly say that? I was Lexi Marshall—a multi-published author. Women adored my books. They devoured them. This malicious statement insulted every fiber of my being.

My temperature began to rise as bewilderment changed to anger. Ms. Editor handed me my disc, then ripped some sheets from a legal pad and shoved those at me, too. They were filled top to bottom with chicken scratch.

"I made notes for you. Revise and have it back to me in two weeks."

Finally finding the confidence and attitude I'd possessed before entering her office, I asked, "And what if I refuse?"

"Then you can try and sell your garbage to another publisher."

* * * *

I left the office, stomping down the street with my jaw clenched tight like a pit bull's. I expected the pressure to crumble my teeth, but instead it gave me a massive atom-bomb-like headache.

How could this happen? Women everywhere loved my books. This Sheila had no friggin' clue. Who the hell was she to tell me how to write my novel? An archaic, styleless shrew couldn't possibly know what today's fashion forward woman wanted to read.

I seethed and walked on, remembering my massage appointment. The thought of hot rocks being rubbed on my skin sounded excruciatingly painful. I just wanted to go home and drown myself in a bottle of my favorite cabernet. The fact that it was only ten o'clock in the morning meant zero to me.

I keyed into my apartment and Cha Cha ran up to me, jumping around, her tiny painted nails scratching at my leg. A hyper dog was the last thing I needed to deal with. Pushing her away, I grabbed the wine from the kitchen and walked toward the bedroom. My body yearned for the high-powered jets of the whirlpool tub.

As I approached the door, high and low pitched moans sounded from behind it like a porno flick on full volume. Were Betty and Floyd screwing again? My eighty-year-old neighbor's bedroom butted up against mine. It wouldn't be the first time I'd heard them getting it on mid-day, but they'd never been this loud before. I walked into my bedroom and found Brenda spread eagle on top of my velvet duvet wearing my black hooker boots. Zak's hairless, perfectly tanned ass pumped up and down and neither of them even noticed me there. I threw the bottle of wine on the floor, shattering it on the hardwood.

"Oh my God, Lexi!" Brenda exclaimed, covering up her pierced nipples with a purple beaded bolster pillow. My boyfriend lay naked between her thighs and her first thought was to cover her flabby tits?

Zak jumped off the bed. "It's not what it looks like."

"Oh, so you weren't fucking Brenda just now? I didn't hear her screaming your name?"

He stood there, a bright pink condom still standing erect. He looked to the floor and I took this simple action as an admission of guilt.

"How could you?" I managed to ask, looking from Zak to Brenda. "And in my boots!"

I turned and ran from the apartment, flew down three flights of stairs to the street and kept on running. I didn't know where to go, but I had to get away.

As my feet pounded on the pavement, I heard the laughing again, this time even louder. Could everyone on the street hear it, or just me?

Surely I looked like a crazy woman as I ran down the sidewalk dodging in and around pedestrians, nearly taking a header into a produce stand. I slowed down after that—last thing I needed was a concussion. Couples walked past, holding hands, cuddling. Yeah, they looked all mushy and lovey-dovey on the outside but I bet those women didn't know. The guys were probably screwing their girlfriends' friends on the side, too. I scowled at a passing male and when I wasn't paying attention, the heel of my favorite pair of Manolos caught in a sidewalk vent and snapped off.

"Can this day get any worse?" I asked the gods, an invitation for more disaster. As the words came out of my mouth the sky darkened and a feeling of doom enveloped me. A truck zoomed by, splashing my cream cashmere coat with the dirtiest, grime-filled muck water imaginable.

Hobbling down the street with black water dripping from my hem, I thought about this catastrophic morning. It had started so well—complete perfection. Over the course of an hour, it had all been royally screwed up. I hailed a cab to Maxine's, the restaurant where Rachel waitressed. Her cheeriness, although sometimes annoying, helped in times like these.

Rachel sat me at a private booth, immediately knowing from my miserable expression and bedraggled attire that something was very wrong.

"I walked in on Zak and Brenda fucking on my bed," I spit out.

"Oh no," she responded and turned her glance to the window, suddenly entranced with the ass crack of a construction worker.

"Wait, you knew about this, didn't you?"

"Lexi, I'm sorry. I was stuck in the middle. I've been telling her for months to stop!"

"Months! This has been going on for months? Oh my God! I can't believe this." I got up and limped toward the door.

"Wait. Let's talk!"

"No. I don't need a back stabber. There's nothing to talk about."

Tears welled in my eyes but I would not allow the wait staff at Maxine's to see me cry like a weak baby. I waved down another cab and when the driver asked if I was okay, I gave him the evilest look I could muster.

"I'm fine! Just drive!"

With the meter running, he drove in circles, waiting for me to give him a destination. But I didn't know where to go. As the meter closed in on fifty dollars, I gave him the address for Marcus's office.

"Lex, what the hell happened? You look awful!"

"Thanks," I tried to say sarcastically, but it came out with heaps of tears. Marcus hugged me and smoothed my wind-blown hair. We sat on the couch in his office and in between bursts of sobs and swigs from the flask he kept in his bottom desk drawer, I told him my depressing tale. He cancelled his appointments for the day and insisted on lunch at my favorite place.

Under no circumstance could I go anywhere looking the way I did.

"Well, I suppose this means a visit to the spa and a new outfit. My treat. What do ya say?"

He always knew exactly how to cheer me up. While Marcus made one last phone call, my cell rang in my purse. The boring bell tone rang as opposed to one of the cute songs I'd specifically picked for each member of my directory. The plain old ring meant my caller's identity was a surprise.

"Ms. Marshall?" the deep voice asked. "This is Lieutenant Eckerson with the fire department. There's been a fire at your apartment."

Marcus and I rushed out of his office. The cab moved at a glacial pace, tires crawling on the asphalt rather than rolling. Visions of my wardrobe and shoes in flames flashed across my eyes. I could even hear my beloveds screaming in sheer agony.

Upon entering the building, we immediately smelled the smoke and dampness. The higher we climbed the stairs, the worse the smell became. The Lieutenant stood in the blackened hallway when we reached my floor.

"What happened?" Peering into my home, I could barely make out any of my possessions. Anything that wasn't burnt to an unidentifiable lump was a water-logged mess.

"It appears some candles were burning in the bedroom. Did you know this when you left the apartment?"

"No, my boyfriend must have been burning them while he was fucking his whore this morning."

He stared at me, eyes wide in a dazed sort of state. Like so many others, he didn't know what to do with my bluntness. Then over his shoulder I saw a vision of a woman sitting on the charred remains of my kitchen counter. Her ruby red lips formed a devilish grin and she held a lit match between her manicured fingertips. She seductively blew it out, then disappeared, but I had recognized her. This ghostly form was the reflection from my dream the night before. And it was her laugh I'd heard earlier.

A crazy concept burst into my mind. These visions weren't just hallucinations; they meant something. Had the universe sent this woman to carry out my karma? Was she Karma?

I didn't get it. I'd never burned anyone's house down or stolen anyone's job. And I'd certainly never had sex with my friend's boyfriend—well, not technically. One time I fooled around with a friend's guy, but the penis and vagina did not meet. I repeat, penis and vagina did not meet! That ten-minute grope session in the darkened back corner of The Purple Pineapple, a now defunct college party bar, happened ages ago and it didn't count anyway. He told me he was breaking up with her. In his mind they were already over.

"Oh, um, well," the fire chief continued, and I snapped back to my disaster of a reality. "Here is an accident report for your renter's insurance." He handed me some paperwork.

"Renter's insurance?"

"Oh, Lex, don't tell me." Marcus explained what it meant to not have the insurance.

I slumped to the soot-covered floor in the hall, wondering what could possibly be next. The day still held plenty of light.

"Oh my God! Cha Cha!" I screamed and bawled my eyes out.

Chapter 4

Marcus took me in his arms and let me cry and snot on his thousand dollar suit. After arriving at his apartment and changing into the most comfortable pair of pajamas he owned, I plopped onto his bed. He brought me a half dozen pillows and a mug of cocoa spiked with Baileys. My angel in Armani.

Marcus joined me in bed and we spent the day watching old movies and eating Chinese take-out. We also popped a couple bottles of wine.

"How could I be so blind?" I asked. "How could I not know he was getting some ass on the side?'

"I don't know. Sometimes we're oblivious to the obvious. I thought maybe he was cheating on you, but Brenda? That shocked me. Never would have guessed the piercings and tattoos would be a turn-on for him."

"Don't even get me started on that bitch. It kills me because she never even liked the dickwad—her word, not mine."

I finished off my sixth or maybe eighth glass and felt the room spin just a little bit, like the slow final rotation on the Tilt-a-Whirl after the power had been cut. My judgment was clouded, I knew that, but Marcus looked pretty damn sexy lying next to me.

After more than three full decades of friendship, Marcus knew everything about me, all my faults, all my idiosyncrasies, and he loved me anyway. He sat up in the bed, propped with expensive feather pillows. I snuggled into him, rubbing my hand over his defined pec muscles. The flicker of the black and white movie on the TV in front of us illuminated his face and without even knowing why, I kissed him. My tongue slid past his lips, making it much more than one of our friendly pecks.

Of course he pulled away. "Lex, what the hell are you doing?"

"Marcus, I want you," I replied and climbed on top of him.

"Come on, we're just friends."

"You know it's more than that."

I kissed him again, feeling far less hesitation this time. For a few blissful seconds, his arms wrapped around my body and I reveled in his delicious nibbles.

But then he gently pushed me off of him and stared me dead in the eyes.

"Listen to me. You are a mess. You're vulnerable and you don't know what you're saying. You'll hate yourself afterward."

"No, I won't. Please Marcus, make love to me. I need you. You can't tell me you don't want me too. I know you'd be lying."

He lay there speechless and I knew there'd be no more fighting. I took my shirt off and crawled back to him. He pushed the hair away from my face and kissed me the way I knew he'd dreamt of for so long.

* * * *

When I woke the next morning, Marcus had already gone to work. I couldn't stay there, in his bed, wearing only his pajama top. Embarrassment filled me as I recalled the evening—throwing myself at him, preying on his feelings for me. He'd always wanted our relationship to step past its platonic level. I was the one who'd decided it best to stay just friends. But now we'd had sex, a simple act of desperation for me—to him it probably meant the world.

I had to get out of there and for obvious reasons, my apartment was out. The friend list was rather short. Non-existent, actually. Only pure hopelessness could lead my brain to even consider this last option. As much as I hated it, spending some time at my parents' house was inevitable.

Dressed in my dirty clothes, the ones I'd worn the day my life fell apart, I climbed into a cab. After a forty-five minute ride, I keyed into my childhood home and knew I'd hit the bottom. At least my next move would be up. It had to be, right?

The house seemed empty, with the exception of the TV blaring in my brother's room. Not much had changed. I lived less than an hour away, but rarely made a visit. My mother's sickening June Cleaver impersonation made me want to hurl.

Every knick-knack sat in its correct place and every lace doily lay perfectly where it belonged. It smelled like Pine Sol, the same scent she's used since the dawn of my existence.

I heard Andy's obnoxious snort of a laugh over the noise of the TV. My twin, a complete loser, still lived at home and still worked at the same pizza joint he'd worked at in high school. How did we come from the same womb? We shared amniotic fluid, for God's sake!

I brewed myself some strong coffee and flipped on the tube. Mom's Victorian-style floral couch lent little in the way of comfort, but I curled myself up on it anyway. As I caught up with the ladies on The View, my eyelids slowly closed. I pushed them open only to repeat the same sequence three more times before giving in completely to my exhaustion.

"Alexandra, honey," I heard first, then Oprah's voice lecturing her viewers on the dangers of fad diets.

"Sweetie, wake up," the mousy voice spoke again and I felt my arm being gently shaken.

I peeked one eye open, then the other.

My mother's beaming face stared at me, her perfect white teeth matching the pearls around her neck. "What are you doing here, dear?"

"I need to stay a few days, okay?"

"Of course! Is everything all right?"

"I don't want to get into it."

"Okay. You know you can stay as long as you like. Your room is always ready for you."

Most parents, upon gaining an extra space in their home, convert it to an exercise room or sewing room. Not my mother. When I left fourteen years ago, she kept the room for me, but returned it to its feminine glory of pink walls and floral print bedding—the décor of the days before I had a say.

At exactly six on the dot, we gathered at mom's formal dining table for a traditional Marshall Family meal: meatloaf and mashed potatoes. Mom and Dad exchanged small talk as we ate. I knew the topic of conversation would turn to me eventually.

"So, dear, where is Zachary? It's been ages since we've seen him. How is he? I thought of him just the other day. I came across the cutest birthday card at the supermarket. It had a cartoon on the front of it with a golfer and I know how much Zachary likes to play golf. I couldn't remember the exact date of his birthday, but I planned on calling to ask you." Clueless to the fact that I'd tuned her out, she could babble on and on about the most mundane things. "So, has there been any talk of a wedding for the two of you?" she asked next.

I stared at her as she awaited my answer, her eyebrows raised in anticipation. I knew what she hoped and prayed for. In my mother's eyes, I was an old maid.

"No, Mom. He's been having an affair with Brenda behind my back for months."

"No! He wouldn't do that! He's such a nice boy. Are you sure?"

"Yes, Mom. I walked into my apartment and saw his penis inside her."

My use of the "p" word at the dinner table flabbergasted her. She never could handle my bluntness. "Oh, well, um..." She stood and cleared away some dishes from the table.

"Do you need to be so graphic with your mother?" Dad asked once Mom had entered the safety of her kitchen oasis.

"Hey, I could have told her I walked in and saw him fucking her brains out. I thought my original statement had significantly more tact."

He just shook his head.

Andy, as usual, laughed his ass off as he shoveled more food into his mouth.

* * * *

For the next few days, I threw myself the biggest pity party ever. I borrowed some of Mom's perfectly matching sweat suits and basically sat my ass on the couch and didn't move, drowning my sorrows in high-calorie, high-fat, high-carb foods. Dr. Pepper and Chester Cheetah soon became my best friends.

I watched old re-runs of Jerry Springer and new episodes of Judge Judy, flipped on some soap operas to see if anyone's life came even close to the grand level of patheticness of mine. Some came close, but not quite.

My cellphone rang only once, though I refused to answer it. Rachel left me a voice mail begging me to call her so she could apologize. I didn't feel like hearing it. I prayed to hear The Rembrandts I'll Be There for You ring tone, the special song for Marcus. Not only did the words fit us, but we'd made a date every Thursday night from 1994 though 2004 to watch the ins and outs of our favorite "friends" on TV.

I wanted to talk with Marcus, but sheer terror prevented me from calling him myself. He'd been right about the night we were together. I was vulnerable, but even worse, I wanted to get back at Zak and I'm sure he knew that, too. My insides churned when I thought of what I'd done. If only he'd forget it ever happened. I longed for our together-forever-always-be-there-for-you friendship but deep down, I feared a permanent annihilation.

Mom walked in the door with armloads of groceries. "Alexandra! Guess what?" she said enthusiastically.

"What is all the excitement?" I asked gaily, but she didn't pick up on my sarcasm.

"I was at the market, trying to pick out some oranges, when Pastor John came up to me. He said 'Hello Maryanne, orange you glad to see me?' Isn't he so witty? I invited him over for supper tonight so you can meet him."

My dull, "Hooray" didn't phase her one bit.

"He's been our pastor for six months now and we haven't had him over yet. He's only thirty-four you know, never been married. Such a shame. It's so hard to believe this nice man is having a hard time finding a woman to spend his life with. He told me he loves to play tennis. Remember when you played tennis in high school?"

"Mom, you can't be serious. Are you really trying to set me up with your pastor?"

"Oh, no! I simply thought he'd enjoy a meal with our family." Her animated face glittered like a tinsel-covered Christmas tree. I knew my mother. At that moment, images of Pastor John and me walking down the aisle were flashing in front of her eyes. I could even hear the wedding bells chiming in her brain.

An hour later, I forced myself out of the indent I'd made in the couch to freshen up for dinner. I looked in the mirror, noticing a chocolate smudge on the hot pink sweatshirt I wore and decided on a wardrobe change. Mom lent me one of her button-down sweaters and a pair of slacks. God help me, I was wearing slacks. The waist came up so high I could almost tuck my boobs into it and the pleats and tapered legs did nothing to show off my figure.

Pastor John arrived right on time, bearing a bottle of sparkling grape juice. He rattled off another corny fruit joke as Mom showed him into the dining room. She giggled like a schoolgirl and I searched for an inconspicuous place to throw up if need be.

Mom introduced Pastor John to me and his eyes popped out of their sockets as they casually glanced at my boobs. Isn't it against the rules of heaven or the pastorhood for him to look at my chest? He shook my hand leaving it covered in sweat.

We sat for dinner and Pastor John and Mom kept their conversation going. He tried to come up with as many witty food jokes as he could and Mom ate up each and every one.

"Alexandra, honey, isn't he just a hoot?"

I murmured an "Ummm hmmm" while my inner monologue answered with, "Yep, what a prize. I can see why there's a line of ladies waiting to get in his pants."

Dinner finished and we took seats in the living room with glasses of the grape juice. While Mom sat engrossed with Pastor John's story of church drama and Dad pretended to listen, I opened the liquor cabinet and doctored my drink with a shot or two of vodka. Or maybe it was three. It's hard to guesstimate when trying to keep one's alcohol abuse on the down-low.

I sipped my concoction and Mom brought up every topic she could think of that remotely interested me, trying to get the Pastor and I to talk. After some two-minute stretches of conversation about tennis, Mexican food and the color aubergine, he announced the need for a good night's sleep. The awkward evening finally ended with Mom telling Pastor John we'd see him Sunday at church, including me. I hadn't stepped foot in that church since my rebellion against organized religion in the early nineties. No way was I going now, not with my mother playing matchmaker with Mr. Holy himself.

* * * *

I knew my self-pitying funk had come to an end when the feel of cotton fleece on my skin felt like a million ants crawling all over my body. Mom lent me her Volvo for an emergency shopping spree. I couldn't afford a whole new wardrobe on 5th Avenue, so Target would have to do. The store's bright red bull's-eye logo scared me, but once inside, I took comfort in its quaintness and found quite a few decent things. Some of the clothing lines actually came from real designers and the fabrics consisted of only minimal amounts of polyester.

I strolled past the lingerie department, spying cute bra and panty sets and grabbed one. But before tossing it my cart, I realized it was a pointless purchase. I didn't have anyone to sex it up for anymore. Granny panties and Cross Your Heart bras were the only lingerie items in my future.

As relieving as it was to wear something other than coordinating sweatshirts and pants, shopping wasn't the same without Marcus to tell me if something looked good on me or not. I missed him so much. We'd never gone this long without talking. I decided to suck it up and call him, or at least call his cellphone when I knew it would be off and leave a voice mail.

After cashing out, I took a seat at the mini Starbucks near the exit of Target. Who knew you could get a damn good Chai Tea Latte at the same place where they sold jumper cables, Barbie dolls and toothpaste?

I dialed Marcus's number. It went straight to voicemail, just like I knew it would.

"Hi, Marcus, it's Lexi. I, um, miss you. Please call me."

A huge weight had been lifted as I took the first step toward getting some of my life back. Once I secured one piece of normalcy, everything else would fall back into place.

I felt good—the best I had in a week—and decided to treat myself to a cut and color touch-up that I desperately needed. Only one huge problem with that plan: my loyalty to Brenda for the past six years left me terrified to trust my locks to anyone else. Trying a new stylist was far more nerve-wracking than sleeping with a guy for the first time. With the guy, I expected it to be awkward, messy and uncoordinated, and more times than not, I was left far from satisfied. But there was an easy fix for that, a glass of wine and my favorite vibrator. If I got a bad haircut, it ruined my week, maybe even my month. At this point in my life, the last thing I needed was hair drama.

I drove around town searching for the trendiest looking salon, all about judging the book by its cover. That was my life. A stunning cover was crucial.

I settled on Le Salon Magnifique. French equals class. How could I go wrong?

The place radiated elegance and sophistication. Clients lounged in chrome chairs while stylists in sleek black robes wove their hair magic. Soft music played, accented by the trickle of a water fountain, giving the place a very Zen-like ambience.

I walked up to the counter. "Give me the works!"

A pedicure, manicure and facial later, I sat regally on my throne. The stylist walked over and I gave her my instructions.

She regally drew a pair of gleaming scissors from her station and dove into her work like an artist. I closed my eyes and let her hands work their magic. Just like those silly shampoo commercials, I lost myself in the orgasmic feeling that descended over me, promising myself I would not moan out in ecstasy.

My dye job came next and once the foils were in place, I sat at the dryer flipping through the latest Cosmo for half an hour. The stylist unwrapped my head and began blow drying my damp locks. The color looked a little off and the more she dried it, the brighter it became. My beautiful chestnut hair now resembled the sickening shade of the traffic cones on the street outside. Horrified, my stomach turn upside down and I suppressed the urge to vomit. I stood and stepped closer to the mirror. Maybe if I blinked real hard, when I opened my eyes it would be back to normal.

Nope, I still looked like Carrot Top.

"What the hell did you do to me?" I demanded.

"Uh, I don't know."

"What do you mean you don't know? It's completely fucked up!"

"Maybe there was something wrong with the dye," she answered smugly and snapped her bubble gum.

My anger morphed into intense sadness and I used every last ounce of energy to hold in my tears. While further inspecting my fiery locks, I spotted her reflection in the mirror. Behind me was that Karma Bitch. She lay sprawled across the counter, head back, laughing so hard she couldn't breathe. In her hand she held a tube of bright orange hair dye.

"Unbelievable!" I said, ripping off my smock, tears long gone, and stormed out.

I drove home and found a Mercedes parked in the driveway. I stomped into the house with my fire-colored hair frizzing in every direction.

"Lexi!" my bubbly blond little sister screamed and skipped over to me, throwing her arms around me. "I'm so happy you're here!"

"Yay, let's throw a party."

Abby lived a perfect Super Suburban Barbie lifestyle. Even as kids, I always knew she'd grow up to be just like Mom, pearls and all. Daniel, her boyfriend, made big bucks doing only God knows what. He'd explained it before, but boredom overcame me three-point-five seconds into the spiel. Abby's job as a Kindergarten teacher had been her dream since the first day she hung her backpack in a kindergarten cubby.

We stood there in the foyer, Abby hugging me way longer than necessary. Why had they come, unannounced, in the middle of the week to visit Mom and Dad?

"Alexandra, dinner will be ready soon," Mom said, walking into the foyer. She noticed my huge hair. "Oh dear. What happened?"

"Small problem at the salon today," I said gritting my teeth.

Andy walked in next. "What's up, Bozo?"

I wanted to pummel him like I had when we were kids, but my inner lady refused to make a spectacle of myself. With a mumbled "fuck you" under my breath, I walked past.

Once in my room, I worked some product in and managed to smooth my hair into a bun sort of thing. All tucked away, it looked somewhat better. I changed into one of my new outfits and made my way to the dining room. Each place setting held the necessary silverware, a fancy folded linen napkin, water glass, wine glass, bread plate and dinner plate. Mom's good china, only brought out on holidays or other major fetes, stared up at me. What was the occasion?

Abby led the same old dinner conversation, going on and on about her school kids and every other boring detail of her life. I zoned in and out, but caught when Abby screamed, "We're engaged!"

Chapter 5

Mom jumped up out of her seat with tears flowing down her cheeks. "I just knew it!" she exclaimed and hugged Abby, then Daniel.

Abby showed off her gargantuan diamond. From the looks of it, Daniel was making up for some sort of shortcoming.

"Are you happy for me, Lexi?" Abby stared at me, her smile wide as a Cinderella-style wedding gown skirt.

"Oh, uh, yeah, of course. Congrats." I raised my glass and chugged the rest of my wine.

"A wedding to plan! How exciting!" Mom squealed like a five-year-old. She'd been waiting for this day since the doctor spanked my ass and yelled, "It's a girl!"

I liked the spanking part of that deal, not the girly things that usually came with owning a vagina.

Even though I despised the gaiety of wedding hoopla, I did want to get married some day. I wanted the security of a penis at my beck and call and to know I'd never be alone. That is what scared me most of all, growing old and gray and ugly and having no one to be miserable with. I'd thought Zak would be the crotchety old fart rocking next to me in fifty years. Apparently, he had other thoughts on whom he wanted to grow old with. I bet those tattoos will look spectacular when her skin's all wrinkly.

I grabbed the half-empty bottle of wine, took it to my room, chugged from it and plopped onto the bed. A vision of Zak's face burst into my brain. Maybe I could forgive him and we could go on like it never happened. So he'd slept with my friend, lied to me for months. What's a little infidelity between friends? There wasn't anything wrong with being insecure, timid, a doormat of a woman. Except for the fact that I hated those women—the ones afraid to stand up to their man for fear of losing him. I wasn't that desperate, was I?

I grabbed the phone and dialed Zak's cell number. I needed answers and the wine had given me the courage to ask the questions.

"Why Brenda?" I spat before he had a chance to say anything beside a hesitant, "Hello?"

"Lex, is that you?"

"Answer me," I demanded, but stayed calm.

"Dammit, I don't know. She was something different."

"Couldn't you find something different in a girl I didn't know?"

"It just happened," he answered. "We never meant to hurt you."

"A one night stand just happens. A two month affair is bullshit."

"I know. It never should have gone on as long as it did."

"Zak, it never should have gone on at all!" My face heated and my voice rose. "You can't tell me I didn't make things spicy enough for you. I came to your office and fucked you in your desk chair! How's that for something different?"

Suddenly a thought bounced into my head. He'd said Ruth left the nail file on his desk that day. Her idea of a manicure was making sure each nail was gnawed to the same length as the others. No possible way did she own a professional grade file and buffer.

"Brenda was there, wasn't she?"

Zak's silence answered my question.

"You bastard!"

"Lexi, what did you want me to do? Have Ruth tell you not to come in? I didn't know you were going to be naked underneath your jacket."

"Where was she hiding?"

"In the bathroom."

"Perfect place for a piece of shit, I suppose."

"Can't we be civil?"

"Civility went out the door when you fucked another woman in my bed and burned my apartment to the ground. Oh, and once I tally it up, I'll be sending you a bill for the damages." I pressed End on my phone, wishing I'd called him on the ancient rotary in my parents' basement. When you slammed the receiver of one of those down, it made an impression.

I'd thought reaming Zak out would make me feel better, but it didn't. I wanted another bottle of wine and maybe a whole package of Oreos, double stuffed and covered in chocolate. Instead, I made my way down the hall to Andy's room for something a bit stronger and less likely to add inches to my thighs.

"What?" he growled after I knocked on his door several times.

"Open the damn door, asshole."

He opened it a mere six inches. Even when we were kids, he allowed no one the privilege or misery of entering his private domain. "What?"

"Gimme some of your shit. I know you got it."

"I don't know what you're talking about," he said and tried to close the door in my face. Having anticipated this reaction, I'd wedged my foot between the door and its frame.

"Now, asshole. You don't want to fuck with me."

Maybe I saw a glimpse of brotherly love or maybe he knew the problems I could cause for him. Either way, he gave me what I wanted. I walked back to my room and locked the door.

I pressed the Open button on the old bookshelf stereo I'd used as a teen. Nirvana's Nevermind CD stared at me. I pushed it back in and pressed the play button. The opening chords of Smells Like Teen Spirit thundered into my chest as I opened the window and squished into my hot pink pleather beanbag chair.

I inhaled a long drag. Were smoking a joint and listening to the songs of a man who'd committed suicide in my best interest? My sanity balanced on the edge of my window sill, its vulnerability increasing with each puff as it teetered closer to the autumn air. But it had been ages since I got high, and it felt damn good. I reminisced about college, when I didn't care about much besides the next party. But as mature adults, we get to a point where drug use seems like such a loser thing to do. Did this mean I thought myself a loser?

* * * *

The light of day blasted my hung-over face as my body still lay sprawled across my beanbag chair. I stumbled down the stairs in search of nourishment. My mother stood preparing her roast for dinner and informed me of the get-together she'd planned. Apparently my stay with them was "a wonderful opportunity" to catch up with my distant kin. I had no desire to make small talk across the dinner table with people I saw every five years at funerals or weddings. And like most things in my life, my mother didn't get it and made the phone calls anyway. She said she knew "just what I needed," a night to relax and forget about my problems. If she really wanted to give me what I needed, she would hand me a pair of dull rusty scissors and Zak's penis.

At six sharp the next evening, the doorbell rang and in trudged my cousin Wendy, her husband Randy and their three brats.

"Wendy Lynn, it's been ages!" Mom squealed and threw her arms around her. Mom always addressed our family members by their first and middle names like we lived five states to the south. "Alexandra, come say hello to your cousin!"

I forced myself toward the foyer to greet them, almost losing a toe when the oldest boy brat came running at me and stomped on my foot. Holding in what I really wanted to say, I spouted an emotionless, "Hello," and flashed my fake smile.

"I'll leave you girls to catch up! I'm sure there's so much you need to talk about!" Mom giggled. "You two used to be such great friends as children!"

Friends? Um, no. I was more like her prisoner, held captive in her bedroom while she bragged about her extensive toy collection, demonstrating each and every one but never allowing me to touch or play with them. Her parents had spoiled her rotten and given her a superiority complex. As we got older, I realized I did not have to sit there and take her bull so I began avoiding her as much as possible.

After brief small talk, dinner was served. I somehow had the misfortune of being seated next to the youngest brat. I watched him shove peas in his nose, his parents oblivious as they carried on with adult conversation. He sprawled across the table to grab a breaded pork chop off the serving platter, dragging it across Great Grandma Louise's lace tablecloth to his plate. He speared it with his fork and began biting off of it.

"Jake, baby, don't do that!" Wendy called and the mini brat slammed the chop back onto his plate. "Lexi, be a dear, and cut that up for him."

I looked down and he glared back, flames filling his pupils. Surely he came from the devil's loins. If I didn't cut up his pork chop, would his head spin and sparks come flying out his ears? That might actually bring some life to this dull affair.

After completing my good deed for the day, I turned my attention back to my plate. I savored the homemade scalloped potatoes and sipped on my wine. As I closed my eyes to wonder how much longer this night would last, I heard a gagging sound coming from the seat next to me.

"Oh my God!" Wendy screamed and Randy jumped up to smack Jake on the back. He coughed up a hunk of pork chop.

"Lexi, what is wrong with you?" Wendy scowled at me.

"What did I do?"

"He's a child! He can't eat pieces of meat that big! Why didn't you cut them smaller?"

"How am I supposed to know how big to cut his meat? He's not my kid!"

"Yeah, that's the answer I'd expect from a selfish single woman."

The meal continued in silence with the exception of the kids, who decided it necessary to make flatulence sounds at the dinner table. Owen began banging his fork on anything and everything around him, seemingly silent to everyone's ears except mine. Bang! Bang! Bang! on his glass, and then thud. Bright red juice flowed like a river across the table and into my lap.

"You idiotic little cretin! Can't you be more careful?" I scrambled up.

"Don't you dare speak to my child like that!"

I knew what I wanted to say to her, but kept it to myself. It wasn't appropriate for young ears. Amazed at my self restraint, I tossed her a dirty look and walked away from the table as the kids pointed and laughed at the red splotches that covered me.

"Alexandra, where are you going?" Mom asked.

"I'm going to bed."

"But we're playing charades after dinner."

Did a twenty-four-hour sterilization clinic exist? If so, I needed to drive there right away. If I ever found myself with child, they'd better lock me in an insane asylum right from the get-go, cause that's exactly where I'd end up.

* * * *

Sunday morning came and Mom practically dragged me to church. And of course this week my parents were in charge of distributing coffee and doughnuts afterward. I tried to get out of it, knowing I'd come face to face with Pastor Nerd-a-lot, but no dice. I hid in a corner and sipped my coffee in peace, but of course that wasn't good enough for my mother. She nagged until I came into the kitchen, and gave me the job of putting doughnuts on paper plates.

"Good morning, Alexandra," I heard from behind, a nasally voice I could recognize anywhere.

"Hello, Pastor John," I tried to say in my most angelic way.

"Did you enjoy the sermon today?"

I couldn't remember one word of it. I'd tuned it out and stared at the bulletin the entire time, counting how many A's there were, then B's. I only made it to C before boredom consumed me.

"Oh, it was nice," I answered. Was it a sin to lie to a pastor? Probably tiny compared to the whoppers on my list for St. Peter when I sit in front of those pearly gates. Pete will surely have a smile on his face as he reads over my transgressions.

"Forgive me if this is forward," he began. Oh no, a start like that couldn't be good. "Would you mind accompanying me to the Pot Luck Dinner next Saturday?"

What could I say? I almost felt bad for the poor guy. He couldn't help his dorkiness. I almost thought of accepting the invitation out of pity. He desperately needed a good lay and visions floated through my head of all the wacky positions I could contort our bodies into. He'd never be the same again.

"I'm sorry, I can't. I'll be out of town." Lie number two.

"Okay, maybe another time," he said and walked off to chat with his parishioners.

On the way home afterward, Mom asked if I'd accepted the pastor's invitation.

"No, and how did you know about it anyway?"

"Pastor John asked your father and me if we minded. Why ever would you turn him down?"

"He's not my type."

"Alexandra, he is lovely and kind and would make a wonderful husband."

"What? Are you husband shopping for me?"

"Well, if you're asking me if I think you need a little guidance in the area, then yes!"

"This is ridiculous. If I even want to get married, and that's a big if, I can certainly find my own man."

"Apparently you haven't had the best of luck lately."

"Unbelievable! When we get back to the house, I'm outta here. I can't take this anymore."

As soon as we pulled into the driveway, I stomped up to my room and packed up my extremely limited wardrobe. I ran to the only person I hoped would be there for me no matter what—Marcus.

I called him on the cab ride back into the city. He didn't say much, but agreed to meet me at Java House, a coffee shop around the block from his apartment. When I walked in, he sat on a plush leather couch with two lattes in fancy Styrofoam cups with lids. He apologized for not returning the call I'd made to him days before.

I brought Marcus up to speed on my family life and the disastrous visit. He touched my awful hair and had a good little giggle.

We sat quiet for a minute in an awkward silence and I knew what kinds of thoughts flowed through Marcus's brain. Dread filled me and I prayed the thoughts would stay where they were.

"Are we gonna talk about what happened with us?"

"Do we have to?" I grabbed for the newspaper sitting on the table and held the sports section up in front of me, pretending to care about the Giants' latest victory.

Marcus pulled the paper away from me.

"Lex, we need to. I have some things to say."

"Marcus, I already know what you're going say."

"No, you don't."

"I do. I know how much it meant to you. And it did mean something to me too, but not what it did for you. I've known for years how you feel about me. There were times I wished I had the same feelings for you, but I just don't. You are my best friend and I love you like a brother. Well, not like my brother, but how you should love a brother. I don't want to lose you and I hate myself for using you the way I did. I wanted to get back at Zak and you were there, ready and willing."

"Lex, stop. You don't know how off base you are. Trust me, I wasn't the one being used."

"What?"

"I don't quite know how to say this...other than to just say it." Marcus shifted in his seat. He rarely looked nervous about anything in his life, but in that moment he looked nearly terrified. "Lexi...I'm gay."

I stared at him, trying to comprehend his words. Gay? No. I had to have heard him wrong. Marcus was a hot thirty-something guy. Women drooled over him. He'd dated, and also slept with, tons of girls over the years.

"Why are you saying that?" I asked.

"It's true. I've known for some time now, but part of me wasn't sure. I knew I had strong feelings for you, but I didn't know how deep they went. When you came on to me that night, I tried to fight you off. I knew it was best for you. But then I decided to do it. If I could make love to you and feel nothing, then I knew for sure I was gay."

I sat back, trying to process what he'd said.

"Oh, my God." I laughed. I tried to stop myself, but couldn't. "I just realized something," I continued between bursts of giggles. "I get it now. This is karma, a chick lit version of karma. The miserable things I did to those women in my books, they're all coming back on me. That Karma bitch is gettin' me good too! You know, like Rachelle in The Chocolate Lover's Guide to Love. Yeah, she had the cheating boyfriend. The boss from hell, straight out of She Works Hard for the Money. I've written about nagging mothers, hair disasters, and whorish best friends. Abby's wedding is surely my pre-punishment for the wedding themed book I plan to write. And on top of it all, probably the icing on the proverbial cake, I now have the gay best friend who was present in every single story. I'm being punished for writing clichés. This is freakin' hilarious!"

"I'm glad this is amusing you," Marcus replied when I finished my hysterical tirade.

"I'm sorry, but you have to admit, it is funny!" I continued to laugh, deep belly-aching laughs. I couldn't stop myself. I wasn't laughing at Marcus, just at my pathetic life.

"I expected more from you," he said as he stood then walked away.

"Marcus, no, wait!" I yelled after him, laughter still in my voice, but he had already walked out the door. There went my place to crash for the night. My visions of re-entering the warm cocoon of Marcus-ville quickly faded.

Chapter 6

I thought of taking a nap on the comfy leather couch at the coffee shop, but the employees would surely frown upon it and throw my homeless ass on the street. Being completely out of housing options, I gathered up my few belongings and checked into the nearest inexpensive hotel.

Keying into the room felt quite surreal. I walked in and surveyed my surroundings. Its amenities were nice enough: a perfectly made bed that could withstand a quarter bounce, a small table with two chairs, great view of the busy street below. But this hotel room, this place for travelers... I now lived there. It was my home, for lack of a better word. When visiting a hotel in the past, I'd never even taken the time to unpack my suitcase. Part of being on vacation was living out of it. The stay at this hotel was indefinite. I'd be using the dressers, the hangers, the perfectly arranged soaps and maybe even the single serve coffee maker.

After hanging up my minuscule wardrobe, I emptied my purse. Lying on the bed was a small makeup bag, a pick for my hair, Marisol Takes Manhattan on disc, Sheila's notes, my cellphone, wallet, and key chain. Every single thing I owned sat in front of me in a tiny mound. I then allowed myself to mourn the loss of my stuff. Sitting in a quiet vigil, I paid respect to my wardrobe, my gorgeous shoe collection and the copies of my books. And poor Cha Cha too. I loved her bulgy eyes and pointy ears. I prayed the poor thing died quickly.

I grabbed the disc and notes off the bed and tried to decipher Sheila's un-legible scribbles. She rambled on and on about clichés and character flaws and told me her neighbor's screeching parakeet could form better sentences than I did.

Maybe I would leave Smith & Roland, find another publisher who actually valued my talents.

My brain then opened and like a flashback set to sappy music, memories brought forth the years I'd struggled to get published. The only thing worse than the time I'd spent preparing and mailing query letters to agents and publishers was the money I had shelled out to do it. Finally I generated some interest and a few requests for partial manuscripts, only to be rejected yet again. My last-ditch effort was submitting to a small publishing house. Lady Luck reached her hand down, plucked my letter from the slush pile and set it right on Val's desk.

Maybe the whole publishing process would be easier the second time around, since I was already a published author. I knew much more than I had back then. It hurt my head too much to think about. I threw the disc and the notes into the night stand drawer and flipped on the TV.

* * * *

Three days later and probably five more pounds gained, I searched my room for high calorie, high sugar sustenance only to discover my supply had run out. I ran—or rather walked—to the nearest food store. Once there I perused the junk food aisle, examining cookie boxes and bags of imitation cheese-flavored popcorn. Even the package of barbeque pork rinds looked tasty. As I set a package of chocolate covered pretzels in my basket, I noticed the waistband on my pants cutting into my skin. Maybe I should skip the crap and opt for carrot sticks instead. I could even hit the gym on my way back to the hotel.

The self-loathing part of my brain kicked in and told me there was no use. I filled the basket with my favorite chips and a tub of dip and threw in a box of Twinkies and one of those giant pixie sticks.

Standing in line, I wondered how intense the sugar high would be if I ate the entire pixie stick and sucked the cream out of every Twinkie. The momentary rush would be cheaper than a good bottle of wine and it wouldn't leave me with a headache. As I daydreamed of bouncing around on my hotel bed, my cellphone rang Sweet Dreams are Made of These. The sound comforted me almost as much as a Snickers bar dipped in peanut butter. I dug into my purse and answered it as fast as I could.

"How's the revision coming?" Val asked. Her voice was a much-welcomed sound, though the topic of conversation did not interest me much.

"Oh, well, it's not. I'm still not sure what I'm going to do."

"You haven't worked on it at all? Lexi! What are you thinking? Sheila wants it on her desk tomorrow!"

"If I decide to continue my career with Smith and Roland, that bitch can wait 'til I'm ready."

"Lex, you don't understand. They're not fooling around. If you don't submit something to her first thing tomorrow morning, you're done. And trust me, she'll black-ball you from every respectable publisher in the northeast!"

"Oh. I didn't realize it was so serious."

It was partially a lie. I knew Sheila was serious. Part of me really didn't give a shit.

"Let me come help you. I can meet you at your apartment."

"Well, that's not possible. It burned down. It's a long story."

"Okay, I'll come to wherever you and Zak are staying."

"Um, that's another long story. Val, really, it's okay. You have your own career to worry about. I'll be fine." I looked up to find the cashier staring at me, annoyance on her face. "Val, I have to go. Love ya Babe. Thanks for checking up on me."

The cashier gave me a dirty look as I handed her my basket and told her I wouldn't need any of it. Once back at the hotel, Sheila's notes stared up at me with all their viciousness. But I read every word, carefully, instead of skimming them like before. And the more I read, the more they infuriated me. Who the hell was she to tell me I didn't know my character? I made her up! I created her and gave her life.

As furious as I was, I still heard Val's words playing over and over in my head. It killed me to make changes dictated by a woman I didn't know or trust. But I did trust Val and if she thought this was in my best interest, I wasn't going to question it. I asked the desk clerk of the hotel where I could go to use a computer and she directed me to the library.

I hopped the subway to the nearest library and asked the librarian to point me in the direction of the computer lab, then immediately sat myself down and got to work. As much as it pained me to admit, some of the points Sheila made were justified. I'd let some basic fundamentals fall to the wayside, which was quite embarrassing. And every other page had a major grammatical error, a rarity for me—I prided myself on good sentence structure and proper punctuation.

How did this story turn out so awful? How could I be completely oblivious to it? Maybe Marcus was right. Maybe I'd been blind to a lot these past few months.

My fingers typed with an energy they hadn't possessed in a long, long time, trying to catch every thought as it tumbled from my brain. I reached page three hundred out of four-fifty and felt a tap on my shoulder.

"Miss, I'm sorry, but the library is closing now. You have to leave."

"What? No! I'm not finished."

"I'm sorry. You'll have to come back tomorrow. We open at nine."

"That doesn't work for me. I need to have this on my editor's desk at nine."

"I can't help you."

I quickly saved my file and gathered up my things. Where else could I go? I needed a computer immediately. Upon walking into the lobby of the hotel, I found a young guy sitting at the front desk playing Solitaire on the computer. An idea popped into my head.

"Hey, there. Whatcha doin?"

"Oh, uh, nothing," he said getting flustered and I saw the game disappear from the screen. "Can I help you, Miss?"

"I don't know. Maybe you can...Richard," I said looking at his nametag. I unzipped the velour jacket of my matching ensemble to reveal some cleavage and leaned on the counter. "I bet everyone calls you Ricky or Dick, right?"

"Um, yeah… Rich."

"Well, Rich, you can call me Lexi."

"Okay, Lexi. Is there something I can do for you?"

"I have a problem, Rich. I have some major work to do. I'm an author you know, and I need to finish some work for my next book." I tried to work my mojo as best as I could. "The deadline is tomorrow. All I need is access to that computer you got there. What do ya think?"

"Oh, I don't know. This computer is for hotel records and if a guest comes to check in, I'll need it. And if someone sees you and complains to the manager, I could get in a lot of trouble."

"Oh, Rich. Isn't there something you can do for me?" I leaned in closer, giving him a flutter of my eyelashes and the bedroom eyes I had so perfected over the years. My boobs were practically falling out on the counter, their newly inflated size no longer fitting in my 34C bra properly. I was not above showing a little skin to get what I wanted.

"Well, um, maybe you can come in the back here. There's another computer in the office. No one goes in there at night."

I walked around the counter and followed Rich into the back office. He showed me to the desk and I set my things down. I turned back toward him and laid a kiss on his lips.

"Thanks, sweetie. I'll make sure I mention you in my acknowledgments."

He stumbled back a few steps as he went to walk out. Twenty-year-olds were so damn cute. If I didn't have important business to take care of, I could have showed him a thing or two. He'd never want to fool around with a girl his own age again.

* * * *

Rich came back into the office at five-thirty in the morning to tell me his shift ended in half an hour. I had to leave. Luckily I was finished, just re-reading and making sure every comma sat in its proper place and every sentence was worded correctly. There was enough time to get a couple hours of sleep before heading to Sheila's office. But I knew full well I wouldn't sleep. The high was too magnificent to come down now.

"Hey, you wanna get some coffee or something?" I asked Rich.

"Oh, um, sure." His cheeks reddened and the corners of his mouth turned upwards.

"Okay, let me go freshen up and I'll meet you back here in a few."

I walked back to my room and changed out of the velour jogging suit I'd been wearing for almost twenty-four hours, opting for some cute jeans and a flirty top. That's how I felt, flirty. I put on some makeup for the first time in days, and tried to manage my crazy hair.

Rich stood waiting for me in the lobby when I came down. He had also changed clothes, opting for a sleek leather jacket and t-shirt in place of his button-down shirt and hotel logo sport coat. We walked out the main doors and down the street. He didn't say anything, just smiled. It felt nice to make someone smile.

We ordered our coffees and I paid. I told him it was the least I could do after what he'd done for me. We took seats and I fired off my first question.

"So, Rich, how old are you, anyway?"

"Twenty-four."

"Oh, really? I thought you were younger."

His baby face bore a bit of stubble but you could tell his facial hair didn't quite grow in perfectly yet. He had dark brown hair styled in a messy-on-purpose way that kept falling in front of his eyes. Every few minutes he pushed it back with a quick run through with his fingers. He took off his jacket, revealing a cool tattoo around his wrist. His shirt fit snugly and now showed off a nice set of abs.

"Yeah, I get that a lot."

"How long have you been working at the hotel?"

He went on to tell me his uncle managed the hotel and gave him the job a few years back. He got a late start in college, having toured with his band "Eternal" after high school. They never made it big or anything, just small clubs and bars and a couple tours opening for bigger bands. A few of their songs played on local college radio stations but had never grabbed the attention of any serious producers. They gave up the idea of super stardom and he enrolled at NYU, needing a flexible job to accommodate his school schedule.

Impressive. Definitely not the life story I expected out of him. Rich was beyond cute, but my first thought was much more nerd than smokin' lead singer.

"So, you're a writer?" he asked. "Like, what have you written?"

"I've published five chick lit books. Ever hear of The Chocolate Lover's Guide to Love or Make Mine Manolo?"

"Um, no. Sorry."

"That's okay. You're a guy and not my target demographic anyway. You'll have to read my next one though, Marisol Takes Manhattan, seeing as you'll be thanked in the beginning of the book."

"You're not serious about that, are you?"

"Absolutely! I'm thinking it will say, 'A special thanks to Rich, the sexy guy at my hotel, for breaking the rules and helping me finish on time.'"

His cheeks changed their hue once again and I felt a familiar little pang in my chest. I hadn't felt it in weeks—the desire for someone's arms to be around me.

"So, Rich, you got a woman?"

With even more blushing he answered a quiet "no."

I went on to tell him about my disastrous relationship with Zak. I felt comfortable with Rich, like we had been friends for years.

"He's an ass." He laughed. "I can't believe he'd be so stupid to cheat on someone as awesome as you."

I looked at his face. The carefree smile of youth and innocence stretched across it but something else was there, too. If I was reading his body language correctly, he was sending me some serious vibes. The thought of him wanting me fluttered my stomach and if time hadn't been an issue, Rich and I would have made a detour back to my hotel room before I continued on to Sheila's office.

"I guess he wanted something different."

"He's an idiot."

I looked at my watch again. Eight-thirty. I stood up and gathered my things. "I have to go. I can't be late."

"Thanks for the coffee and the conversation," Rich said, standing too.

I stepped to him and kissed his lips, a soft gentle kiss. "Thank you for everything."

Walking out of the coffee shop, I knew I'd made a new friend, maybe more. This adorable guy was way too young for a relationship, but definitely fuckable. Surely it would be sexy and fun and exactly what I needed

Chapter 7

The elevator at Smith & Roland whizzed up to the eighth floor. I reached Sheila's office, Val's old primo corner space, at exactly 9:02 on my watch. Forcing my arm up, I knocked and heard her witchy voice shriek, "Come in!"

"I made revisions," I said in my most unfriendly manor and pulled the disc from my purse.

She typed away at her computer, pausing for half a second to point her boney finger at the basket on the end of the desk.

"Well, don't you want to read it right away?"

She stopped once again, sighed loudly and cast her evil gaze at me. "Do you honestly think you are the only writer in this publishing house that I have to chase after and baby? I'll get to it later and I'll call when I have further revisions."

"Further revisions? You've got to be kidding me."

"We're done here. I have work to do."

Hot molten lava bubbled up inside me and though I wanted to spew it at her, Val's words replayed in my brain and cooled my temper momentarily. But it wouldn't keep for more than five seconds, ten tops. The rage inside my chest would come bursting out if I didn't leave immediately. I spun around and reached for the door knob.

"Oh, Lexi."

"Yes?" I said through gritted teeth using every ounce of will power I had to remain calm. I didn't even turn around to face her.

"I have a girl I want you to mentor. She's my niece, Amanda."

"Excuse me?" I said as I spun my body around. "What does that mean?"

"She's studying Creative Writing at NYU and has an internship here. I want her to talk with a published writer. I'm sure you have a lot of mistakes she can learn from. She's here every Monday, Wednesday and Friday from three to six. I don't have the time to sit with her or guide her. I expect you to be here at least two of those days."

Karma appeared and took a seat on the end of Sheila's desk. She smirked at me and I wished I could claw her collagen-filled lips right off her face.

I ignored the bitch, the one existing only in my imagination, and continued with my rant. "So, basically I have to babysit your niece? You can't make me do that."

"No, I physically can't. But what I can do is throw that sparkly disc of yours into the trash can."

"I believe that's extortion."

"Call it what you will. I'm sure you can learn a few things too."

I stormed out of the she-devil's office. How could this be happening? With every cell in my body, I struggled to get my own life back in order. I had no time, or energy for that matter, to hold the hand of some college kid. This Karma bitch was really fucking with my life and I was ready for her to stop.

* * * *

I swung by my apartment, well, the burnt-up, blackened space that used to resemble an apartment, to grab my mail. My landlord walked into the lobby as I sifted through two weeks' worth of credit card applications and "You May Be A Winner!" envelopes.

"Lexi, I'm glad you're here. It saves me a phone call. I hate to tell you this, but it's going to take about two months to renovate your apartment."

"That long? What am I gonna do? I can't afford to live in a hotel for two months!"

"My insurance is covering it but you know how that goes. I won't see a check for a while and the contractors won't start work until they have half the money. I can't pay it out of pocket. I'm sorry. The best I can do is not charge you rent while the renovation is going on. Hopefully that will help with your hotel stay."

"Thanks," I mumbled, knowing it didn't matter anyway. My name may have been on the lease, but Zak had paid the rent.

Without him, apartment or no apartment, I'd be shelling out the cash.

I walked to the street and once again had no clue what to do or where to go. With my limited funds now paying for my hotel stay, most of my normal forms of entertainment were off limits—facials, massages, shopping for shoes. The tightness of my jeans told me to hit the gym. At least that was already paid for.

I walked into the gym to find its machines gleaming, the sounds of fans blowing and free weights clinking. Muscled masculine bodies and women in teeny tiny sports bras and shorts filled the room. The trainers greeted me with warm "hellos" and "where have you been?" They all knew me. Normally, I spent quite a bit of time there, perfecting my body. My two-week pity party fat binge left me embarrassed to take my sweatshirt off. They'd gasp if they saw the flab that now lived in my midsection. I kept the shirt on and figured the extra sweating would help melt away my fat.

I got on a stepper machine and fell into my familiar exercise rhythm within a few minutes. I stared straight ahead, in my zone, moving my legs as hard and as fast as I could. Sweat dripped down my back as I noticed someone get on the machine right next to mine. Of all the empty ones, why did they have to choose one so close to me? I hated that. From the corner of my eye I recognized the blond hair pulled into a bun, not a single strand out of place.

"Lexi, can we please talk?" Rachel begged of me.

"I don't have anything to say to you," I said through heavy breaths.

"Don't do this, please. It's not my fault."

"You weren't the one actually screwing my boyfriend, but you could have done something about it. You could have told me."

"I wanted to, believe me. I was against the affair the whole time."

Part of me believed her and I did want to forgive her. I knew she wasn't to blame.

"Even before it officially started," Rachel went on," I told Brenda to stay away from Zak. Even when she said you weren't good enough for him, I stuck up for you and she's my best friend in the whole world."

"Wait a minute. She said I wasn't good enough for him? Who the hell is she to say that?" Pissed off again, I climbed faster and faster on my stepper machine.

"I told her she was wrong."

"Damn right! I was the best thing that ever happened to that asshole!"

"And when she told me Zak said she was better in bed than you, I told her it was an awful thing to say."

"What?" As I turned to her, I lost my footing and fell backwards off the machine. My head smacked on a treadmill behind me and everything went dark.

* * * *

I woke to faces all around me. Rachel held my hand, petting it and speaking my name in a soothing tone.

"Get the fuck off of me!" I yelled as my head pounded.

"Lexi, stay calm," one of the trainers said. "We're gonna call the paramedics."

"Paramedics? Come on. That isn't necessary." I tried to sit up and felt something drip down my forehead.

"Oh my God! She's bleeding!" Rachel screamed like I had a huge gaping wound with brains oozing out. One of the trainers handed me a washcloth and I held it to my head.

"I'm going home." I stood up slowly.

"That cut needs to be taken care of," another trainer said. "Let us call someone."

"No, I'm fine. I just need a Band-Aid."

"We're calling an ambulance."

"Do that and I will sue you! Give me a damn Band-Aid and let me go home."

The trainers looked at each and shrugged their shoulders. They pulled open a first aid kit and used some of its contents to clean and patch me up. I left the gym with a huge butterfly bandage on my forehead.

I walked to the subway to catch a ride back to the hotel. Rachel insisted on coming with me for fear that I'd black out and get fondled.

Why couldn't she just leave me the hell alone?

The pitying look on her blemish-free face gave me all the ammunition I needed to execute her. She was just the messenger, but the comment about Brenda being better than me in bed stabbed a huge sharp knife through my ego. I'd always prided myself in being the best lay anyone ever had.

Rachel followed me into the hotel and up to my room. She offered to call into work so she could stay with me but I refused. After downing some Tylenol, I told her I didn't need a watchdog. She got the hint when I turned off the lights and pulled the blankets over my head.

* * * *

Hunger pangs woke me and even with my eyes wide open, the darkness of the room made it feel as if they were still closed. I fumbled for the light, blinded for a few seconds when I finally found the switch. The clock read 9:35 PM. I hadn't eaten a thing all day and a hot, greasy pizza sounded like the perfect meal. I threw on some clothes and marched down to the nearest pizzeria.

When I got back to the hotel, Rich sat at his post looking adorable.

"Hey friend!" I said as I walked in.

"Hi," he replied back and noticed my bandage. "What happened to you?"

"Embarrassing story. I'll tell you over some pizza."

I sat behind the counter with him and shared my Italian sausage, green pepper and onion masterpiece and the story of my fall. As midnight came and went, I felt energized, ready to gab all night. The ten-hour nap had revitalized me, but Rich yawned every two minutes.

"Did you get any sleep today?" I asked.

"A little, not a ton though. I got some in the afternoon. I usually get a few hours after work before classes, but I didn't get to this morning."

"Oh, I'm sorry. Why didn't you tell me 'no' when I invited you for coffee?"

"I couldn't turn you down," he answered as his cheeks blushed.

I left it at that.

"Why don't you go lay down in the back. I'll stay here and if anyone comes, I'll wake you up."

"No, I couldn't and besides, I like sitting with you."

I stayed and talked with Rich the rest of his shift. He told me about his band and how the members were going their separate ways. We talked about our families and how neither of us fit in with them.

I felt such a connection with Rich, on many levels. It surprised me that someone his age could capture my attention so completely. Younger guys had never interested me in the least. When I was a freshman in high school I dated juniors and seniors. When I was a senior in high school I dated college guys. Even upon joining the real world, I had an age requirement for the guys I dated: three to five years older than me. It puzzled me that someone a whole eight years younger could grab me like this.

As six AM approached, Rich's half-closed, bloodshot eyes made him look as if he could fall asleep standing up.

"So, same time tonight?" I asked.

"Um, sure. If you want."

"Yeah. It was really fun. And I have nothing else going on these days."

"Okay, it's a date," he said and gathered up his things, waving as he walked out the door.

Giddiness and energy filled me. I went to the gym early and got in a great workout, avoiding the steppers like the plague. I took in a spin class, trying my best to concentrate on the instructor's words. My thoughts kept finding their way back to Rich, replaying his words over and over, "It's a date." It had been a long time since I'd been on a real date. I knew this was just us sitting and talking at the hotel and the phrase "It's a date" didn't mean a real date. I couldn't help it though and found myself looking forward to the next time I'd see Rich.

As ten o'clock neared, I rummaged through my limited wardrobe to find something to wear. I kept telling myself I didn't need to look good, but the inner diva in me needed to look hot.

I ran for Chinese food and made it back to the hotel by the time Rich took his post at the front desk.

"Hey, look at you all dressed up. I thought you were hanging out with me tonight?"

"I am," I replied and he blushed. A tingle radiated throughout my body.

God, he was so damn cute!

* * * *

I got myself into a whole new routine, sitting with Rich each night for his shift then working out at the gym. After burning tons of calories, I went back to the hotel and slept till two in the afternoon. Wednesdays and Fridays became my days to mentor Amanda.

The first day I met with her, I didn't know what to say or do. We sat in the meeting room and she asked me a couple questions. I showed her around the place and tried to explain the ins and outs of book publication, or at least how I understood it. I shared my experiences with her.

"I just don't know what to write about," she said to me the next time we met up. "Where do you get your story ideas?"

"They come from life. Write what you know, what makes you happy. Write what's in your heart and soul."

"I don't know what's in my soul."

"Okay, well, first off, what kind of books do you like to read?"

"I like your books. I read them all."

"So, you like chick lit?"

"Yeah, I guess."

"What do you like about it?"

"I don't know. Why do you write it?"

"When I started writing I didn't have a genre in mind but I liked telling stories about women who are strong, women who don't let life's disasters get them down. They lead exciting lives and they never settle for less than they deserve."

As the words trailed from my lips, I realized I'd dealt with my stupid karma the exact opposite of how my characters dealt with their disasters. If I wrote my books the way I'd handled my real life, no one would read them. Stories of pathetic women throwing themselves huge pity parties and gaining tons of weight definitely wouldn't sell.

"I like reading about women who are strong and fun and get what they want," Amanda said.

I listened to her words and examined her: crisp white shirt, every last button securely fastened up to her neck. Her sweater vest with corduroy knee-length skirt and beat up loafers added to her ultra conservative appearance. Her dull brown hair hung straight down, every strand cut the same length as the others.

She liked my books because they temporarily whisked her away from her boring world.

"I think you need inspiration," I said to her. "Let's get out of here."

We hailed a cab and it took us to Fifth Avenue. Amanda needed a makeover. No, need wasn't the right word. We had a life or death situation on our hands.

"How much cash do you have?" I asked as we walked into the first boutique and inhaled the scent of new clothes. The high I felt far surpassed the home-grown variety I'd scored from my brother.

"Not much. Maybe thirty dollars."

I frowned. Thirty bucks would only get her a pair of underwear and a scented drawer sachet, if she was lucky.

"But I have my dad's credit card for emergencies!"

"Perfect! This is definitely an emergency. Tell him you had to pay an unexpected lab fee for school or something like that. Ooh, or intern expenses!"

I grabbed several things for her to try on and ushered her into a changing room. A small sparkle of light shone in her eyes and grew as she tried on outfit after outfit of gorgeous, trendy clothes. Together we chose a few things for her to purchase, then headed to the shoe store.

Shoe therapy was an absolute must. No one on this earth could slip into a pair of Manolo Blahniks and not feel sexy and fabulous. After testing tons of flirty little strappy shoes, we decided on a must have for fall—the black boot.

Next stop: the salon. We ordered facials for two and had our makeup done. The stylist returned my hair to its fabulous chestnut shade.

I gave her carte blanche on Amanda, who seemed extremely nervous and closed her eyes to shield them from the horror happening in the mirror in front of her as her long stringy locks fell to the floor. If her hands weren't trapped under the smock, I'm sure they would have been pressed tightly across her eyes, her fingers not even spread for peeking.

When the stylist spun her around to see her new auburn lowlights and cute layered bob, I practically had to pull her eyelids open for her.

One eye popped open at a time. Amanda stared at her reflection, mouth in a straight line, eyes wide. I'd hoped for a better reaction and prayed she wouldn't start bawling or something. I wasn't even sure she was breathing.

The corners of her lips turned upwards and her eyes twinkled with excitement. She slipped out of the salon chair and toward the mirror to get a better look, touching her new hair. It looked like she wanted to cry, but from joy rather than sorrow.

"Lexi! Thank you so much!" She threw her arms around me.

We ended our afternoon at Friday happy hour.

"I'll get us some drinks," I said, then leaned down and whispered to her, "How old are you?"

"Nineteen," she whispered back.

"Well, today you're twenty-one."

I came back with two Cosmos we sipped as we compared the cute executives. A wide-eyed smile was plastered across Amanda's face and I took some pride in helping put it there. Her protective shell had been broken down—my good deed for the day. Maybe it would help me in the karma department. I could certainly use all the good karma I could get.

"Are you more inspired now?" I asked her.

"Most definitely!"

Chapter 8

Amanda got a little tipsy after her one drink so I made sure she got to her dorm room okay before making my way back to the hotel. Excitement grew inside me as I walked past the front desk, where Rich and I spent our nights together, and waved to the clerk who worked the shift before his. I still had two hours before he came on duty and I didn't like waiting for anything, food, my turn in the bank line, not even through the previews before a movie. Waiting for Rich was pure torture.

After watching some unbearable reality TV, I freshened up and walked to the lobby of the hotel. Rich sat there waiting for me, smiling as I made my way over to him.

"Well, hello! What have ya got planned for me tonight?" I wondered. Most of our nights flashed by with non-stop conversation. We tried to play cards or some other activity but never made it very far. We just had too much to talk about.

"Tonight, I'm taking you to the movies!" he said matter-of-factly.

"Don't ya think that will be kinda hard to do if you're keeping watch over the front desk?"

"No, I got the new Tom Cruise movie on DVD and I thought we could watch it here on the laptop."

"Didn't that movie just open in theaters last weekend? How did you get it?"

"I have connections," he answered back with a wink.

Rich and I set up our comfy leather office chairs at the front desk with a big bowl of microwave popcorn in between us. Ten minutes into the movie, right in the middle of Tom's action sequence, our hands met in the popcorn bowl and entwined themselves together. I felt a flutter in my stomach as our salted buttery fingers rubbed together. We sat for the rest of the movie holding hands inside the bowl.

* * * *

As the sun rose over the city, I helped Rich clean up after our night at the movies. It had been one of those magical first date nights and I didn't want it to end. My body didn't want to turn and walk away from him. It wanted to be as near to him as possible, feeling like a giddy teenager. I made up a stupid story about being exhausted and asked Rich to walk me back to my hotel room.

When we reached my door, I keyed in and pushed it open.

"Well, this is it then." I stared up at him. "I guess I'll see you tonight?"

Rich stood there, barely a foot away, both hands stuffed into his pockets. "Um, yep, tonight."

The anticipation made my heart beat fast and my whole body tingle. Would he just kiss me already! And what was holding me back? Normally I took what I wanted rather than sitting back and waiting for whatever to come to me. Why couldn't I do that with Rich?

"Um, okay. I guess I'll go into my room." But I stayed put, leaning against the doorframe.

"Um, yeah, I should go too."

Rich shifted his weight from one foot to the other and it looked like he was leaning into me. My stomach flipped around inside my body and my heart raced waiting for his lips to press into mine. Instead he stepped backwards and away from me.

"Okay, goodbye."

Sadness filled my entire body as I watched him walk away. I couldn't be mistaking the intensity between us. There was something there, something strong. Why wouldn't he act on it?

* * * *

Over the course of the next week, Amanda and I spent some time together and she asked me a million questions, not a single one of them referring to writing a novel or selling books. She interrogated me on fashion and makeup and insisted I show her how to wear her hair. Once I'd schooled her in achieving a fabulous exterior, we moved on to the most important topic— how to talk to a man. I gave her all my best pointers. She gobbled up the info, jotting down almost every word I said.

"Lexi, you are my hero!"

"Oh, I wouldn't go that far!" I said as we browsed a couple boutiques.

"No, you are! You are so awesome and I want to be just like you."

"That's flattering, but you need to keep your own identity. If you're going to write great stories, they have to be from you, your own original voice, your own unique experiences. I can show you how to dress nicer and help you be more extroverted, but I don't want to change who you are."

"The old me was boring."

"No, not boring. Maybe a little bit on the safe side. Okay, maybe a lot on the safe side!" I laughed. "You need to find comfort in your own skin. Inspiration will follow."

* * * *

Rich and I reached the three-week marker since meeting and the flirting between us raged out of control. Our steamy almost-kiss at my door a week earlier had only intensified the feelings between us. Every second together turned the heat up a degree and every brush of his hand sent surges of electricity up and down my body. I knew he wanted to kiss me but wanting was as far as it went. No hugging, kissing, nothing. And I couldn't take it anymore. I'd already masturbated to the mental picture of his face a dozen times but that didn't give me the level of satisfaction I craved. I needed to have the real him, in the flesh, his voice in my ears as we made love.

No more fooling around. We weren't kids. I wanted Rich and I would have him. I showered and shaved every inch of myself and coated my body with a sweet yet intoxicating scent sure to bring any man to his knees. I changed into the new outfit I'd bought with Amanda and planned the night in my head. The hotel lobby was a ghost town after midnight, with exception of the occasional late night partier coming in for the night. The couch in the back office would be perfect. No one would see us and we could hear if anyone came into the lobby.

I'd gotten to know Rich's Uncle Walt, the general manager of the hotel, pretty well. He knew what the hotel was like overnight and didn't mind me hanging out as long as the phones were answered and his guests were taken care of. If Rich stayed awake, Uncle Walt stayed happy.

Rich and I sat playing cards at the front desk while my brain flashed me pictures of what it thought he looked like naked. I wanted his tight sexy body wrapped around mine, his hands igniting my skin as he rubbed me up and down, his lips on my neck, breasts, stomach, not stopping till every single inch had been kissed. Thinking about my immediate future raised my body temperature a few degrees and I felt the unmistakable drip of moisture in my lacy purple panties. I looked at the clock. 11:47. Close enough. I laid my cards down.

"Hey," Rich said, "don't quit because I'm winning!"

"I'm not. I'm quitting cause I can't sit here another minute without jumping out of my seat and kissing you."

He looked at me, trying to form words, and turned a sexy shade of crimson. I stood and leaned over him, pressing my lips to his, pushing my tongue into his mouth. He returned the kiss until I pulled away.

"Come with me," I said, reaching my hand to him. He took it and obeyed without speaking a word. Anticipation tingled throughout my body as each step took us closer to my visions of how the night would play out. Before the door had even clicked shut, I wound my arms around his neck. I kissed him the way I'd wanted for weeks, running my hands up and down his body, feeling every curve, every tight muscle. Rich's lips and mouth devoured mine with urgency, proving what I'd known all along—he wanted me just as much as I wanted him. Passion had ignited deep within each of us the moment we met, growing and filling every cell of our being until this moment. Now it was exploding all around us.

I tugged Rich's jacket off and unbuttoned his shirt with my lips still firmly attached to his. Pulling away for a moment, I examined the skin I hadn't yet seen. His back and chest were decorated with tattoos that mirrored the one on his wrist. The inked designs turned me on more than I'd ever imagined they could.

I stared into the eyes of the dragon that adorned Rich's chest. The spiky tail of the black tribal-style design curled around a pierced nipple. I kissed the beast, tracing my lips down its body, and flicked the piece of shiny silver with my tongue.

A simple suckling of his nipple seemed to flip a switch inside Rich. He yanked off my shirt and bra in two swift motions, then tossed them to the floor and covered my breasts with his hands and mouth. He took over the lead, something I wasn't quite used to. Usually I was the one in control, choosing the positions, setting the pace. But that night, I let him take control. I wanted him to ravish me.

As an experienced woman in her early thirties, I'd never expected someone this young to be so unselfish in bed. Rich's hands caressed all the right places, slowly, sensually, lingering in certain ones like he already knew my erotic weaknesses. He brought me to the peak of exhilaration not once but twice before allowing himself to orgasm.

We lay in each other's arms, our heavy breaths mirroring one another's, as an utter giddiness overcame me. The feel of Rich's naked body on mine, the sound of his voice while we made love, all of it… it was beyond my every expectation.

He kissed me once again, then gazed into my eyes. I wished I could jump into those deep cerulean oceans, submerging myself in his beauty. He traced the outline of my lips with his finger. I'd never described any man as dreamy, but in that moment, his features so warm and caring, that was exactly how he looked. This feeling of adoration was quite foreign to me.

"Lexi, I want to be with you. I've never felt this way about anyone. I can't get enough of you. Whenever I'm not with you, I can't wait 'til I am. This wasn't some one-time thing for me. I want to take you out and show you off." His hand graced my cheek.

I took it in mine and kissed his fingers.

He continued, "I want to be more than just your friend. And I don't care that you're older than me. It doesn't matter that—"

I interrupted his grand speech by pressing my lips to his once again. I didn't need to hear a syllable more. It was already exactly what I needed to hear.

"I want this too. I want to be with you. A real shot at something."

Rich's lips formed an impossible smile, one he couldn't hide even if he wanted. This was the start of something new and different for me. I didn't know how I'd be at it, if I'd be any good at a relationship like this, but I wanted to try.

As his shift came to an end, instead of leaving and going home, Rich came to my hotel room with me to sleep. I laid in his arms, completely and totally safe. Zak and I had never spooned or cuddled in any way. He had a certain way of sleeping and it didn't leave any space for me. At the time I hadn't cared. Girly stuff like that was for needy, clingy women, not me. But this was different. I wanted to feel Rich's arms around me, holding me tight. His breath on my neck, the warmth of his embrace… it felt nice to know he was there.

* * * *

The bright autumn sun shone on my face and I opened my eyes to find an empty space beside me.

Where did Rich go? Why would he leave me? Had I dreamed our night of glorious sex?

The bathroom door creaked open and he walked out wearing only his boxer briefs. He noticed me awake and climbed back into bed.

"Hello." He kissed me. "I didn't want to wake you. You looked too peaceful."

We kissed and I found myself getting lost in him all over again.

"What do you want to do today?" he asked after pulling away from a very unhappy set of lips. "It's gorgeous outside."

"This right here is all I need," I said and began tugging at his underwear.

Rich just flashed his perfectly white teeth and stepped out of bed, leading me to the bathroom. Two hours later, after a rather long and steamy shower, we got dressed. It was Saturday and the whole day stretched before us. Nowhere to be, not one thing to do. How would we spend our first day as an official couple? I didn't care as long as long as my hand intertwined with his.

Before we spent the day gallivanting, I had a few things to tend to. First was a stop at my apartment building to retrieve my mail. After tossing a huge pile of junk, I reached for my credit card bill. The envelope felt a bit heavier than my previous one and I envisioned the transaction list trailing to the floor and rolling down the hallway. Instead of facing that embarrassment in front of Rich, I simply peeked at the balance, holding in a gasp when the number surpassed my normal balance by a few dollars. Okay, maybe a few thousand more than normal. Shoving it into my purse, I decided to worry about it later and moved on to a pretty pink envelope with my parents' address neatly penned in the top left hand corner.

"Uh, I can't believe this."

"What?" Rich asked. "Bad news?"

"I guess you could say that. It's an invitation for my sister's engagement party. It's in three weeks. The thought of standing around while a bunch of people coo over her is revolting."

"I can go with you. Maybe it won't be so bad."

"You will?" I asked, almost wanting to cry. Where was this sappiness coming from?

"Yeah, if you want me there. Where else would I be?"

How the hell did I win the boyfriend lottery? If I was still with Zak and showed him the invitation, he would have scoffed at it and refused to go. He hated my family and truthfully I couldn't blame him. I could barely stand them myself.

Next we made a stop at the apartment Rich shared with two friends. Consumed with curiosity, I couldn't wait to see where he lived, ate, slept, dreamt of me. Surely it was no Park Avenue Penthouse. I knew the trials of college life, working full time and surviving on the little money you scraped up after bills. For me it had been especially hard, dealing with a newly diagnosed addiction to designer shoes.

When we walked in, two guys sat on a dusty plaid couch playing video games while two others sat in the kitchen area smoking cigarettes and eating cold pizza. The ashtrays overflowed with snubbed Marlboros and maybe the remains of a joint. Take-out boxes cluttered the counter and coffee table.

"What's up, kid? Haven't seen you in days!" one of the smokers yelled and slapped hands with Rich. The gamers paused the action and came into the kitchen to greet us. They grabbed beers from the fridge, offering them to us. I shook my head "no."

"Guys, this is Lexi." Rich turned and looked at me. "My girlfriend."

"Oh, so this is the hot chick you've been going on and on about for weeks. She's graduated to girlfriend status, no longer just the face you whack it to everyday?" one of the guys commented.

"Gryz, you're an ass."

I pulled Rich close to me. "Yeah, those days of jerking off are way over now that you've got me."

After giving me a squeeze, he began doling out introductions. Two were bandmates and the other two were guys who tagged along for the ride. I hadn't heard any of the music the band played, but by the look of this tattooed, pierced, spiky-haired bunch, I could only guess it was some form of punk or rock.

Rich changed into new clothes and we headed out, holding hands as we walked down the street. I felt like a kid again, giddy and happy and feeling like I'd just won a major award.

He apologized for his friends and told me a little about them. It surprised me to hear one was pre-med and another would soon have his MBA. After my hair disaster, meeting Rich, and now meeting his friends, I began to wonder if my thoughts on judging book covers were very wrong.

We spent the day walking around Central Park, talking and laughing. I'd done it millions of times, but with him the experience felt new and different.

"Do you want to go out tonight, to a club or something?" he asked after we'd played on the swing set like a pair of kindergarten sweethearts.

"Oh, I don't know. I'm too old for that stuff. I haven't been to a club in years."

"Come on, it will be fun."

I agreed, but only if I could buy a new outfit and shoes. Even if my next credit card bill needed a mile of paper, I wanted to look hot for Rich. And if I made all the girls hate me for not only having the most gorgeous guy there but being quite sexy myself, so be it.

We walked to one of my favorite trendy boutiques. I grabbed several short, sexy dresses and took them in back to try on. Rich sat uncomfortably in a chair and waited.

I put on eight size four dresses, my normal size, and not a single one fit. Asking the fitting room attendant for a bigger size went against every fiber of my being. After claiming I didn't like any of them, we proceeded to the next store. I hesitantly reached for the dreaded size six, which fit, albeit snugly. It was definitely time to stop gorging myself on fatty greasy food.

Next came shoe time, another store I knew Rich felt uncomfortable in. He snickered when Tristan came running to me and kissed both my cheeks energetically.

"I take it you're a regular here?" Rich asked as Tristan pranced to the back of the store searching for shoes to go with my outfit.

"I guess you could say that." I smiled.

Tristan came back with a fabulous little pair of Pradas, a perfect match for the new dress.

"What do you think?" I asked as I modeled the shoes, but Rich was distracted with the box.

"Lex, those shoes are four hundred dollars."

"Yeah, I know."

"Is that normal?"

"Uh, yeah."

"Wow. I heard of women and shoe obsessions, but I had no idea."

"These shoes are stunning. They're more than something I throw on my feet. They give confidence and sophistication. Any women can wear them and feel like royalty. I saw these same shoes in People magazine and yeah, guess who was wearing them? Fergie. But not the Black Eyed Peas, Fergie. The British Fergie, as in 'Duchess'. Honest to goodness royalty."

"Okay, I get it!" He stood and kissed me right in the middle of the store.

Zak had always shunned PDA.

* * * *

We waltzed into Club Infinity, dressed to the nines. I knew I looked hot, but standing next to stick girls in size zero, I felt self-conscious. Rich and I found a quiet corner booth and ordered some drinks. We made out like high school kids as I tried my best to keep it PG-13. In my mind though, we teetered between NC-17 and porn.

After a never-ending techno song finally ended, the DJ spun a sultry R&B tune. Rich led me to the dance floor where we rubbed and grinded, moving in a perfect motion as we mirrored our movements from the night before. Flashes of Rich and I having sex crept into my brain once again.

"We need to get out of here," I said to him.

"Why? Is everything okay?" He stopped dancing, eyebrows raised, and a look of concern crossed his gorgeous face.

"Yeah, but if we don't leave soon, I'm going to rip your clothes off right here in the middle of this dance floor."

Rich's eyes widened, then narrowed and became accompanied by a sly smirk. He reached for my hand and escorted me from the club. We took a cab back to the hotel, barely making it off the elevator before half our clothes were off. Once inside the room, his masculine body crawled on top of mine.

"No," I said and sat up, pushing him down onto his back. "It's my turn."

Chapter 9

Rich and I lay in bed after hours of love making, tired and sweaty. Physical exhaustion claimed us but we weren't ready to sleep just yet. For us it was still early, only four o'clock in the morning. I normally didn't go to bed until seven or eight.

Moonlight illuminated his face and aside from a few prickly stubbles, his skin felt baby-ass soft and completely blemish free. His nose looked like a picture in a plastic surgeon's catalog. As I continued to admire his facial perfection, I wondered how many other women had stared up at it after making love with him.

"So, now that we're officially a couple, I need to ask. How many women have you been with?"

"Oh," he said and even in the dimness of the moonlit room, I could see his blushed cheeks. "I don't know. I'm not sure."

"Not sure because it's a high number?" I giggled a bit.

"Lex, you have to understand what it's like. I sang lead in a band. We toured on and off for almost three years. I'm sure you have some idea what that lifestyle is like."

"Well, not particularly. Enlighten me."

"It varied, but we probably averaged like two or three shows a week. I guess do the math."

"And you fucked a different girl every one of those nights?"

"Not every night. Please don't be mad at me," he said, sensing my tone.

"Okay, that's like..." I paused to calculate in my head. "Three hundred girls?"

"No! Well...probably not. I really don't know."

"Oh my God!" I sat up in bed, clutching the thin sheet to my breasts.

"Have you ever been tested for diseases?"

"After we came home and decided we were done touring, yeah! I went for like two years, every six months just to be sure. I'm clean, you can trust me on that."

I relaxed somewhat as he continued.

"It was so insane back then. I hate even thinking about it. I did a lot of stuff I'm not proud of."

"Like drugs?" Did I want the answer to another personal question?

"Yeah. Coke, X, it's all part of the job description of a rock star. Hard to stay away when it's everywhere. It's way in the past though. Haven't done anything in years. Few drinks here and there but that's it. And I haven't been with any girls since then either."

"Really?"

"Yeah, I couldn't be with anyone until I knew without a doubt I was clean and once that happened I couldn't do the casual sex thing anymore."

I felt a little better, but the possibility of three hundred different pussies on his dick over the years did not sit well with me.

"What about you?" he asked next. "How many guys have you slept with?"

"My insignificant number is no comparison."

"Come on, tell me."

"It's like thirty. No, wait, that was Zak. Marcus makes thirty-one and you, thirty-two."

"You slept with your gay best friend?" He laughed.

"Yes, the night I found Zak in bed with Brenda. I was desperate for some affection, okay!" I hit him with a pillow. "And I didn't know he was gay then."

After some playful pillow fighting, Rich pinned me and his lips made their way downtown. Zak had always refused, said he couldn't stand the taste. I soared to heaven with orgasm number three for the night and decided the three hundred girls didn't matter. They had only one forgettable night with him, one shot at nameless sex. I had Rich now and he was all mine, to be with over and over again.

* * * *

Now that Rich and I had become an official item, our schedule changed slightly. Instead of me going back to my room alone to masturbate after his shift ended, he came with me and we spent the time making love to each other and not the images in our heads. When he left at nine-thirty for class, I went to the gym. After a good workout, I slept till Rich came back to the hotel after his classes. He handed over his laptop before going to sleep. I went to work editing *Marisol Takes Manhattan* and started the next installation, *Marisol in Love*.

A few weeks later, Sheila called to tell me she'd re-read the newly updated *Marisol Takes Manhattan*. Even though I'd pushed it closer to perfection, it still needed work. I made a few more changes and handed it back to her. While I waited for her reply I kept my fingers on the keys, creating the next volume of Marisol's life.

The words flowed from my brain faster than my fingers could type them. Inspiration struck me and I had a feeling it was all Rich's doing. He filled me with a happiness I hadn't experienced in a long time, years probably, if ever. I'd thought Zak made me happy. But looking back now, he was just there—a security blanket. He was stiff and rigid. Downright rude and tactless.

Why did I fall in love with him, again? Abs, eyes, money—something like that.

But now I knew a fat bank account and anally-tended-to stomach muscles were not what I wanted to spend my life with. At least not anymore.

And what about Rich? Could he be the man I wanted to grow old with? How could I be thinking such thoughts, only knowing him for six weeks? After what had happened with Joe so many years ago, I'd sworn off love at first sight. Maybe I was wrong about this, like the dozens of other things in my life.

Another evening began as I put away the laptop and Rich woke in time to punch in for his shift. I ran for our dinner and by the time we finished our grilled chicken salads, midnight had come and gone. Like most weeknights, we were the only forms of life the lobby saw. We slipped into the back office for some X-rated fun but just as our clothes started to peel off, the bell on the desk chimed. Rich quickly buttoned himself up, leaving his shirt untucked to hide his protruding bulge.

"Yes, sir. How can I help you?"

"I need a room for the night," the man answered. Sitting alone and half-naked in the back office did not satisfy me in the least and being in a frisky mood, I crawled out to surprise Rich under the counter. I quietly unzipped his pants tooth by tooth and freed his huge cock from the confines of his khakis.

"Oh," Rich moaned as my lips wrapped around him. His fingers continued tapping at the keyboard. "Yes sir, we have a room for you."

I continued with my task as he did with his, working ever so slowly, not wanting to get him off. My tongue tickled and circled the head as he handed the man his room key and wished him a peaceful stay at the Luxury Inn. Rich then ducked under the counter with me.

"You are crazy!" he said and pulled me on top of him.

"And you love it!"

He looked at me, expressionless, our faces only a few inches apart, and pushed my hair back. He stared deep into my eyes. "Yeah, I think I do."

The comment surprised me and I didn't know what to say. I couldn't go there, not yet. I kissed him and pushed his hardness into me, rocking my pelvis until we both cried in ecstasy. I couldn't deal with the L-word yet.

* * * *

Friday afternoons became pampering day for Amanda and me. Even if we didn't buy anything, trying on trendy clothes helped get us in the right state of mind for writing stories about fabulous women. We ended the afternoon with martinis at the same happy hour each week. Our goal this week was to get Amanda a date with one of the hot guys who also frequented the place.

"Okay, how about that one?" I asked, pointing to a twenty-something in a pinstripe suit with a pink shirt and matching tie.

"He's wearing pink. I don't know if he's quite my type, if you know what I mean."

"Hey, real men wear pink! Only a completely confident man can wear that color and make it look good! Okay, now stare at him a little as you sip your drink. But not stalker staring, sexy staring. See if he catches your eye."

"Lexi, I can't do that."

"Yes, you can. You look amazing today. You are a smart and beautiful woman. How are you ever supposed to write stories about hot, sexy passion if you never experience it for yourself?"

"Okay, I'll try. But if he comes over and tells me he's getting a restraining order against me, it's all your fault."

She did as I said and within a few minutes, he caught her eye. She smiled at him and he flirtatiously smiled back. Excitement burst through my veins as I relived my youth vicariously through Amanda. Dozens of free drinks had come from this perfected sexy stare-down move.

"Oh my God. He's coming over, Lexi. What do I do?"

"Say hi and whatever you do, don't tell him you're only nineteen."

The cute blond-haired guy sat next to Amanda and introduced himself. They chatted back and forth and he asked to buy her a drink. I urged her to go with him and watched her the whole time. She barely made eye contact and kept looking down at her hands while they talked. There was so much she needed to learn.

After giving them fifteen minutes, I walked up and told her we had to leave. He asked for her phone number, just as I expected and we walked out.

"Lexi, why did we have to leave? I thought it was going really well."

"Yes, perfect actually! You left him hanging, so it will make him want to call you and find out more. See what I mean?"

"I guess."

"Just wait. Within a few days, he'll call and when he does, he'll ask you for a date."

Amanda and I hugged, then went our separate ways. I needed to get a present for Abby's stupid engagement party. What the hell do you even get for an engagement gift? If you ask me, the shindig is just a ploy to get people to spend their money on you. Next comes the bridal shower—more money—and finally the wedding—even more of my hard earned moolah.

I perused the aisles at Bed, Bath and Beyond and assumed anything sold there would not be good enough for Abby and Daniel's tastes. Surely Tiffany & Co. would be tops on their list for a registry location. My limited budget for engagement party gift-giving only allowed for a silver picture frame from Macy's. It would have to suffice. I paid, then walked to the gift-wrapping counter, where I chose a cutsey wedding type of paper that Abby would swoon over, and of course a frilly bow for the top.

The gift-wrapping woman asked if I wanted to attach a card. I grabbed one of the free enclosure cards off the rack and scribbled down the first short, to-the-point thought that sprang into my head.

Congrats,

Lexi

Maybe I should do something a bit more personal. I reached for a new card and began to write in my nicest penmanship.

To my loving sister and brother in-law to be,

I wish you joy and peace in your new life together.

Love Always,

Lexi

The first was boring, but the second had way too much mush. I didn't do mush. As the woman gave me a look of impatience, I reached for yet another free enclosure card and settled on a combination of simple and sincere.

Congratulations and best wishes.

Love,

Lexi

I stuck the card in the envelope and before licking it, paused and wondered if I should include Rich's name or not. We were in a serious committed relationship, despite its newness. We spent most of our waking moments together, plus the unconscious ones. There were no signs of it ending anytime soon. Wouldn't it be rude of me not to include him, since he'd be a guest of the party? I pulled the card back out, adding & Rich after my name.

* * * *

Saturday afternoon, Rich and I borrowed Uncle Walt's Caddy and drove to my parents' house. I fidgeted with my dress and checked my watch repeatedly as nervousness set in, but I didn't know why. I didn't care what my family thought of him. They could go fuck themselves for all I cared. Maybe I was scared of what they'd do and what Rich would think. He had family issues too; hopefully he could handle anything mine dished out.

Up until this time, no one had met Rich. I hadn't seen Marcus since his big gay reveal. It had taken some time, but he'd realized my outburst of laughter was not me reacting to his news, just hysteria about my own life. We'd talked on the phone a few times, patching things up and I'd mentioned my new beau.

I instructed Rich to take a left and then a right and we were mere blocks away from introducing him to people as my boyfriend. Even if it was just my family, it would make our relationship a bit more real and validated.

We pulled up to the house well before the party's official start time, so I could give the introduction before the hoards of people arrived.

I squeezed Rich's hand as we walked up the path, hoping he wouldn't run screaming from house, stranding me there.

Chapter 10

I took Rich's coat and hung it in the hall closet with mine. Mom walked into the foyer wearing her lace trimmed gingham-checked apron.

"Alexandra!" she said hugging me. "I didn't realize you were bringing a friend."

"Um, yeah, Mom, this is Rich, my boyfriend."

He shook her hand. "It's a pleasure, Mrs. Marshall."

Her eyes lit up and I could instantly see the wheels turning in her brain.

"Robert, come meet Alexandra's new boyfriend!" Mom called out and we took seats in the living room.

Dad walked in and shook Rich's hand.

"So, Richard, what do you do for a living?" she asked.

"Mom, come on! We've barely been here two minutes. Don't start that already."

"Dear, it was just a question."

"Lex, it's okay," Rich said calmly. "Actually, ma'am, I have another semester to finish at New York University for my Bachelor's degree in Music Business. I currently work as the assistant night manager at the Luxury Hotel and Suites."

"What exactly do you do with a degree in Music Business?" Her ridiculous questions irritated the shit out of me. They weren't for casual conversation. She was prying for information to see if he'd make a suitable husband.

"I'm not quite sure yet. I'd like to manage a few bands, find new talent, maybe get into producing music later on. I have time to figure it out."

Dad left the room and came back with two bottles of beer and handed one to Rich. My mother's eyes almost popped out of her head when she saw the tattoo on his wrist peeking out from his shirtsleeve.

"I see you have a tattoo there," she said next.

"Maryanne, leave the boy alone," Dad piped up.

"Well, I have to get back to the kitchen anyway. Hors d'oeuvres for fifty people aren't going to prepare themselves."

Abby came flying down the stairs. "Lexi!" she screamed and hugged me tightly. "And who is this handsome gentleman?"

I introduced Rich to Abby and Daniel. He congratulated them on their engagement. Guests began arriving and Abby left to greet them, doing that annoying thing newly engaged women do—assume everyone wants to stare at the penis supplement on their finger.

As more guests arrived at the house, Rich and I mingled around and I introduced him to the few family members I could stand to talk to. Aunt Matilda was my favorite, probably because she drank too much and did not possess a filter for the thoughts that spilled from her mouth. She was the only person in the family that I resembled at all, in looks or personality.

"Hello, Aunt Matilda."

"You're not gonna hug me are you? I'm already hugged out."

I laughed. "No, of course not. I want you to meet my boyfriend. This is Rich."

"Hello," he said and shook her hand.

"Nice to meet you. Be a good boy and fetch me another vodka tonic."

Rich did as he was told and after talking with Aunt Matilda, I noticed Andy had decided to join the party.

"Oh, there's my brother," I said to Rich.

"Your twin?"

"Yeah, I know, funny isn't it? The whole blond hair blued-eyed thing skipped me even though we shared a womb."

I took Rich over and introduced them.

"Huh huh," Andy snickered. "What are you, like twelve?"

Could my brother not be a retard for just one night? "You're a fuckin asshole."

"Kids, kids," Mom said and ushered us both out of the room. Before she could give us a good talking to, the doorbell rang. Mom rushed to it and there stood Pastor John.

"Maryanne, I sincerely apologize for being late. Youth group at the church ran over this evening."

"Oh, it's quite all right! Please come in."

"Hello, Alexandra!" he said as Rich appeared at my side, just in the nick of time.

"Oh, hello, Pastor John. I want you to meet my boyfriend Rich."

They shook hands and I thought I saw the Pastor glare at Rich. It had to be my imagination.

The party continued on, with everyone oohing and aahing over Abby and the ring and the plans for the wedding. I already dreaded it all. I'd definitely be sitting at the bar with Aunt Matilda getting plastered off the free top shelf liquor.

As Rich started up a conversation with my dad and Uncle Lou, I tip-toed into the kitchen for a slice of Mom's triple layer chocolate cake before it disappeared. In spite of all the things I despised about my mom's 1950's way of life—and there were many—I did envy her baking skills. It couldn't be legal to create such decadent masterpieces out of a few cups of flour and butter.

"Oh, I see you've gotten into the cake. I know it's your favorite!" Mom squealed and sat next to me. "Have you talked with Pastor John? He's looking mighty handsome tonight. I love his argyle sweater! The green really brings out his eyes, don't you think?"

"Are you serious? Mom, I'm here with Rich, remember? My new boyfriend."

"Well, dear, Richard seems like a nice boy, but you can't possibly build a life with him."

"I'll build a life with whoever I damn well please."

"Alexandra, I'm looking out for your best interests. He is still in school and doesn't even have a career picked out. How can he take care of you? And besides, that tattoo gives me the willies."

"Don't you ever stop? When are you going to realize I don't want your life or the perfect little dreams you have imagined for me? I choose where my life goes and who I spend it with." I stood. "And for the record, that's not the only tattoo he has. He's got a couple on his back and a real nice one on his chest that I stare at when I'm fucking him."

As she gawked at me, motionless, I walked out, knowing my last comment would get her. Sometimes I needed to say things like that. They reminded her I'm not the perfect angel Abby is.

I took Rich by the hand, saving him from an awkward-looking conversation with Pastor John, and grabbed our coats.

Within thirty seconds the Caddy was shifted into drive and we were on our way back to where things made some kind of sense.

"Is everything okay?" Rich asked once we drove away.

"Oh, just peachy," I said as I rubbed my temples, an attempt at massaging away my migraine. "My mother was being her normal nagging self and I couldn't take it anymore. It's the same shit every time I visit. That's why I rarely do anymore."

"You should meet my family. Talk about white trash. I never fit in with them either. When I was a kid, I spent every waking minute at Gryz's house with the band. At least your family cares about you. Mine never gave two shits where I was or what I was doing. I got out of there as soon as I could and never went back. I see them maybe once a year."

"Did I interrupt some important Godly conversation with Pastor John?"

A grin lit Rich's face as he shook his head. "That guy has major hots for you!"

"Oh, no!"

"He told me how special you are. 'A beautiful gift from the hands of God.' Then he gave me the third degree and told me the Lord would be watching."

While I laughed at the thought of Pastor John getting tough with Rich, The Rembrandts resonated from my purse.

"Hi," I answered still laughing.

"What's so funny?" Marcus asked.

"Oh, nothing. We're on our way back to the city from Abby's engagement party at my parents' house."

"Laughter is a good sign, right?"

"Uh, what do you think?"

"I guess that's a 'no.' You definitely need a drink then! Come meet us at Marti's."

"Us, as in who?"

"Kevin and I."

"Oh, um, who's Kevin?" I asked, already kinda knowing the answer.

"Lex, he's my new boyfriend!" he replied.

Marcus just came out of the closet and he already had a boyfriend? I didn't know if I could handle seeing him flirting and acting all cutesy boyfriend-boyfriend with someone. I had no issues with gays, but this was my Marcus.

"Um, well, okay. I guess we could stop for a few drinks."

"Great! I'm dying to meet Rich!"

* * * *

As Rich and I approached the bar, I debated walking past and not even stopping. The thought of seeing Marcus with a man scared me, though I didn't exactly know why. If I refused to see him with a man, maybe his gayness wouldn't really exist. I knew it sounded stupid, that if a tree falls in the forest analogy, but to me it seemed to make some sort of sense.

Rich and I walked in and right away I saw Marcus stand and wave us over. The man sitting next to him must be Kevin. His skin was bronzed and he had short, well-groomed blond hair. He was very good looking, the kind of guy I'd probably check out thinking he was straight, until he spoke.

"Hi! You must be Lexi! Marcus told me soooo much about you!"

"Yes, I'm Lexi the Infamous." I took my coat off and hung it on the back of the chair, grabbed the specialty drink menu off the table and flipped through it looking for something extra strong.

"Hi," Rich said stretching out his hand to Marcus. "I'm Rich, the Forgotten."

"Oh my God, I'm so sorry," I said.

"I know. Your brain is fried at the moment."

"Yeah, family get-togethers do that to her," Marcus added with a chuckle. "Was it horrible?"

"Well, take Abby and her disgustingly huge diamond, add a few annoying relatives, my nagging mother, my retard brother and throw in Pastor John. What do you think?" Hopefully my family drama masked my uneasiness about meeting Marcus's new love interest.

"Disaster!" Marcus said and pulled me in for a hug.

"Rich is adorable!" he whispered into my ear with a tinge of flamboyancy. It boggled my mind that Marcus had been out of the closet for barely a couple months and so much had changed in his demeanor. I had no problems with flaming homosexuals— they were great fun at parties. It was just beyond weird for Marcus to be one.

Chapter 11

A few days later, Rich got a call from his pre-med band mate, begging him to play for a charity concert benefiting the Children's hospital he interned at. A band had dropped out and they needed someone last minute to fill in. Eternal hadn't played together in over two years and Rich couldn't pass up the opportunity. Raising money for the hospital was a great thing to do, but I knew he missed playing the music.

For three full days before the show, Rich became a completely different person. Normally he was a pretty happy guy, but this was true bliss. It showed on his face when he came to see me after band practice and carried over into the bedroom. Both of us found ourselves in a state of euphoria.

Laying naked in his arms after a quite enthusiastic love-making session, I asked if the reunion would be a permanent one for the band.

"No, I don't think so."

"Why not? You seem so happy!"

"I've got too many things going on right now. So do the other guys."

"Well, if their girlfriends are even half as satisfied in bed as I have been the past few days, they might be trying to convince them too!"

The day of the show I took the title of "groupie" with my special backstage pass lanyard, and looked forward to hearing the music. Rich sang lead vocals and had written a lot of the songs himself.

I watched as he tuned his guitar before the show, fingers twisting tuning pegs and plucking at the strings. His hands massaged up and down the neck of his black and silver metallic Fender Stratocaster. Needless to say, my panties were moist. Aside from an Eddie Vedder crush in my teenage days, the whole rock star image had never really turned me on. It was safe to say that had changed significantly.

Amid thunderous applause, the guys took the stage. I watched from the side of the stage instead of the sardine-packed crowd and as soon as Rich played the first chord, I was hooked. He turned to me as he sang the chorus, his lips fighting a smile as he winked at me. His voice echoed throughout my body and the base line thumped in my chest. A serene calm come over me and I became lost in his words. They swirled around me, a gentle sort of tornado, as I stood in the center. They tickled my ear drums and caressed me from head to toe.

If I would have known Rich and the band back when they were touring, I would have definitely been first in line to sleep with him.

* * * *

The next week, I had an appointment with my gynecologist. I'd developed an annoying feminine itch, most likely a yeast infection, latex condoms being the culprit. I hadn't had that problem with Zak; we'd never used them. Long before we got together, he decided he never wanted kids and as a thirtieth birthday present to himself, had a vasectomy.

Rich lay sleeping peacefully while I quietly showered and dressed myself in my plainest underwear and bra. I always felt the need to wear my most modest lingerie when I went to the girly doctor.

I sat in the waiting room flipping through the only non-mom magazine in the whole place, an ancient issue of National Geographic. My cellphone rang and every eye in the place shot me daggers. I quietly answered it in the hallway.

"Hey hon, what's going on?" Marcus asked.

"Honestly, I'm pretty sure I have a yeast infection and I'm about to have my snatch looked at. How are you?"

"Fantastic! You got plans with Sir Hunk-a-lot tonight?"

Sir Hunk-a-lot? Marcus had basically told me he thought my boyfriend was hot. We'd shared almost everything two friends could, and now opinions on men? This was going to take some getting used to.

"Um, not sure. He doesn't have to work, but he has a ton of school work to do."

"Okay, let me know. Kevin and I are doing dinner at The Bistro and wanted you to come. It's so great that we're both in a couple now! But if Rich can't come, you should still join us."

"I'll think about it. I gotta go. They're calling me."

"Ciao, babe!"

I turned off my phone and followed the nurse to the exam room. She gave me a paper gown to wear and told me the doctor would be in soon.

I hated the gynecologist more than any other doctor. As much as I liked my vagina being touched, having a cold metal instrument crank it open like a mechanic working on a car wasn't exactly pleasurable.

The doctor came in and greeted me, then asked what was going on. After describing my burning and itching symptoms, she took a look under my hood.

"Alexandra, when was your last period?" she asked.

I laid quiet for a minute thinking about it. "I'm not sure. A few months ago, I think."

"It's been that long and you're not concerned?"

"No, my cycle's been that way for as long as I can remember."

"What forms of birth control have you been using?"

"Condoms."

"Every time?"

"Yes." Where was she going with this? I didn't need the safe sex talk like a horny sixteen-year-old full of raging hormones.

"Well, I think you might be pregnant."

"That's impossible. We're very careful."

"Is he your only partner?"

"For the past couple months, yes."

"And before him?"

"My last boyfriend had a vasectomy." As the words came out of my mouth, I remembered my one night with Marcus. We didn't use anything at all.

"Let's do a urine test and see what we get."

My heart beat fast and the sound echoed throughout my body. I thought I could actually see it thumping up and down beneath my skin, like a bizarre scene from one of those crazy cartoons I'd watched as a kid.

My hand shook as I caught some of my pee in a plastic Dixie cup. After handing it to the nurse, I walked back to my exam room and sat on the table to await my results. The second hand on the clock above me clicked in slow motion, seeming like three for every one. How long did these things take? It had been years since the last time I took one, way before Zak. I clearly remembered the panic that filled me, thinking an oopsie with my boyfriend du jour had caused morning sickness. After the negative test and a conversation with Brenda later that day, we realized a pint of sweet 'n' sour pork shared the night before had led to both our heads hanging over the toilet rim.

I looked to the clock, but only a minute had passed. Surely these tests were better than they were years ago? Shouldn't the results be instantaneous?

When the doctor finally came back in, I tried to read her face as she sat down on her rolling stool.

"Lexi, you're pregnant."

I followed her statement with a blank stare and gaped mouth.

"Are you okay?" she asked.

I didn't know what the proper answer was. Was it okay that I didn't want kids probably ever? Was it okay that I'd finally bounced back from being in the lowest place I'd ever been in my entire life and now had this to deal with? Was it okay that I had no clue whatsoever who the father even was? There were three options: my cheating ex, my gay best friend, or the twenty-something college student I was now dating.

An annoying cackle interrupted my thoughts. She'd left me alone for a while, but here she was again. That bitch, Karma, back in my face and getting off on fucking up my life. She'd let me believe I deserved happiness only to mock me and tell me how ridiculous I was to think for even a moment that I deserved any of it.

"I have to go," I managed and hopped off the examination table.

"Take this prescription for prenatal vitamins," she said, handing me a small sheet of paper. "And make your ultrasound appointment on the way out."

"Why?"

"We need to monitor the baby's progress and determine your due date."

"Oh, well, I'll only need that information if I, um, take this pregnancy to term."

"Oh," she said after realizing what I meant.

"If I do the ultrasound, will it tell me when I got pregnant?" It would be nice if it could also tell me whose sperm had invaded my egg.

"It can give us a round about date, but not exactly. We can narrow it down to a week."

"That would help, I think."

* * * *

I walked the long way back to the hotel. The look of late November deceived New Yorkers. Its sun shone brighter than most summer days but the chill permeated even the thickest of wool. I tucked my hands way into my pockets, pulling my coat close to me, and stopped to watch some kids playing at a park.

Memories flooded my brain, forcing me to think about Joe Kelly. My first love, my first everything. After years of pushing every notion of him to the deepest darkest corner of my soul, his face sat front and center once again.

My sophomore year, he was a senior and I fell in love with him the minute he stepped foot in my English class. As Mr. All-Star, captain of the football and baseball teams, his celebrity status made him a shoe-in for Prom King. He had a dozen Ivy League college acceptation letters, most accompanied by full-ride scholarship offers.

I was never a wall flower, but Joe's popularity brought me to the peak of teenage notoriety. Everyone knew who we were and no party could be called a success without our presence.

When my secret drug store purchase produced a plus-sign, it naturally upset me. The parties I'd miss, the clothes I couldn't wear. The shock wore off and I envisioned the future and the three of us being a family. Our happily ever after began with Joe as the highest paid Yankee or Giant. I'd be the dedicated wife sitting in the stands, cheering till my lungs collapsed. Junior would sit on my lap in a miniature version of his jersey.

When I told Joe about the baby and my dreams for our future, he accused me of cheating on him and wanted nothing more to do with me. He completely smashed my heart, leaving me alone and afraid. Marcus was the only other person I ever told. He held my hand during my abortion and promised to keep my secret forever.

Now in a similar situation, I was just as clueless as ever. Were all my dreams going to be smashed again?

Without knowing an approximate conception date, there was no way of knowing who the father was. Obviously, if I got pregnant before Marcus and I were together, somehow Zak's vasectomy got screwed up. I'd read stories of botched surgeries and shady doctors who collected the money but didn't do the snip. Granted, they were fictional stories, but still. Fiction story ideas have to come from somewhere.

Rich could be the father, even though we used condoms every time. One could have broken. They only have like an eighty-five percent rate of prevention.

And then there was Marcus—my best friend who slept with me just to make sure he preferred the penis.

I watched a little girl in a cute red pea coat climb up a slide and zoom down it into her mother's arms. It was an adorable scene to watch, nothing like my cousin Wendy's brats. This pair had a true mother-daughter bond, giggling as they chased each other around, both happy as could be. I couldn't picture myself doing it though, not even for a moment. Zak had told me right at the start, kids were never part of his life plan and made sure he wouldn't have any accidents. The news didn't bother me one bit. Spit-up and story time didn't exactly fit into my busy lifestyle either. My idea of entering mid-life involved lots of extravagant vacations and many days spent at the spa, not attending class plays and dance recitals.

I sat and thought and sat some more, still with no clue what to do. There was no point in saying anything to anyone until I at least knew what kind of pregnancy timeline we were dealing with and therefore, which daddy had won the baby lotto. With an excruciating week to wait, I'd go out of my mind debating the possible outcomes.

I shifted on the bench and the itch in my crotch reminding me that the doctor had never given an official diagnosis on the yeast infection. Damnnit! Just one more thing to irritate the shit out of me.

I pulled out my cellphone, turned it on, and listened to a voicemail from Mr. Gibson, my landlord. The message informed me my apartment would be ready on the fifteenth of December. Part of me was happy, but the other didn't care. Life was convenient for Rich and me, living right where he worked. A second message came from Marcus telling me the restaurant had changed to Mario's. I called him and told him I wasn't in the mood for going out.

After hanging up, I glanced at the time on my phone. The last thing I wanted to do on this depressing Wednesday afternoon was hang out with Amanda. But Sheila had me by the proverbial balls. If I screwed up with her she'd take a blowtorch to my career and lose not one second of sleep by doing it.

Amanda would at least be a momentary distraction from the disaster known as my life. She ran up to me the minute she saw me. "Lexi! He called!"

"Who?"

"Chad! You know, Mr. Pink Shirt from happy hour last Friday."

"Oh, that's great! How did it go?"

"It went okay, I think. He asked me out on a date!"

"See. Didn't I tell you? Now let's get to work." We sat down and wrote an outline for a scene. Leading lady X gets asked out on a date. I told Amanda to envision what her fabulous inner self would do on this date and outline it on paper. Within an hour's time, she'd written the entire scene.

"See," I said, "you start living the life and the words come naturally." As I thought of my advice to her, I wondered what my upcoming books would be about. If I kept this baby, they'd go from sexy glamorous page-turners to novels boring enough to put to sleep the crankiest of babies.

* * * *

As each day dragged on, I spent a good amount of time wondering what to do about the baby. It didn't matter whose DNA surged through its body, I still had a life to consider besides my own. I yearned for the normalcy I'd had days earlier, the new happiness I'd found. This little creature was going to screw everything up no matter what the ultrasound revealed.

I left Rich fast asleep in the hotel room as I crept out to my appointment. Before I closed the door behind me I took one last look at his angelic face. We had built something great the past two months. I walked out knowing my life would never again mirror the simplicity that Rich and I shared; it didn't matter who the father was or if I kept the baby or not.

The receptionist at my doctor's office took me to another part of the building, a separate waiting area for the ultrasounds. Surrounding me were expectant mothers and fathers, all excited to see the first glimpses of their precious cargo.

When my name was called, I followed the nurse to a small, dimly lit exam room. She gave me a paper sheet and instructed me to disrobe from the waist down.

The technician entered a few minutes later and introduced herself. She pulled out a strange looking wand thing and put a miniature condom on it. After she inserted the thin penis-looking object into me, a form appeared on the screen.

"There's your baby," she said and went on to point out its beating heart, head and arms. "I estimate the fetus to be ten weeks old."

Immediately, I asked for a calendar. As she handed it over, she told me my due date was June twenty-first. Little did she know I had other reasons for needing the calendar. I counted back ten weeks and that took me to the night with Marcus.

"Can I ask a question?" I said to the technician.

"Of course!"

"How effective is a vasectomy?"

"As long as the patient did sufficient testing afterward and got negative results, they're as close to a hundred percent as you can get. The tube that carries sperm from the testicle is completely severed."

Zak wasn't one to leave things to chance. I'm sure he went for testing. "So, have you ever heard of malpractice? You know, like, a doctor collects the money, knocks the patient out, skips the actual procedure but tells them their sample is negative."

The technician laughed and removed the wand from my vagina. "That only happens on TV." She then handed me a small piece of paper. "Here's your baby's first snapshot."

"Oh, okay," I replied and shoved it into my purse.

As I walked out of the room and toward the main door, I heard my name being called.

"You need to make appointments for your prenatal visits."

I kept walking without looking back.

Chapter 12

I saw no point in keeping the baby news from Marcus. He needed to know and I needed to tell someone. We met at one of our favorite lunch places, but even the baby field greens salad with mouth-watering lemon basil vinaigrette turned my stomach. Was it morning sickness or just my nerves?

Marcus, who normally sensed every emotion of mine, sat quite oblivious as he went on and on about his new life. "I think I'm in love!" he said dreamily.

"What? With Kevin?"

"Yes! I've never felt this way before. The feelings I had for you, as strong as they were, were not like this."

"That's great and all Marcus, but this is your first gay relationship. Don't you think you should get out there and ya know, test out the other colorful fish in the sea?"

"Lexi, this may be my first gay relationship but you can't seriously think he's my first gay lover?"

I sat there astounded. Kevin was not his first male lover? When did this happen? Where the hell was I that I didn't know my best friend was getting some man-on-man action? I thought to ask the question but I really didn't need the details of the notches on Marcus's rainbow decorated bed post.

"Don't you think you should try dating some more men before you settle down?"

"I don't even want to. Kevin says the same thing and he's been around the gay block a few times."

"Oh? How many times are we talking here?"

"Lex, don't worry. He's completely clean. Trust me, I've seen the test results. I would never be with someone that wasn't."

"I know."

"I'm happier than I ever thought I could be. I never felt this way for a woman. Lexi, you know I love you, but it's a different kind of love. What I feel for Kevin is so much bigger. And I know it's the same as how you feel for Rich."

"Oh, I don't know."

"Lex, I can see it in your eyes. In both yours and his. You're crazy about each other. You were never like this with Zak, ever. Regardless of his age, Rich makes you happy and I can honestly see you building a future with him."

"Marcus, I'm pregnant and the kid is yours."

He laughed—a sort of Scooby Doo type chuckle—and immediately began chewing the nail on his index finger.

"It's not funny. I'm completely serious."

"That's impossible. We were only together once."

"We didn't use a condom and I know I don't have to give you a Sex Ed lesson."

"Rich has to be the daddy, not me."

"I'm ten weeks pregnant. Count backwards. I didn't even know him then."

"It has to be Zak's"

"Wrong again. He's fixed, remember?"

Marcus turned white.

"I'm not sure what I'm going to do yet," I told him, "if I'll even let the pregnancy continue."

"Um, I have to go," he said and threw forty dollars on the table. He turned and walked out, not one glance back at me.

* * * *

Thanksgiving, the holiday known for eating too much and succumbing to L-tryptophan before dessert is even served, had never been a big deal to me. My family always gathered at my mother's sister's house and I usually came up with some kind of excuse to skip it. After the disaster at Abby's engagement party, I had no desire to be around them again so soon.

Rich had a few days break from school for the holiday and after sleeping in on Thanksgiving Day, we bundled up to brave the icy cold for the Macy's Parade. It wasn't something I normally did. The whole parade thing seemed kind of corny to me but Rich thought it would be fun.

High school marching bands and Rockettes in glittering costumes walked past us as cartoon characters flew high above, bobbing and weaving with the swirling wind. I'd watched the parade on TV a few times but in person, the gargantuan floats looming overhead instilled both fear and a weird sort of joy within me. I snuggled myself into Rich and he kissed my frozen nose.

"I have plans for us for today. I hope it's okay," he said to me.

"Of course. I'm up for anything," I answered, forgetting for a moment that being up for anything wasn't completely accurate. What would I say if he wanted to go out and get completely piss-drunk? I hadn't decided what to do about the kid yet but I knew for sure I didn't want to harm it any more than I already had.

When the parade finished and onlookers began to scatter, we walked a few blocks, stopping in front of a swanky hotel.

"Here we are," Rich said as he pulled me through the rotating brass doors. I instantly felt like an actress in a 1920's movie—an incredibly underdressed actress. Important looking people in designer suits and fur coats sauntered through the bustling lobby while bell hops in uniforms toted expensive luggage. A dazzling crystal chandelier cast glittering illumination on the entire room and its rich dark wood tables and leather furniture with nail-head trim.

Rich strode up to the counter and gave his name. After only a few moments, the desk clerk handed him a room key. How on earth he could afford a room in such an expensive hotel?

We rode a mirror-clad elevator car to the tenth floor and the operator politely held the door for us. Rich keyed into our room, a suite with an amazing view of the city and a bedroom with a Jacuzzi. The king-sized bed looked like it sat four feet off the ground, draped in lush burgundy tapestry sewn with gold thread. It even had steps leading up to it.

"How did you ever afford this?" I threw my arms around him.

"The owners of this hotel own our hotel, too. I lucked out and they had a room available at employee rate."

After lounging in the Jacuzzi, among doing other more kinky things in the bubbly water, we donned our fancy hotel bathrobes. Rich took a seat on the chaise near the windows, pulling me onto his lap.

"Has this been anything like you thought today would be?"

"Not exactly," I answered then kissed him, tasting the sweet remains of the Belgian chocolate that once lay on his pillow. A knock came to our suite door.

"Perfect!" Rich said jumping up. He ran to the door and a waiter rolled in a fancy cart topped with shiny domed plates, champagne in an ice bucket and a vase with a single red rose.

Rich thanked the young man and slipped him some cash. He moved the cart's contents to the small dining table in our room. I took a seat as Rich regally drew the lids off the plates. With a burst of steam, the smells of roast turkey, fresh cranberries and cornbread stuffing filled my nostrils. I about died and went to heaven.

"I can't believe you did all this," I said, looking up at him.

"I haven't spent a holiday with anyone worthwhile in a long time. I wanted it to be special. I'm hoping it's the first in a long line of special holiday moments for us."

I smiled as my eyes blurred with moisture but quickly blinked it away. Rich uncorked the bubbly and poured two glasses. He handed me one and sat down across from me.

"Happy Thanksgiving," he said and clinked his glass with mine.

I returned the sentiment, then lifted the glass to my lips. I let the sweet liquid touch them for just a second. When Rich wasn't looking I poured the contents into the ice bucket.

We enjoyed our meal together, rehashing each of our own holiday horror stories with our families. We laughed together while in the back of my mind I prayed this wasn't the only holiday we'd spend together.

* * * *

Once the Thanksgiving festivities were over, I threw myself into my work. I had nothing better to do and needed to keep my mind off the thing growing inside me. I met with Sheila and again she told me my manuscript for Marisol Takes Manhattan lacked something.

"I've given her everything I have!" I said to her, practically yelling.

"She has no heart. Readers are sick of one dimensional, fashion-obsessed prima donnas. Make her more real or I'm trashing the whole project."

"You can't do that."

"Don't test me. You know I can," she said, glaring at me through her black so-five-years-ago plastic framed glasses.

I left the office and saw Amanda walking toward me. "Lexi," she cried out and burst into tears. I pulled her into the bathroom and cleaned her up. When she calmed down she explained what happened.

"I went out with Chad last night. It was horrendous! He's probably telling all his friends what an awful date I am and they're telling their friends and now half of New York probably thinks I'm a total loser!"

"Oh, come on. It couldn't have been that bad."

She went on to tell me every gory detail: tripping in her new Jimmy Choos and spilling wine on him, nervous, awkward conversation about her dead dog's bodily functions and lastly the dreaded handshake good night followed by an, "I'll call you."

"Ooh, that's not good."

"It was such a disaster. It started bad and kept getting worse. And no matter what I did I could not stop saying stupid things! I've never been so embarrassed in my life."

"Okay. The first bad date is out of the way. It can only get better from here. We'll go to happy hour today and find a new guy for you."

"Oh no! I can never go to that bar again. What if Chad is there? I can't face him!"

"Amanda, the worst thing for you to do right now is run and hide. You have to make sure he sees you with a new guy, looking even hotter and more amazing than you did last week. We have to make him wish he never left you with a pussy hand shake."

I fixed up her makeup and hair and we headed out. We took seats near the bar to be in the middle of the action. I ordered Amanda's drink and we scoped out the guys. We spotted Chad and she started to panic.

"Relax. If he sees you in distress, he'll know he won. Come on," I said and pulled her toward a group of guys standing within earshot of Chad. I worked them like I hadn't done in a long time. They were eating out of my hands. I got another drink for Amanda. The more she drank, the less her nerves affected her.

As she talked with a twenty-something in a clean black suit, I walked off to the bar to get myself a club soda. "I'll have whatever she's having," one of the guys from the group said as he sat down next to me.

"Are you sure? It's just a club soda."

"Absolutely. Who needs liquor to have a good time?" he answered and paid for the drinks.

He continued talking, not trying one bit to hide his flirtation. He was the perfect specimen of a man I normally went for—tall, dark and handsome, wearing a sexy smile and an expensive suit.

He had great taste or a great stylist and I could tell he made big bucks.

"Why don't we get out of here and continue this conversation over dinner?"

"Oh, I can't," I said as the vision of Rich's face flashed into my brain. "I'm in a relationship."

I slipped off my bar stool and politely added, "Thank you for the drink and the conversation." I turned to walk away but heard him speak out as I did.

"Five dollar soda wasted on a tease."

I turned right around and splashed the remaining contents of my glass in his face. I so wished I would have ordered a drink. A glass of red wine would have looked spectacular dripping down onto his crisp white shirt.

"If you think a club soda was gonna get your dick in my pants, you are surely mistaken."

I grabbed my coat and walked out onto the street. Amanda followed behind me.

"That was so awesome. Can I please use that in my book?"

"Sure, glad I can be your muse."

Normally a scene like that would have left me energized, ready to take on a world of assholes and idiots. I am woman, hear me roar! Only now, I felt used and disgusting. I wanted to curl up in Rich's arms and breathe him in. I walked into the room at the hotel. He lay there asleep after his classes for the day, but I didn't care. I needed him. I took my clothes off and crawled in next to him, kissing him until he woke.

"Please make love to me," I said. Without even a question, he did, softly and tenderly.

* * * *

The semester crept closer to its end and I barely saw Rich for five minutes without his nose in a book. I couldn't wait for finals to be over.

The solitude left me a lot of time to think about the baby. When I'd gotten pregnant the first time, a child of fifteen and abandoned by the baby's father, abortion seemed the only logical option for me. At thirty-two, I had a whole world of choices. But I still didn't know if I wanted to be a mother now or ever. Would I want to damage my body for a baby I planned on giving away? Could I even give my baby away to strangers?

And if I did decide to keep it, was I on my own? Marcus's reaction didn't exactly give me warm fuzzies. I pulled out the crumpled ultrasound picture. I could barely make out the form of a head. How could this thing be inside me, moving and growing, its little heart beating?

I thought about Rich. How would he handle it? Would I lose the one guy I was truly starting to love?

My cellphone interrupted my musings when it rang the familiar I'll Be There for You melody.

* * * *

I met Marcus at the coffee shop near his office.

"How are you feeling?" he asked as I sat down.

"Okay, I guess."

"I'm sorry I ran out on you last week. I feel horrible. That was the worst thing I could have possibly done to you, especially after the way Joe treated you all those years ago."

"It's okay. I know how unexpected it was to hear. You needed time to process it. Hell, I need time to process it all. I still don't know what I'm doing yet, keeping it or, ya know, doing what I did last time." I couldn't bring myself to say the actual word out loud.

"Lex, things are different now than they were years ago. You're not a teenager and you have people who love you and support you."

"Who?" I asked sarcastically.

"Well, I know you don't get along with your family but you know your mom would be head over heels for a little one."

"I doubt she'd be jumping for joy over her oldest daughter having a child out of wedlock with her gay best friend." Hearing the statement actually come out of my mouth made both of us giggle a bit.

"What about Rich?"

"I haven't told him yet."

"Why on earth not?"

"I'm scared of how he'll react."

"He's not a selfish jackass like Joe was."

"I know. But I can't expect him to hang around and become an instant step-daddy."

"You've got me."

"I know. You're always here when I need anything at all."

He looked up at me with a seriousness in his eyes. "I want this baby."

"What?"

"I want to be a dad and this might be my only chance. You don't have to raise him or her if you don't want. I can take the baby after it's born and give it everything it needs. You'll never have to be more than cool Aunt Lexi."

Marcus's last statement hit me kind of hard and my brain flashed Aunt Matilda's face in front of my eyes. She was sixty-five years old and alone. She never married, never had kids and now she had no one. Did I want that life for myself? I'd always wanted my life to be meaningful. I thought writing novels, being semi-famous and living a fabulous life was what I was meant to do. Like so many other things in my life, maybe I was wrong about this too.

I had never thought of myself as the motherly type. I would probably be the suckiest mom on the planet but maybe I could try. A tiny human being would need me for everything. Sometimes I could barely take care of myself. How in the world would I ever raise a normal, functioning person? The kid would surely end up in therapy.

But he'd have Marcus too. He'd be a great dad. He was the levelheaded one, the one who planned things and kept my head out of the clouds. Maybe we could balance each other out. Maybe this kid stood a chance.

"I don't think I want to be cool Aunt Lexi," I told him.

"This is your decision. But please, I'm begging you. Don't kill this baby."

"You're not getting what I'm saying Marcus. I don't want to be its aunt." I paused and a few tears rolled down my cheeks, a rarity for me. "I want to be its mom."

"You do?" He threw both arms around me tight. "Thank you so much!"

I knew it wasn't going to be easy, in fact, it was going to be hard as hell but I had Marcus. He'd never leave me. We could do this together.

As Marcus cried sobs of joy into my ear, I thought of Rich. How would he fit into all of this? I loved him and never wanted to be without him. My only hope was that he loved me enough to stick around.

I shook off the uneasy feeling in the pit of my stomach. "It better be a boy! I don't know if I can handle pig tails and saddle shoes!"

"Don't worry, I can take care of that stuff!" he said, hugging me again.

Chapter 13

Friday came and I felt like crap. Three weeks ago I didn't have one clue I was pregnant. Now my body experienced one weird thing after another and none of my clothes fit right, not even the bigger ones I'd bought when I thought I was getting fat for no reason. Regardless of how much sleep I got, exhaustion took over and the smell of tuna repulsed me. I realized this after sitting next to a woman at the deli who dined on tuna on rye. The smell enticed me until the stomach acids crept into the back of my mouth and saliva pooled. Luckily the fresh air outside had revived me.

The thought of Friday Happy Hour with Amanda made me want to curl into a ball, pull the covers over my head and never come out. I asked her if we could hang out at the office instead. We worked on her manuscript while I yawned continuously.

"No sleep today?" she asked.

"Actually I just woke up from a nap. I only got out of bed to come here."

"Oh, are you all right?"

"Um, yeah, well..." I paused, having no reason to keep it hidden anymore. "I'm pregnant."

"Wow! Congratulations! Rich must be super excited!"

"Um... he's not the father." Her dumbfounded look meant I needed to give some sort of an explanation. "I got pregnant before I met him. I'm like two and a half months along. I didn't know 'til recently."

"So, who's the father?"

"You're being pretty nosey, don't you think?"

"Sorry, I thought we were friends." She looked down and continued reading over her work.

"Yes, Amanda, we are. I'm sorry I was so bitchy. I can really use all the friends I can get right now."

She looked up and smiled.

"Marcus is the father," I confessed.

"Your gay best friend Marcus?"

"Yes...this is going to be really awful to explain to people. We had a one-night thing, okay, before I knew he was gay. Actually before he knew for sure he was gay. But anyway, we talked and we're going to raise the baby together."

"Wow! That's so wonderful! Hey, can I use this in my book?"

"No! You most certainly can not!" I laughed and gave her a playful punch on the arm.

As Amanda and I worked, I felt better, or at least distracted for a while. Rich sent me a text to tell me he had finished his last exam.

i want to celebrate. when you coming back to the hotel?

I texted him back.

almost finished here. be home by 5:30

great c-ya then!

* * * *

I walked into the hotel ready to crash. My feet killed. Pregnancy and Manolos must not go together. I waved to the desk clerk and made my way to my room. As I keyed in, I heard soft music playing. Candlelight illuminated the room, at least a hundred tiny flickering flames, covering every table, counter and ledge. Bouquets of red roses decorated the room and petals were scattered on the floor and bed. Rich stood holding a single rose, looking completely sexy in a rock star version of a suit and tie. He wore his perfected messy-hair-on-purpose and even in my state of complete exhaustion, I wanted to rip all his clothes off.

"What's this for?" I asked.

"To celebrate." He handed me the rose and took my free hand in his. We sat on the bed and I expected him to cover me with kisses and peel my clothing off one piece at a time. Sometimes we made a sexy little game of it. But this time he just kissed me, a simple meeting of the lips, then pulled away smiling.

"Lexi, I love you."

Hearing the words fluttered my heart. He wasn't the first man to tell me he loved me but maybe he was the first to truly mean it. I wanted to kiss him and hold him and tell him I loved him too and live with him happily ever after like the whimsical fairy tale stories I used to gag over.

My body shook, both from excitement and sheer terror. Would his love for me be enough to make it through what I had to tell him? Tears began trickling from my eyes. Maybe the pregnancy hormones were kicking in. Maybe not.

"I've never seen you cry. What's going on?"

"I love you too," I said and a grin covered his entire face. He kissed me again and his body began pressing mine toward the bed but I stopped him. "Wait, we need to talk."

"I want you naked, to feel your skin on mine and make love to you. We can talk later."

"No, Rich, we need to talk now."

He immediately stopped and sat up on the bed, his eyes staring at me with bright red flashing hearts in them. "What is so important that it can't wait?" he asked, not a care in the world.

"Oh my God. I don't know how to say this to you."

"It's okay. Whatever it is ,we'll deal with it. Do you have more crazy relatives or a secret identity?" He laughed at the joke.

My hands felt clammy and trembled even more. "Rich, I'm pregnant."

He stared at me, eyes wide open, mouth trying to form words.

"Oh, wow," he finally got out. "That was not what I was expecting at all."

"I know. I was just as shocked myself."

"When? How? We were careful every time."

My tears started to fall again. This was going to crush him. "The baby isn't yours. I got pregnant before we even met. I swear I never knew."

He said nothing as I burst into tears. He held me tight and I cried as hard as I had seventeen years ago. It had been that long since I'd felt such despair or let myself feel any real sadness.

I calmed down and waited for the question I knew he would ask next.

"Have you told Zak yet?"

"It's not Zak's either."

"Then who?"

"Marcus."

"The one night thing?" Rich asked and I nodded my head. "Does he know?"

I nodded again. "At first I wasn't even sure if I was going through with the pregnancy or not. But I decided to keep the baby and Marcus and I are going to raise it together."

Rich sat quiet and expressionless. It worried me.

"So badly I wanted this baby to be yours. You have to know that." I brought his hand to my lips, kissing his palm. "I love you, and I need you in my life and the baby's life. Please tell me there's hope for us."

"I don't know," he said, then stood up. "I just don't know."

He walked out of the room leaving me to wonder where he was going and what he'd be doing. Would he come back? Would he stand by me? Did he really love me like he said he did?

I lay on the bed a crying mess, preparing myself for a life without Rich. Visions flashed through my head, a montage set to sappy music. It showcased the things he and I did together as a couple, things I now imagined doing alone or not at all. Would I ever walk through the park and not envision the two of us having a picnic and making out like teenagers? Whenever I passed the Empire State Building, I'd always think of the time he sang quietly in my ear as we slow danced on the outside promenade of the eighty-sixth floor. Playing gin rummy at three AM, fighting for the last spoonful of mint chocolate chip ice cream, watching reruns of seventies sitcoms. These were the simple silly pleasures that Rich introduced me to, the things that made up our life together.

My mind wanted to think positively. He'd just declared his love for me. That had to count for something, right? Maybe he could accept this and we'd live happily ever after.

It was past midnight when I woke to the door opening. I must have cried myself right to sleep. Rich sat down next to me on the bed, the smell of liquor and smoke radiating from his clothing. His face stayed emotionless.

"I can't do this. I'm sorry."

"I thought you loved me?"

"I do but I can't deal with all this...stuff."

"Stuff? As in, the kid that's growing inside of me?"

"Um, well, yeah."

"I thought you were different. I thought you wanted to be with me and support me through anything."

"It's not even my kid!"

"It's not about that. It's about us and you being a man and being here for me!"

"What do you want from me?"

I looked at him and as much as I did love him, I knew he didn't love me unconditionally and that's what I needed.

"Nothing."

Rich walked out of the room and the click of the door echoed in my ears. It sounded so final. I cried my eyes out again; nothing else seemed appropriate. My body had suddenly been sucked into a time warp—fifteen again and rejected by the man I loved.

Then I heard the laugh. After all she'd done to me already, Karma still sought her revenge for those poor women in my books. Or maybe there was more. It hurt my head too much to think about it.

Marcus came right away and helped me pack my things, insisting that I let him take care of me. My mental state allowed me no objections but I promised him I'd be out the second my apartment was ready. There'd be no furniture or even a pillow to rest my head on, but at least I'd have my own home back.

Marcus asked what happened with Rich and I told him the whole story, sob for sob. Rich's reaction surprised him. I'd never expected it to go that badly either. We went from being completely in love to broken up in a matter of hours.

* * * *

The next week I saw Amanda before she flew home to Ohio to spend Christmas with her family. She was my only girlfriend and I knew I'd miss her. Instead of sitting and reading through her manuscript, we went out for a late lunch.

"Here, I have something for you," she said, handing me a Tiffany's gift bag.

"What's this for?" I asked and pulled out the gift, a silver baby rattle.

"Your baby needs fabulous stuff, so here's a start!"

Amanda didn't know any of the drama—the abort-or-don't-abort debate, the shared arrangement between Marcus and me or the break up with Rich. It was a simple act of friendship and I truly appreciated it.

"Thank you. But how did you ever pay for this?"

"I used Daddy's credit card and if he asks, I'll tell him it was a gift for my favorite teacher."

I hugged Amanda before she left the restaurant and gave her my cellphone number, insisting she call me over the break. I punched her number into my address book with the ring tone That's What Friends are For.

Chapter 14

My days of mooching off Marcus came to an end when Mr. Gibson called to tell me the apartment was ready a day early. Even though I'd known the move was inevitable, I wasn't quite prepared. My credit card balance steadily climbed toward the heavens while my savings account plummeted toward the zero mark. I had no idea how I would pay the rent.

Having no other money source, I needed to find a job and I hated that. Being a full time novelist was my dream job, so when I'd waltzed away from my marketing career years ago, I'd never imagined falling back on it. Returning to it now felt like accepting a failure of sorts. I wasn't a failure, at my writing anyway, just a failure at life.

I checked out my apartment and it mainly looked the same, but different too. And that made me happy. I couldn't imagine living there the way it was, the memories of seeing Zak with Brenda and the chaos that followed. This new place would be a fresh start.

Every inch of the apartment gleamed with stellar whiteness. Even my posh gray marble countertops were gone, replaced with substandard Formica in the same luminous white as the rest of the place. So much needed to be done to make the place livable. The only problem with an apartment re-decorating project was the lack of funds to do it.

I did need some essentials though, and after a call to my credit card company for a five-thousand-dollar raise on my limit, I set out shopping. Marcus and Kevin came with me and I watched the two of them acting cutesy together. I missed Rich more than ever and found myself stifling tears in the middle of Pottery Barn. In the past when a relationship ended, I was off and looking for a new warm body within forty-eight hours. This time I had no desire.

After purchasing a bed, mattress and couch that fit into my extremely modest budget, we hit the appliance store for the essentials: microwave and coffee pot. Marcus and Kevin looked at chic appliances far out of my affordability, pointing out the ones they liked and could get when they moved in together.

"Hey, what was that I heard?"

"Oh, well..." Kevin stopped and looked at Marcus, unsure if he should go on.

"Lex, we're moving in together," Marcus answered.

"Oh, wow. That's um...great," I replied, trying to sound enthused. I hoped he knew what he was doing. I couldn't talk, though. Before the whole baby thing came about, I'd pondered the idea of asking Rich to move into my apartment with me when it was finished. Marcus and Kevin's relationship was no different.

* * * *

I met with Sheila once again to discuss Marisol Takes Manhattan. This was it. Either it satisfied her or she still hated it, dumping the project and my career in one effortless swoop.

"Lexi, I don't know what has been going on in your personal life, although I have heard rumors. Whatever it is, it's had a tremendous affect on your writing."

Was this a good thing or a bad thing? Her facial expressions were hard to decipher.

"You have finally given me what I always knew you could."

"Are you saying you like the revisions?"

"Yes! Marisol finally has a heart. She can love and be loved and feel earth-wrenching heartbreak. She's a real person."

I thought about my own heart. I'd finally opened mine up to some new forms of love, forms I hadn't thought existed for me.

"Thank you, Sheila."

"Don't thank me yet. I want Marisol in Love in two months."

"I've gotten a good start on it."

"Good!" she said transferring her eyes back to her computer. Did I actually see a semi-smile on her face? As I turned to walk out of the office, she spoke again.

"Oh, I'm sending Marisol Takes Manhattan to line edits, then it will be ready for the printers. I'll need your acknowledgment page ASAP. Have a good holiday."

* * * *

I sat myself down with a cup of tea, pen in hand. Usually my acknowledgement page was easy. I gushed love for Val and Zak, my girlfriends and Marcus. This time I had different people to thank and even though Rich and I were over, I still needed to include him. The book wouldn't exist without him. He'd helped me in so many ways to write it. He'd opened up my heart to real love, if only for a short time, and then of course true heartbreak. He made me experience these new emotions and helped me evolve into a more mature person and writer. I'd always be thankful for that. As much as it hurt that he left me, I couldn't blame him. He had too much life to live to be bogged down with an instant family.

My first thank you is for Rich. This book wouldn't exist without you. The profound impact you had on my life has changed everything. I'm a better person and a better writer because of you. Secondly is Marcus, my life long friend. Thank you babe, and thank you for everything you'll be doing in the future. Amanda, you're a true friend and an inspiration. Sheila, my editor from hell, thank you for pushing me to be the writer I didn't know existed.

* * * *

A cab took me to my parents' house for the mandatory family get together for the holidays. I hadn't seen them since the engagement party and my mother had only called me once to invite me to Christmas Eve dinner. Dread filled me as I anticipated telling them about the baby. I could already hear the ranting and raving my mother would do. In her eyes I was surely going to hell for getting myself knocked up outside the holy bonds of wedlock.

Mom answered the door and seemed to have forgotten our last conversation about Rich. She hugged me and cheerfully asked where he was.

"I'm sure you'll be pleased to know we broke up."

"Oh, dear. I'm sorry."

"Sure you are."

"Alexandra, he may not have been a suitable husband for you but it still pains me to see you heart broken."

Unsure of her sincerity, I muttered a simple, "Thanks".

Mom slipped her favorite Christmas CD into the stereo, humming along with Nat King Cole as he sang I'm Dreaming of a White Christmas. She sashayed and pirouetted into the kitchen, her holly print apron fluttering as she spun, and put on pots of water for potatoes and vegetables. Dad pulled the ham out of the oven and basted it.

I stared at the perfectly shaped Christmas tree in the living room, draped in tacky tinsel just like when we were kids. Mom's treasured Nativity scene lay underneath atop Great Grandma Marshall's hand-stitched tree skirt. I pulled the baby Jesus out of his manger and examined his tiny face.

"Isn't that burning a hole in your hand?" Andy asked sarcastically. "Like a vampire with a cross?"

I wanted to chuck the baby right at his head but instead I laid him gently back in his soft bed.

Abby and Daniel burst into the house shouting an annoyingly chipper, "Merry Christmas, everyone!" After setting down the mounds of presents they'd brought in, she came right over to me with her wedding bible: the fattest binder I'd ever seen, jam-packed with bridal barf, some of it oozing out the sides. She flipped it open to show me a picture of a form-fitted bubblegum pink frock.

"This is the dress you'll be wearing for my wedding!" she squealed.

"I'm in your wedding?"

"Of course! Who else would be my Maid of Honor?"

"Um, perhaps one of your friends that you actually like."

"Lexi! Don't be silly! You're my sister, and I love you!"

"Well, I don't know. Besides, a dress like that will never fit me in April."

"Oh, didn't Mom tell you? The wedding's been pushed back a couple months. I really want to be a June bride! The new date is June twenty-first."

"That's not going to work at all. That's the day I'm..." I stopped myself before the baby news came spilling out

"When you're what?"

"Oh, nothing, never mind. It's fine."

* * * *

We sat at the dining room table devouring Mom's traditional Christmas Eve dinner, complete with honey-glazed ham, mashed potatoes and a green bean casserole. I didn't know how or when to make my announcement. This was probably as good as it was gonna get.

"Okay, before everyone gets busy with the festive holiday crap, I want to tell you all I'm pregnant. It's not a big deal, so go on with what you're doing. I just wanted you to know."

I continued eating my meal, as I was completely starved, but everyone sat staring at me like I'd suddenly grown horns and a third eye.

"No big deal?" Mom asked. "Of course it's a big deal." I couldn't tell if she was happy or appalled. "Where is Richard for this?"

"Mom, I told you we broke up."

"But dear, how could he leave you when he's going to be a father?"

"He's not the father. I got pregnant before we met."

"Oh, thank God!" Mom exclaimed. "You must be back together with Zachary then. Oh, how exciting! We can plan a double wedding! Both my girls can get married together!"

The evil look Abby shot her could have burned the entire house down. Mom must've forgotten her hatred for spotlight-sharing.

"Mom, relax! Zak's not the father either. It's Marcus."

Andy almost choked on his mashed potatoes. "Isn't he gay?" He laughed hysterically next to me.

I punched him in the arm.

"Alexandra, not in your condition!"

"Oh my God! You've got to be fucking kidding me," I mumbled.

"Okay, honey, let me get this straight," Mom said and Andy chuckled again. "You are carrying Marcus's child? I thought you two were just friends?"

"Yes, Mom, we are."

"I'm confused."

"It doesn't take much."

"Lexi, please," Dad said. "Don't make this harder than it is."

"For who, you and Mom? I think I'm the one has to push this kid out and take care of it. How is any of this hard for you?"

"Please explain it to your mother as simply as possible."

"Fine," I said and turned to Mom.

"Mom, I had sex with Marcus. It was a one-time thing. We obviously were not careful. I got pregnant. We're going to raise the baby together. I'm due on June twenty-first."

"June twenty-first?" Abby interjected, finally commenting in the situation. "That's impossible! How are you going to be at my wedding? You have Maid of Honor duties to attend to!"

Could she be any stupider?

"Abby, you know where babies come from and the whole labor and delivery process. If this kid wants to come out the day of your wedding, there is nothing I can do about it. If you want to guarantee that I am there, you have to change the date."

"Why? I'm not changing the date for you!"

"You know, I can't win here!"

Tears ran down my cheeks as I rose from my seat. Damn these pregnancy hormones! I stomped into the kitchen and without even thinking grabbed a bottle of wine and poured a glass. How good would it feel to down the entire bottle right about now? I breathed in deeply then exhaled, and emptied the glass into the sink even though I wanted to smash it on the floor.

Dad came into the kitchen behind me.

"You know, from the moment you were born, I never worried about you. As a kid you ran with the boys and never cried when you fell. You never let anyone take advantage of you and you never let anyone get away with putting you down. You were always the strongest of my kids."

"And?"

"And I know you'll make it through this too, no matter what anyone says to you. When you're determined to do something, there's not a goddamn person on this earth who can stop you. I've always loved that strength."

"Really?"

"Yes. And I love Abby because she's sweet and always wants to include everyone in everything. She likes things to be perfect and when a wrench gets thrown in, well, you know how she can get. Then there's Andy. I love him because...well, I'm still figuring that one out." We both laughed. "But you get my point."

"So what about Mom?"

"She's old fashioned. She doesn't nag you because she wants to make you miserable, it's very much the contrary. She wants you to be happy and in her mind, being married and living the family life is happiness. It's her happiness and she is wrong to push it on you."

"Well, I do want that too. I didn't used to, but I do now."

"You seemed happy with Rich. I'm guessing he didn't take the news well?"

I shook my head. "He's young and I didn't expect him to hang around."

"You know we're here for you."

"Yeah, I do," I said and he took me in his arms. It reminded me of stormy nights as a kid. Dad's hug made the thunder much less frightening. And now as an adult, it still had the same effect.

Mom walked into the kitchen and I wiped away my tears before facing her.

"Alexandra, I didn't mean to upset you."

"I know, Mom."

"Abigail said she will discuss the wedding plans with their coordinator and see if it will be possible to move the wedding up a month."

"She doesn't have to do that."

"Yes, I do Lexi," Abby said as she appeared in the kitchen. "I'm sorry I yelled at you. I want you there and I know you can't control when your baby is born. It was a stupid thing for me to say."

Abby hugged me and the arrow on my family-love-crap-o-meter had reached its max. Any more and I'd surely puke from the over-joyification.

"Okay then," I said, wiping away my last remaining tear. "Is it time for dessert?"

Everyone laughed and Mom brought out her famous cherry cheesecake and apple pie. The rest of the evening went remarkably well. We laughed and talked and it almost felt surreal. I couldn't remember the last time I'd spent a pleasant evening with my family. Even some of Andy's dumb-ass comments made me laugh.

Chapter 15

Once the gifts had been opened, Abby and Daniel left for home and Mom, Dad and Andy retired to their rooms. I sat in the living room alone. The tree remained lit while the rest of the house was dark. I curled up on the couch with a mug of cocoa and watched the snowflakes gracefully float to earth outside the window.

In rare moments of peace and serenity, I thought of Rich and imagined what it would feel like to have him sitting next to me. And that usually led to tears.

Stop this! He's gone, not coming back, ever.

I longed for him and felt ridiculous coming to such a pathetic realization. The fabulous Lexi Marshall had never longed for anything in her life. Occasionally I did have trouble finding my heart's desire, like the rare Manolos a few years back. Tristan had only gotten one pair in the shop and they were sold before he could hide them for me. It had been sad, but I didn't dwell on it. I had moved on to something else.

But this time instead of moving on, I sat there with my eyes closed, imagining Rich's arms around me, his kisses on my forehead, cheeks, lips. Replaying in my mind were the things he used to whisper to me after we made love and the one and only time he told me he loved me.

I pulled out my cellphone and looked at his picture—the only one I had and just couldn't bring myself to delete. The desperate woman inside me wanted to call him and beg him to come back. My thumb hovered above the keypad. I knew I could find the numbers without even looking at them.

Instead I opened my contact list and clicked send when I got to Amanda's name. Never did I think I'd be calling a nineteen-year-old to cry my eyes out to.

"Lexi, merry Christmas! How are you?"

"Miserable!"

"Oh my God! What's wrong?"

"Rich left me."

"On Christmas Eve! That bastard!"

"No, it was weeks ago. I never told you. I couldn't talk about it then."

"What happened?"

I told her the story.

"Lex, if I could, I'd jump on a plane right now and come and hug you."

"I know you would. I feel better after talking to you though. I'll let you go. Have a merry Christmas, okay?"

I went up to my room and opened my suitcase, pulling out a sweatshirt of Rich's that somehow ended up with my things. I put it on and the smell comforted me. His arms were wrapped around me once again and I drifted into the best night's sleep in weeks.

* * * *

Christmas morning, Mom made breakfast complete with bacon, eggs and pancakes. She casually mentioned me going to Christmas service with them.

"Mom, I really don't want to, okay?"

"Alexandra, it's Christmas, the birth of our Lord. Shouldn't you go and celebrate Him?"

The last thing I wanted was to come face to face with Pastor John again, but with the busyness of the holiday he would surely be distracted.

I went and made my mother happy.

The church seemed ready to burst as happy parishioners packed in, dressed in their holiday best. I actually listened to parts of the sermon this time. Pastor John spoke about being thankful for what we had in our lives instead of emphasizing what we didn't. He made sense. Rich was no longer part of my life, no matter how badly I wanted him to be. I needed to focus on the positive things in my life, the few that there were.

After the service I stood in the back of the church while Mom insisted on waiting to wish Pastor John a merry Christmas. They talked, then looked at me, then back at each other and it gave me a weird feeling. Mom walked over with Pastor John right at her heels.

"Alexandra, I invited the Pastor over for supper tomorrow night. I figured the two of you could spend some time together."

"Mom, are you serious?"

"Yes, dear. Of course."

I tried to be as quiet as possible. We were in a house of God after all. "Are you still trying to set us up?"

"If you spend some time together, maybe you'll find you have a lot in common."

"Mom, stop this, okay? I am fine. I don't need you to play matchmaker." I tried to remain as calm as possible.

The Pastor stood right behind her but I was sure she didn't realize it.

"Who's going to take care of you and this baby?" she asked and motioned to my stomach. "You need a husband and your baby needs a father!"

Pastor John's mouth dropped open and his eyes tripled in size. He turned and ran to the front of the church in two seconds flat.

"It has a father—Marcus!"

"It won't be the same. Your baby won't have a proper life."

"Mom, I can do this. Marcus will help me. I can take care of myself and anything else that comes along. Why can't you accept the fact that I'm not you? I'll never be you and I don't want to be."

She walked away speechless.

Dad put his arm around me and walked me outside. "Don't mind what she said."

We drove home in silence. I'd planned to stay for a couple days, but now I wasn't sure I wanted to anymore. But if I went back to the city I'd be completely alone. Marcus had gone with Kevin to his parents' house in Maine for holiday festivities.

As Christmas Day came to an end, I sat watching It's A Wonderful Life on TV. Mom came in and sat next to me on the couch. She held a knitted blanket in her arms.

"This is for you," she said handing it to me.

"It's beautiful. What is it?"

"It's the blanket I wrapped you in when I brought you home from the hospital. I saved it all these years to give to you for your own child."

I didn't know what to say.

"Alexandra, I know you're not like me. I knew that the minute the doctor laid you in my arms."

"Then why do you keep trying over and over again to make me be something I'm not?"

"I don't know. Maybe I'm afraid for you. I want you to have a full and happy life. I'm starting to realize your idea of a full and happy life is not the same as mine."

"Thank you. It means a lot to hear you say that."

"I can't stop worrying about you and hoping you're happy. You'll understand that soon enough with your own son or daughter. I want to help, if you'll let me. I promise to try very hard to take your thoughts and feelings into consideration."

We'd reached a new level. She finally accepted me for me instead of squishing me, kicking and screaming, into her mold.

* * * *

After spending a few days with my family, as nice as it turned out to be, it was time to go home. I had work to do. Sheila had found some editing work and other freelance stuff for me. It wouldn't give me wads of dough to roll around in but it would help diminish my mounting debt.

Plus, if volume two of Marisol's life was ever going to be finished on time, I had better get writing.

Marcus called me barely five minutes after I walked in the door of my apartment.

"So, you're back from la la land?"

"Yeah, it wasn't too bad though, this time anyway."

"Wow. I'm shocked."

"Yeah, so am I. Oh, I wanted to tell you. I have my prenatal appointment next week. Did you, like, want to come or something? I heard some dads like to do that kind of thing."

"Yes! Of course! Is it okay if Kevin comes along?"

"Why?"

"Well, he's going to be a big part of this baby's life too."

"I don't know, Marcus. I'm not sure what this appointment is going to entail and I don't know Kevin all that well yet."

"I understand."

"How was Christmas with his family?" I asked, changing the subject.

"It was fantastic!" He gave me the complete rundown: the food, the gifts, the Christmas sing-a-longs and meeting Kevin's entire extended family. He went on and on about how wonderful Kevin's parents were. They'd known of Kevin's sexuality for years and were open and accepting about it. Marcus still hadn't told his parents yet. They were the blissfully ignorant type who rarely embraced anything outside their comfort zone. He needed to do it soon if he and Kevin were moving in together and he'd better tell them about the baby, preferably some time before it popped out.

* * * *

As New Years Eve neared, I wondered how I would celebrate. For at least the past eight years, New Years Eve involved a fancy dress, lots of champagne and a gorgeous guy to kiss at midnight. The champagne was out and surely I'd look hideous in any dress I tried to squeeze my bloated self into. The gorgeous guy... nope again. It seemed my big celebration would be with Dick Clark this year, if I could even stay awake 'til midnight.

At seven o'clock on December thirty-first I plopped myself on the couch with my down comforter, some snacks and my remote control. Of course the phone rang, forcing me out of my warm, comfy cocoon. It was the one thing I'd failed to bring onto the couch.

"Lex, you almost ready? We'll be leaving in ten minutes to come get you," Marcus's voice boomed through my cellphone.

"What are you talking about? I'm not going anywhere."

"Why not?"

"I have nothing to wear, I can't drink and most importantly, I don't feel like it."

"I've never known you to be a party pooper. Come on! It's just a simple party at Kevin's sister's house. You have to meet Jeanette. She's perfectly sweet and I won't take no for an answer."

"Rrrr," I growled at him, accepting my defeat. "I can't promise I'll look good."

I rushed around to find something decent to wear, settling on a gold wrap sweater with metallic thread woven through it. The impulse bargain purchase looked ultra-trendy in the store but at home, in normal lightning, I understood why it was fifty percent off. But it was New Years Eve and in my opinion, that gives one the right to wear overly shiny metallic clothing. I threw it on with the only pair of pants I owned that were stretchy and still somewhat fit. My hair decided to do a weird frizzing thing so it was forced into a twisted do and secured with a clip. When the buzzer rang I needed only a few swipes of my mascara wand.

Marcus, Kevin and I shared a cab, and during the ride they filled me in on all things Jeanette. She had the two kids and the super successful husband. She spent her days volunteering with the PTA and doing other Park Avenue housewife things.

We walked into an apartment of wall-to-wall people, far more extensive than the simple house party Marcus had lured me with. Marcus and Kevin led me around as they greeted and air kissed a ton of people I'd never laid eyes on before. Finally I got to meet the super sister. Jeanette did seem very nice and right away showed us to the buffet. By that time, starvation consumed my body and the simple act put her at number one on my list of favorite people.

I watched Jeanette work the room, ensuring every guest was comfortable and happy and had a full glass of whatever drink they fancied. She reminded me of a cooler, more sophisticated version of my mother. She came to check on me and sat down for a minute.

"Kevin tells me you are pregnant! How exciting!"

"Yeah, it's definitely something."

"I can't wait to see my brother as a father, well step-father, I guess," she said, a genuine look of happiness on her face.

"So, Kevin and Marcus are pretty serious about one another, huh?" I asked her.

"I've never seen my brother so happy."

"I've never seen Marcus this way either. I worry though, it being his first gay relationship and all."

"The heart knows. I truly believe that. I knew within an hour of meeting Jeff that he was the man I was going to spend my life with."

"Wow, that's really something." Was that how true love worked? Maybe there was something to that love at first sight thing. I'd felt an instant connection with Rich.

"You should come meet him," she said, and we walked over to a group of men standing and laughing. I thought I heard a familiar laugh in the bunch but brushed it off. Jeanette introduced me to Jeff.

"Oh, great to finally meet you," he said and shook my hand. "It's nice to put a face with the oven."

I forced a laugh at his "bun in the oven" joke. He went on to introduce the men in the group, ending with Zak. We glared at each other, exchanging looks of "What the fuck are you doing here?"

"Oh, do you two know each other?" Jeff asked.

"Yeah, you could say that," I answered, still scowling at Zak.

"Wow, what a small world!" Jeff said next. "How do you know each other?"

"Oh, I'll take this one," I said, turning to the rest of the group. "Zak and I dated for over three years. I came home a few months ago and found him screwing one of my best friends on our bed. He then burned down my apartment, destroying every last thing I owned, and killed my dog." I turned back to him. "That about sums it up, right?"

Zak was left speechless and embarrassed, exactly what I'd hoped to accomplish. He excused himself and walked away.

"I guess I'm a bit bitter," I said to the rest of the group and laughed.

Marcus pulled me away.

"What were you doing?"

"Nothing, just talking. I'm really starting to have a fun time!"

"Please stay away from Zak."

"Hey, I was taken over to him."

"I don't want you to start any trouble."

"Me? Start trouble?"

Marcus stuck by me like a watchdog, either protecting me or making sure I didn't make a scene and embarrass him. He introduced me to his new friends in his new gay circle. Periodically I'd glance around to check on Zak and see what he was doing and who with. It seemed he was alone. Definitely no Brenda and I didn't notice a replacement bimbo on his arm either.

Marcus walked away when Kevin needed to talk to him. I felt a hand on my arm and as I turned, saw it was Zak's. He must have waited until my guard left his post to make his move.

"We need to talk."

"I don't need to do anything with you," I said, jerking my arm away.

"Lex, please."

Visions of me going Kill Bill on his ass brought a smile to my face but ultimately my curiosity won out.

"Fine," I said, and we walked to a quieter spot and sat down.

"Are you pregnant?" he asked right away.

"How is it any of your concern if I am?"

"Who's the father?"

"That is most certainly none of your damn business."

"It's Marcus, isn't it?"

"Yeah, and?"

He laughed. "How the hell'd you end up in his bed?"

"He comforted me when I needed it most because he's a real man who knows how to take care of the people he loves. We're going to raise this baby together and Kevin's going to be part of our family too."

Zak laughed again, harder this time. "A real man? I see Marcus finally came out of the closet. I always knew that guy wanted a dick in his mouth!"

"You're a real asshole, you know that?" I stood up.

"Don't leave," he said as his face went serious. "I haven't said what I wanted to yet."

"What?" I asked impatiently.

"I'm sorry."

"For what?"

"For Brenda."

Looking into his eyes, I sensed a shred of sincerity. I sat back down next to him.

"We've been over for a while now and I've had time to think. I did a shitty thing to you. I guess I was bored in our relationship and with my life in general. It wasn't about the sex. I don't think it was about you at all. But instead of talking to you I went out and screwed somebody else."

"I can't believe you're owning up to your mistake."

"Yeah, I am and I really regret that I hurt you."

I'd have expected an alien invasion before hearing those words come from Zak's mouth.

"We could have ended the relationship in a better way," I said, "but it did need to end. I'm much better off now."

"Good. I hope you're happy with your baby. I can't believe you're pregnant though! Can you even imagine yourself as a mother?"

"Not yet but I hope to."

Zak and I went our separate ways and back to our friends at the party. I felt good. The relationship had finally been given the closure it needed. I enjoyed the party and laughed with Marcus and Kevin and felt better than I had in a long time.

As midnight approached, the countdown began and I thought of all the new things that awaited me. My life would never be the same again. The numbers decreased three, two, one and everyone screamed "Happy New Year!" Couples around me kissed and I thought of Rich, wondering if his lips were on someone else's at that very moment. I felt a pull on my arm. Zak stood there and before I could say anything, he kissed me.

Chapter 16

Zak's kiss warmed my body and took me to a comforting place that I easily slid into. He may not have been the man I dreamed of kissing at midnight, but he was there and it was exactly what I needed. He led me into a bedroom and closed the door behind us. We kissed as his hands wandered up my sweater then tugged at my pants. I instinctively did the same to his as we fell onto a bed covered in coats.

The moment swept me away and it only felt natural to make love with him. The motions were incredibly familiar and for a second they sucked me into a comfy world of nostalgia where I was held and caressed and didn't care whose hands were doing the caressing. But then Rich's face burst into my brain and I remembered it was Zak's hands on my breasts and Zak's dick inside me. Though he was no longer a part of my life, it still felt like I was cheating on Rich. My heart hadn't let go of him yet.

"My sexy Lexi, you're so fuckin' hot!" Zak said as his tongue slimed my plump breasts, the pregnancy making them much bigger than the last time he felt them. "Get on top and ride me, baby."

Zak's dirty talk repulsed me and I couldn't go on a second longer. We rolled over and I straddled him, then climbed off.

"What are you doing?" he asked as I pulled my underwear back on.

"I'm going home."

"Why? Is this some sort of payback?"

"No, it's not. I don't love you. I don't want to be with you and having sex with you isn't doing either of us any good."

I left him lying on the bed with his dick still hard, a feeling of complete freedom washing over me and it had nothing to do with payback. I hugged Marcus and Kevin, wishing them both a Happy New Year and said my goodbyes to Jeanette and Jeff. My bed was calling and I couldn't wait for the night of sleep that awaited me.

A few days later, I retrieved my mail and came across an envelope addressed to me in Zak's handwriting.

Lexi,

You know I'm not good at apologies, but here goes anyway. I'm sorry for what happened at the party. I know I fucked up what we had and for a minute I wanted it back. I know that's not what you want and it's not what I deserve. I hope we can one day be friends.

Zak

PS- I hope this can replace part of what I destroyed. I'm sure half of this amount was shoes alone. Ha Ha.

Enclosed was a check for fifteen thousand dollars.

* * * *

Marcus met me outside my doctor's office for the prenatal appointment. He'd taken the whole day off and devoted it to me. After the doctor we'd do lunch. Kevin would meet us and then we'd go shopping. I was in desperate need of clothing, having already stretched out every last article I owned. The check from Zak gave me the perfect excuse to splurge on some new things, after paying some bills, of course.

Marcus and I sat together in the waiting room and he nudged my arm as a gigantically pregnant woman struggled to get out of her chair.

"That's gonna be you!" he whispered, looking completely giddy.

I'd never realized how much Marcus wanted a family.

A nurse called out my name and the two of us trekked into the exam room. She weighed me and slid the marker seven notches past my last weight measurement.

"Oh my God! Seven pounds in a month!"

"That's normal weight gain for this part of the pregnancy," the nurse said. "A pound a week is standard, but seven is fine too."

I made a mental note to eat more veggies and less Doritos.

When the doctor came in, she took a tape measure to my stomach and informed us she was measuring my uterus. My belly now looked like a hard bump, rather than the muffin top that refused to go away even after doing five-hundred crunches every day for a month. The doctor then held the monitor to my stomach to find the baby's heart beat. Marcus almost burst into tears.

"There really is a baby in there!" he said, squeezing my hand. Hearing it this time had a much different impact on me. I even got a bit misty-eyed.

"So, before you leave, do you have any questions?"

"Actually, I do. I guess it's more of a concern than anything else." I paused before continuing. "Well, I didn't find out I was pregnant until I was ten weeks along. During those first ten weeks I drank alcohol, rather a lot, and also, um, smoked some marijuana."

"Lexi!" Marcus gasped.

"It was one time when I was staying at my parents' house. My mother kept nagging me to find a husband, Abby announced her engagement and after downing a bottle of wine I found the courage to call Zak and confront him. After that I was feeling pretty low and well, getting high sounded like a fine idea."

"Okay, okay, nuff said," Marcus replied.

"Well," the doctor said with wide eyes. She blinked a few times then continued, "I'm assuming this alcohol and drug use has stopped?"

"Oh yes! Not one sip of anything alcoholic since you told me I was pregnant. And the weed thing, I normally don't do that. Really, it was a one time thing, complete desperation. I swear, never again." I held up my right hand like I was giving the Girl Scouts oath. She needed to know I cared about my baby.

"Okay. While alcohol and drugs during pregnancy can be detrimental to an unborn baby, chances are he or she is fine. We'll be able to tell more once we do the next ultrasound."

On our way out of the office we made an appointment for the ultrasound. Until then, I'd be left to wonder if my self-indulgence had harmed my growing fetus. I knew Marcus wanted to lecture me more but he also understood why I had done it. He knew the depth of my depression during that time and instead focused on the good parts of the ultrasound. He couldn't wait to actually see the baby and find out if we'd be parents of a boy or girl. That part actually excited me a little bit too.

We met Kevin at the restaurant for lunch. We ordered and Marcus gave Kevin a play by play of the entire doctor appointment. As I watched Kevin's eyes get teary too, I decided I would let him have more of a part in this pregnancy.

"Kevin and I have some great news!"

"Yeah, what?"

"We found an apartment! It's got natural wood work, hardwood floors, eat in kitchen, dining room, fireplace..."

"Bay windows with a view of the park." Kevin butted in. "Walking distance to great shops and restaurants..."

"And three bedrooms," Marcus added next.

"Oh, wow," I said. "Why so many?"

"Well, Lex, one for Kevin and I, one for the baby...and one for you."

My brow furled. "Are we having slumber parties or something?"

"We both want you to move in with us. We can be a family. There's no point in us living in separate places. And in all honesty, I don't think I could bear an every-other-weekend thing with the baby. I want to tuck him or her into bed every night."

I hadn't given even one thought to a visitation schedule.

He continued, "You can have all the freedom you need and you can even have the big bedroom."

I didn't know what to say. Living alone did suck and having the twenty-four-hour help when the baby came would be nice too. Marcus then threw out the money saving aspect. In my current economic status I could barely buy Ramen noodles and tap water on my tiny budget after paying rent.

But I hadn't lived as part of a family in years. People always around, no quiet time alone, someone always stealing the last of the Oreos. Could I go back to that?

"I don't know. What about privacy? For me and for you. You're still in the honeymoon phase of your relationship. You won't want me around to interrupt your romantic moments."

"We've already discussed this. Kevin and I are comfortable enough in our relationship to know neither of us are going anywhere. We can make time for romance. We don't need to break out the strawberries and champagne every night of the week or make love on the living room rug to show our feelings for one another."

I giggled at the mental picture of Marcus and Kevin in the middle of a romance novel sex scene, complete with burning loins and unfulfilled desires.

"This baby is already a part of our lives," Marcus continued. "Of course it means big changes for you, but it means big changes for us too. We want to make sure you know you're not alone and you don't have to do it on your own. Living together will make it easier on everyone."

"Okay, but what if down the road I want to bring someone home, you know, like a man or something?"

"As long as we have time to plan, Kevin and I can take the baby out of the house for the night. We can get completely out of your way."

"I don't know. I don't want us to hate each other because we're forced into tight corners."

"Lexi, trust us, this apartment is far from tight corners!" Kevin laughed.

"We'll be a family and being a family does mean we'll argue once in a while," Marcus added next. "I love you enough to work things out and make the best life possible for all of us. Come on! You know this will be perfect!"

"Okay, okay! You had me at bay windows and fireplace! Let's do this. When do we move in?"

* * * *

I explained the situation to my landlord Mr. Gibson and he understood. He was ecstatic, actually. He had a waiting list for the building so filling the spot wouldn't be a problem. And he could fill that spot with a tenant willing to pay a much higher rent.

Marcus hired some movers to empty out my apartment. If this had taken place four months ago, it would have taken a tractor-trailer to haul my stuff. These days my belongings were quite limited.

As I surveyed the apartment—a last look for nostalgia's sake—my eyes glazed. I'd lived there for a good portion of my adult life and recalled many happy memories from that time. Some not so great memories too, but they'd led me to my current life. I now stood with a future ahead of me that I'd never planned for. It seemed kind of exciting, along with terrifying beyond belief. Life would never again be dull.

I breathed deep and let out a content sigh. I set the keys on the counter and closed the door behind me. Marcus stood waiting in the lobby.

"Ready to go?" he asked.

I answered with a definitive "yes" and meant it.

We walked into the new place, boxes everywhere. The movers brought in my things and further covered the shiny hardwood floors. Kevin happily fluttered about the apartment unpacking and organizing.

"You're here!" he exclaimed and hugged me. "This is going to be so great!"

I got to work and picked up a box with my name on it.

"Oh my God! What are you thinking?" Marcus shrieked.

"What?"

"I've been reading up on pregnancy. You shouldn't be lifting anything."

"Marcus, it's a box filled with pillows. I think I can handle it."

"Well, okay, but that's it. We'll carry everything else in."

I checked out my new digs and found my bedroom. Marcus and Kevin had given me the master like they promised, with its whirlpool tub in a private bathroom and a super huge walk-in closet. My eyes panned the rest of the room. The bed and dressers sat in perfect spots. Sunlight shone in from the bay window, complete with bench. I could already envision myself curled up there with a good book, maybe even reading nursery rhymes to the baby. I then remembered the really thick, really expensive cashmere blanket I used to have—perfect for snuggling with on a cold day. It was bright red, not matching one thing in my old apartment. I decided to buy another just like it and decorate my new bedroom around it. A black and white floral comforter would look fantastic with a few red pillows thrown on top for a splash of color.

The spare bedroom, the baby's room, was right outside my door. Its bare white walls and shiny hard wood were nice, but I didn't feel any decorative inspiration when I walked in. Marcus came up behind and hugged me.

"If it's a boy, we can paint this room beige, with a red and black striped border underneath crown molding, giving it almost a Burberry color scheme. If it's a girl, no sissy pink princess crap. I'm thinking soft aqua and lilac. It will be a serene feminine oasis."

I pulled his arms tighter around me. "You really are wonderful, you know that?"

"I do."

"The ultrasound is tomorrow. Are you leaning either way, boy or girl?" I asked.

"As long as it's healthy, I'm happy."

"Oh, cut the bull! Everyone says that but they all secretly want one or the other. I'm rooting for boy."

"Honestly, I can see myself playing ball with a boy and dolls with a girl. I really don't have a preference."

"At least we won't have to wait much longer to find out."

"I know! And then we can start buying stuff!"

* * * *

I invited Kevin to tag along to the ultrasound appointment and he threw both arms around me tight and thanked me. Marcus beamed from ear to ear and his happiness made me happy. This new age family thing could actually work out.

Later at the doctor's office, my name was called and the three of us stood and walked over to the nurse. She led us to the exam room and I climbed up onto the table to wait for the technician to come in.

After brief small talk, I was instructed to pull my shirt up and the ultrasound tech squirted some cold gel onto my stomach. When she pressed the ultrasound wand to it, we immediately heard the whump whump whump of the baby's heartbeat. Marcus squeezed my hand and I saw him squeeze Kevin's as well. The technician moved the wand around and within a few seconds the baby—our baby!—appeared on the screen. The picture was dark and grainy but I could see how much it had grown and changed. Its arms and legs were fully developed and it actually looked like a real baby, not just a blob. We could see its eyes, nose and lips and it even appeared to smile at us. I looked to Marcus and watched a tear roll down his cheek.

The tech took her measurements and noted them in the computer.

"Is everything okay?" I asked, concerned that my moment of marijuana weakness had affected my baby, stunting its growth, or worse, causing it to grow an extra appendage.

"Yes. He or she is right on schedule! Everything looks perfect!"

Marcus and I both let out a sigh of relief.

"Can we know the sex?" he asked excitedly.

"Let's see," she said and moved the wand around. "Hmmm, well, it appears he or she has curled up in a ball and I can't get a look at the genitalia. The baby is being quite modest and does not want us to take a peek."

"Modesty...we know that trait didn't come from you, Lexi!" Marcus laughed.

"Gee, thanks!" I said with a laugh of my own.

"So, what does this mean?" Kevin asked the technician.

"Stock up on yellow and green clothing," the tech answered. "Unless there's a problem, you won't have another ultrasound and the sex of the baby will be a surprise on delivery day!"

We left with pics in our hands of our little one. Marcus demanded we head straight to the chicest baby boutique in the city. Until that day, I hadn't given so much as a sly glance at a crib or baby blanket. Marcus seemed to know the store like the back of his hand and gave a warm "Hello" to the girls at the front counter. He took me right over to the Ferrari of all cribs in a gorgeous mahogany wood, reached for a butter yellow blanket from a shelf nearby, and hung it over the rail of the crib.

"Look, it's neutral and still stylish." He grabbed some sheets and things in varying shades of yellow and put them together. "I'm seeing the walls done in stripes, a few shades of pale yellow, just a tint or two off. Very subtle. The crown molding can match the crib and that armoire over there is a must-have."

Marcus dashed off to check out its drawers, then something else caught his eye. Kevin followed behind and I watched them ooh and aah over miscellaneous baby items. I sat down in a comfy glider rocker that matched the crib. Its cushy memory foam pads formed to my pregnant body as I rocked. For the first time since finding out I was pregnant, I imagined myself holding my baby in my arms and cuddling it. Marcus could paint the room pink and orange hound's-tooth if he wanted and buy every ostentatious baby gadget made, but I had to have that rocker.

Chapter 17

I paid for my rocking chair and a burly delivery man brought it by the next afternoon. He set it up in the bare baby room right near the window. I sat in it and gazed outside. Snow blanketed the earth while gusty winds picked up individual flakes and threw them onto rosy-cheeked faces. New Yorkers rushed past, pulling their scarves tight to their necks and their hats over their red ears and I felt relieved that junior's arrival would be after the cold disappeared for the season. The warmth of summer would be upon us and I was certainly glad I wouldn't have to worry about keeping him warm when he was so little.

Worry. Not an affliction I experienced often. I rarely worried about a thing in my life: not about myself, the future, the consequences. But now would I be filled with worry every minute of every day? Would I constantly be fearful of something bad happening to my baby or me? What would he do without me? What if something happened to him? Would I be able to survive without him?

* * * *

I finished the first draft of Marisol in Love and made an appointment with Sheila to drop it off. Then I'd wait for either her approval or more likely, disapproval and editing notes. I knocked on her door and she grumbled from behind it. It somewhat sounded like "come in" but most times I found her caveman-esque dialect hard to decipher.

"Oh, it's only you."

"Okay, nice to see you too, Sheila," I said and set my disc on her desk.

"That better be good. I don't have time to screw around like we did with the last one," she said without looking up at me, tapping away at her keyboard.

"Okay, enjoy," I said with my famed sarcastic tone and rolled my eyes. Obviously the she-devil had returned.

"Fuck!" then a thump. Sheila's forehead lay pressed to the desk.

I thought of just walking away but for some odd reason I didn't. "Um, are you okay?" I asked.

"I'm fine," she snarled.

"Okay." I started to walk out but again felt the need to turn back around. "Do you want to go get some coffee or lunch or something?" My concern for Sheila's mental health surprised even me.

"Are you serious? Don't answer. No. I don't have time for that crap."

"You need to take a break. Come on, let's go. I insist."

She looked up at me. "You are pregnant, aren't you? You've become motherly all of a sudden."

"Yeah, and I'm hormonal too, so don't piss me off. Get your coat. Now."

We walked silently to the restaurant. After being seated, Sheila ordered a glass of red wine and I asked for tea to warm myself up. Once our lunch orders were placed and Sheila'd drank half her wine, she started to speak.

"I was married once, you know. Even pregnant."

Our relationship to date hadn't gone much past the initial introductions and silent fuck yous. I wasn't quite sure how to react to the first piece of personal information she'd ever shared with me.

"But you know how it goes," she continued, "…you lose the baby and sometimes the husband too."

"Oh, I'm sorry."

"Don't be. It was for the best. I needed that time for my career anyway. What about you? Can you handle motherhood and a career?"

"I'm sure as hell gonna try."

"And the father? Is he a good man?"

"Yep, the best. His boyfriend is great too."

She gave me the look—the same amused but confused look everyone got when I spit that line at them.

"Yes, my baby's father is gay," I said with a laugh.

Sheila let out a quiet cackle and downed the rest of her wine, ordering another.

"How in the world did you have sex with a gay man?"

Hearing the question caused an intense hilarity to come over me and I tried to stifle my laughter but the harder I pressed my lips together the worse it became.

"This is a really good story," I got out though giggling bursts. "I was devastated after finding my live-in boyfriend in bed with another woman, one of my best friends mind you, and in desperation came on to my life-long best friend who I thought had this unwavering flame for me. Turns out he just slept with me to find out if he was gay or not!" I laughed even harder. People in the restaurant were staring but I continued with my laughing and the story. "So now he's in his first gay relationship, happy as can be, talking commitment ceremony and I'm having his kid! The new love of my life dumped me because he couldn't handle me being pregnant with another man's child. It doesn't get much more fucked up than that."

"Yeah, you're right!" Sheila joined me in laughing.

"I should be starting this kid with therapy in utero!"

We calmed down and wiped our tears with our linen napkins. Our plates of piping hot food were set down in front of us and I dug right in. I couldn't go long without putting something in my stomach. My arms and hands felt a bit shaky, especially after expending all that energy to laugh like we did.

"I give you a lot of credit," Sheila said. "You most definitely have some balls if you're taking this on and pretty much all on your own."

"I'm not on my own. Marcus has been my best friend since babyhood. He's seen me at my worst and I know he'll never leave me. We're all living together and we'll raise the baby together."

"Hmm, quite an interesting living arrangement. But what about your love life? Don't tell me you're giving up on the happily ever after shit?"

"I don't know anymore. I thought I had it but he couldn't give me unconditional love like I needed. Do you know any man who will want a relationship with a woman, her kid, the kid's gay father and gay dad number two? That's the package deal I come with now."

"You are worlds away from the bratty, self-centered woman I met four months ago."

"That's a compliment, right?"

"Yes, it is."

Pleased with the new friend-ish type relationship we had created, we walked back to the office.

"Oh, before I forget," she started, "Marisol Takes Manhattan should be on shelves the first week of April. I arranged a book signing for you the beginning of May."

"A book signing? Do I really need to do that?"

"Yes! You need to get out there and meet your readers. Don't tell me you've never done one before!"

"Val always told me I didn't need it."

"Well, that is exactly why she's now working two floors down."

My eyes went wide with the bluntness of Val's demotion.

"We'll do a photo shoot and print some posters to advertise," Sheila continued. "I'll call you with the details once the photographer is booked."

I'd always thought doing a book signing would be cool but the way Val described it, it was a waste of a day. She said no one went to those kinds of things and sitting there for only a few readers wasn't worth it. Now that I was finally doing one, I was excited and looked forward to it. Ironically though, I'd waited years to do a book signing and photo shoot and I would be huge and pregnant for it.

I left Sheila's office and heard my name being screamed. Amanda, obviously back from Ohio, ran down the hall and hugged me.

"Oh my God! Look at you!" she exclaimed. "Look at your little baby belly!"

"Yeah, it's out there and none of my clothes fit anymore!"

"Well, you know what that means! It's time to shop!"

After doing some work, we hit one of the coolest maternity stores, Mum's the Word. I picked out a few necessities, browsing through the selection of over-the-belly pants.

"I absolutely cannot see myself wearing these!" I said to Amanda. "They're like huge granny panties." A large pregnant woman stood nearby, meeting eyes with mine and smiled.

"Yeah, they're ugly," the mom-to-be said, "but they're the only ones that stay on! I bought a ton of the cute low rise under belly pants and by the time I made it to seven months they barely stayed up."

"Oh? Wow. Thanks for the tip."

She waddled away and I realized I'd been given my first bit of advice from a fellow mom. It was weird.

After paying for my things, Amanda and I browsed a boutique for her. I sat sulking as she came out of the dressing room time after time wearing something utterly cute and trendy.

What a skinny little bitch. I would have looked way better in that skirt than she did. It was mean to think that, but my pregnancy and temporary fatness gave me license to insult any cute, slender girl I pleased. We preggos had to make ourselves feel better somehow.

Amanda chose a few things to buy, then picked up a pink lacy baby doll top and matching thong.

"What do you think? Should I get it?"

"Why? Do you need it?"

"I slept with three different guys while I was home on break. I could have definitely used something sexy to wear."

"Amanda, are you serious? Why did you do that? Weren't you a virgin?"

"No, I did it once in high school but not since. I'm a different person now. I went home and showed all those losers I went to high school with how much I've changed and how cool and sexy I am now."

"So...you had sex with losers to show them how un-loser you are now?"

"Yep."

"That doesn't make sense."

"Well, I was just doing what you told me."

"Whoa! I never told you to go have sex with losers."

"You taught me to stand up for myself and not let other people intimidate me or look down on me. I showed them I'm not the same shy girl I was back then. I'm mature and independent and fabulous."

"Okay. That's fine and dandy. Just be careful. You don't want to end up like me."

"Why? You're amazing! You're everything I strive to be."

"No, I mean pregnant!"

* * * *

The cold wind whipped my hair around as I walked home. I pulled my scarf over my head trying to avoid a hair disaster. It could turn into a bird's nest in two-point-five seconds if the wind swirled it just right. Curls and snarls were a lethal combination.

A hearty gust blew my scarf, stopping me dead in my tracks. As I reached to fix it I looked up, noticing the sign on the theater in front of me. The marquee read "Eternal—One Night Only—This Friday".

Rich's band was playing a show.

Seeing the band's name like that sent all kinds of emotions through me. I felt tingly and happy for him. After the charity show a few months back, he'd told me he missed playing more than he thought. I encouraged him to keep at it but he rattled off a long list of excuses.

The next few days, I thought a lot about the Eternal show and how much I wanted to go. It would be no big deal. Rich would never see me, especially if I stood in the back. Amanda could tag along with me. I called her up and told her it would be great research for her book. She agreed even though "it really wasn't her scene." Who knew this once timid Ohio transplant, who'd never walked into a bar in her life before meeting me, now had her own scene.

After working on Friday, we went to Happy Hour, then grabbed a quick dinner. The show started at nine and I wanted to be there on time. I didn't want to miss a single second of Rich.

The crowd consisted of mainly rocker types. Amanda and I looked completely out of place waiting in line with our Prada bags and Jimmy Choos. After buying our tickets and finding our way inside through hoards of twenty-somethings dressed head to toe in black, I noticed a table selling t-shirts and CDs. Rich never told me the band had recorded their music. I had to have one.

While I paid, Amanda struck up a conversation with a guy, pierced lip and bright blue hair spiking out in all directions. Tattoos of half-naked women decorated both arms.

"Amanda, let's go inside, okay?"

"Hey babe, give me your number," the guy said.

Amanda fished around in her purse for a pen but I dragged her away.

"Lexi, he is so hot!"

"No, stay away from guys like that!"

"Hey, you dated a guy in a band!"

"Yes, but mine was normal and not high as a kite."

We found a spot to stand with a perfect view of the stage. Rich walked out and my heart melted. I felt like a teenager totally crushing on a rock star. He began to play and his penetrating voice vibrated through my body. Every song felt like a dream, a surreal moment. But I knew I'd wake in the morning and remember them completely and for the rest of my life, not only for those first few seconds when you limbo between sleep and awake.

As one song ended, Rich announced a new song, written a month earlier. This was their first time playing it to an audience. As the words floated out of his mouth, I knew they were about me. He was singing right to me.

How could I give up,
On something barely started.
It was perfect and precious,
My world finally made sense.
I knew where my place was,
It was right beside you.
The circumstances changed us,
There was nothing I could do.
No matter how much I try,
No matter how much I want it,
Doesn't matter what's in my heart,
Even if it's killing me inside,
I can't be the man you need,
Even if I love you,
Endlessly.
I want to be a better man,
I wish I could be something fake.
To give you what you want,
And make everything okay.
It would all be a lie.
I can't go on that way.
It isn't fair to either of us.
I can't do that to you.
No matter how much I try,
No matter how much I want it,
Doesn't matter what's in my heart,
Even if it's killing me inside,
I can't be the man you need,
Even if I love you,
Endlessly.

Hot tears cascaded down my cheeks as I thought of Rich and us and what we had that was now gone forever. Even above the deep base guitar chords I heard a familiar cackle. Again Karma laughed at me in my time of misery. Why was she there? Why was she doing this to me? Or was I doing this to myself?

Amanda put a hand to my shoulder. "Are you okay?"

I looked at her with my tear-streaked face and could only shake my head.

"Let's get out of here."

The cold air blasted us as we pushed our way through the filthy doors. Tears poured down my cheeks the entire cab ride home as Rich's words to me replayed over and over.

Chapter 18

Amanda followed me up to the apartment. When we walked in, Marcus and Kevin sat snuggled up on the couch watching a movie, totally in old married couple mode.

"Lex, what's wrong? What happened?" Marcus asked me as I walked past in a daze. Ignoring his questions, I went straight to my room to draw a warm bath. I threw in some of my favorite bath oil beads and asked Amanda to make me a cup of tea. A nice bottle of wine would have been the perfect way to drown my sorrows but for obvious reasons that wouldn't be possible. Green tea with honey and lemon would have to do.

I put the Eternal CD in my shower stereo and laid with my head back, a warm washcloth over my face. Amanda came in and I instructed her to set the tea on the floor next to the bathtub.

As I soaked, breathing in the scent of Jasmine, I lost myself in Rich's music and lyrics. Getting over him took so much effort and so far I'd been doing a pretty good job of it. Now he was smack in my face again and it was my own fault. I never should have gone to the concert and certainly shouldn't have bought the CD. The best thing would have been to shut it off, but I couldn't. I couldn't shut off Rich's voice. It comforted me, yet made me miserable at the same time.

The water turned a frigid temperature. Decision time: drain and start again or get out. I chose the latter and dressed in my most favorite fuzzy pajamas. It's amazing what pregnancy will do to you. I'd traded silky nighties and sleeping in the nude for flannel and fleece.

Upon taking my empty teacup to the kitchen, I found Amanda in the living room curled up on the chair asleep. Marcus and Kevin were still watching TV.

"Hey, what's she still doing here?"

"She didn't want to leave until she knew you were okay. She must have drifted off."

Poor kid. The last thing she needed was an express train into my mess of a life. I covered her up with a blanket and turned to go back to my room. My pillow beckoned for me.

"Lex, she told us what happened," Marcus said.

I stopped walking but kept my back to him. I didn't want him to see my tears fall.

"I don't want to talk about it, okay?" I said in my most brave voice.

"Why did you go there? You should have known better."

"Marcus, what did I just say?"

"Okay, okay! But you know I'm right."

I walked off and tucked myself into bed. I tried to sleep but kept thinking about Rich. Was he off screwing some groupie right at that moment? There were tons of half-naked girls at the show. Band fuckers. I could see the line out his door, all of them waiting their turn to jump on and ride him.

The thoughts swimming through my brain seemed worse than stabs with a butter knife. I picked up the phone and dialed his cell number. As it rang through to the other end, I panicked that he would notice the caller ID and deem me one of those crazed lunatic ex-girlfriends who calls at one in the morning. My hand started toward the phone's cradle, realizing the call was made from the apartment phone and not my cell. He wouldn't recognize the number.

He picked up after only a couple rings and uttered a confused "Hello?"

That's all I needed, so I hung up. He couldn't answer his phone that quickly if some slut was gyrating her nasty body on his. I slept peacefully knowing Rich was alone in his bed just like I was.

* * * *

The sun radiated into my room as I peeked an eye open to check the time. The January day was barely past seven but I hopped out of bed anyway. Amanda still slept on the living room chair. No sign of Marcus or Kevin. I turned on the coffee pot and tried my hand at something domestic. How hard could it be to make breakfast?

I perused the pantry in search of breakfast fare and found a box of pancake mix and a bottle of syrup. The fridge contained the ingredients for ham and cheese omelets. I began whipping up the pancake mix, following the directions on the box, and after warming the skillet, I poured the thick batter on. While it sizzled I grabbed a mixing bowl and cracked a few eggs into it. Noticing that there were pieces of eggshell floating in the bowl, I fished for them with my finger but the damn things kept getting away from me.

The smell of burnt something-or-other rose to my nose and as I turned toward the stove I knocked the bowl of eggs onto the floor, splattering them on my pajamas and feet. The smoke detector screeched out its annoying beep as my fluffy pancakes turned into unidentifiable black discs.

Marcus and Kevin came running and Amanda jumped out of her chair. I stood there crying, eggs dripping from my hands. As they hurried around me cleaning up the mess and airing out the kitchen, I shuffled to the table, sat down and cried.

"I'm going to be a terrible mother," I sobbed.

"Lexi, no! You'll be fantastic!" Amanda said, trying to console me.

"I can't even make pancakes or eggs. Kids like those kinds of things."

"You'll learn," Marcus said next. "Hell, I can't cook either! That's what I have Kevin for."

Kevin gave him look of faux astonishment, then smiled. "Lexi, we'll do this together. What you're not good at someone else will pitch in and do. I'm sure there's tons you can teach the little guy that we can't."

"Like what? I'm friggin' useless."

"Um, well..." Kevin hesitated.

"You make a mean martini!" Marcus chimed but his attempt at humor failed miserably. They looked to each other, searching for some other worthwhile attribute to console me with.

"Shopping!" Amanda added. "If it's a girl you can show her all the best places, just like you showed me! She'll be the best dressed kid at playgroup!"

"Is that all I'm good at...drinking and shopping?"

"Of course not," Marcus said. "You will teach this baby your art, your writing, and no one on earth will be able to read him a story and bring it to life like you will. He's going to love curling up in that rocker of yours. You'll give him something that will stay with him the rest of his life."

"Really?"

"Yes! And who else can teach him better than you not to take shit from anyone? He or she is going to be the luckiest kid on the planet to have a mom like you."

I was the lucky one. No way in hell I'd survive this parenting thing without my adoring support group.

* * * *

Sheila finally called about the photo shoot, scheduled for the next week, and within two seconds of hanging up I went to the mirror to examine myself. Skin was okay but could definitely use a facial. Eyebrows needed a wax. The hair desperately needed a cut and color touch up.

I debated what to do, having had no luck with either of the last two salons I tried. No matter how many fancy places I went to or how many snobby stylists I let touch my precious locks, no one could do it quite like Brenda. Either pregnancy hormones put you in a forgiving mood or despair had begun to set in. I called and took her first available appointment.

I walked into the salon a few days later and the staff greeted me warmly. By the sly glances and smirks they gave each other, I could tell they knew the nitty gritty of what happened with Brenda and me.

The shampoo girl took me in back and scrubbed my head. I always loved that portion of the whole hair experience. Her fingers moved in circles, big ones, then small ones, massaging every square inch of scalp as the scent of super expensive salon shampoo wafted into my nostrils. They must send those girls to a special school or something. It never felt that good when I washed my own hair.

I took a seat and browsed the latest issue of Vogue while waiting for Brenda.

"Lex, I'm ready for you." Her hair was a more normal shade of brown with subtle red high lights and a simple bob haircut. It was the least ostentatious I'd ever seen Brenda look. Even her clothes were toned down and she seemed to have less metal poking through her skin. I'd gotten so used to the sparkling protrusions that her face looked bare without them. The only piercing I noticed was the one in her nose, a tiny diamond stud having replaced the silver hoop. My mind couldn't help but wonder if she'd kept the ones underneath her clothing.

I followed Brenda to her station in silence and sat down. Unsure where to start, I surprised myself by still being mad at her. I thought I'd let it go. But seeing her in the flesh brought the memories of that day and a vision of her naked body in front of my face and I was much madder than I thought.

"I almost fell over when I saw you on my schedule for today."

"Yeah, I'm surprised myself that I'm here. I'm still really pissed at you."

"Then why are you here?"

"Because I need my hair done for a photo shoot. You're the only one who can do it the way I like."

"What makes you think I won't screw it up on purpose?"

"I know you and I know you won't do that to me."

She paused for a minute, our eyes meeting in the mirror. "You're right. I screwed up your life enough," she said and combed through my wet hair.

"So is this an admission of guilt?"

"I suppose."

"Are you sorry?"

"Sorry I wrecked our friendship, yes. Sorry I broke up your relationship, yes. Sorry I fell in love..." She paused for a second. "No."

"You fell in love with Zak?"

Brenda put down her comb and pulled a chair up next to me. "I did. I don't know how, but I did. I asked myself a million times how I could be so stupid to fall in love with someone like him."

"He's such an asshole," I said. "I didn't realize it when we were together but I do now. He can be good at hiding it."

"Oh, I knew it the whole time and maybe that's what attracted me to him. But how could I fall in love with someone who crapped on his girlfriend and fucked someone else behind her back? He broke my heart even as much as I tried not to let him get to me."

"What happened?"

"Well, when he had nowhere to go, he stayed with me and Rachel a few days. I mentioned us getting a place of our own, since you guys were over. He told me we had no future. I was just something he needed as a distraction. It was fun while it lasted, blah blah blah, we both needed to move on. I fell completely head over heels for him and I couldn't fathom the idea that he didn't love me too."

I could relate to how Brenda felt, the pain of loving someone who wasn't able to love you back the way you needed. That wound was still fresh in my heart. I almost pitied her.

"Even after the way he treated you, you're not sorry you fell in love with him?" I asked.

"No. He at least showed me I was normal and capable of falling in love. Now I'll be smarter about who I fall in love with."

"Good. Zak and I made peace with our relationship. I saw him on New Year's Eve and we talked. He apologized for everything. I can see he's slightly less of an asshole than he used to be."

She got up and continued with my hair. "Aren't you going to ask?"

"What?"

"How I can live with myself for being the back-stabbing slut who fucked her friend's boyfriend?"

"Well, since you brought it up."

"I don't know. I've beat myself up looking for an answer. The only decent one I can come up with is that you were too busy to give Zak what he needed. I was betraying you but at the time, he looked so desperate and I thought I had no choice but to help him. Can love really make you that stupid?"

"True love can make you do things you never thought you would."

"My love for Zak definitely wasn't the true kind but it still made me do things I shouldn't have. It made me a selfish bitch and the worst kind of friend."

"I thought you hated everything about him."

"I did but in my fucked up world I guess hate is equivalent to love."

I sat quiet, not sure what to say. Did anything else need to be said? Brenda continued on with her snipping in silence as I contemplated my feelings. Things would never be the same between us but I no longer saw her as the slut who'd wrecked my life. She'd changed my life forever and mostly it was for the better. How could I hate her?

"So, is it true?" she asked as she finished up my hair.

I knew exactly what she was referring to. "Yes. And yes to the next question—it is Marcus's."

"I hear he's gay now."

"Yep and completely and utterly happy. He's in love."

"I guess it's safe to say he's over you?"

"That would be a yes. We're still close and we're going to raise this baby together. Kevin will be a part of it too. We'll be one weird, eclectic family."

"If you're happy, then I'm happy for you."

"Yeah, I think we will be."

"And are you seeing anyone? In all the years I've known you, I've never seen you single."

"I dated someone for a while but he couldn't handle my being pregnant with another man's child."

"Who needs the bastard?"

"He's young, so part of me knew he wouldn't stick around. The other part was devastated. I thought he loved me enough to handle anything that was thrown at us."

"Who was he?"

"You ever hear of a band called Eternal?"

"Fuck yeah! They're awesome!"

"It was the lead singer. Rich."

"Holy shit! He is so friggin' hot!"

"Yeah, I know. Wait a minute...you've never slept with him, have you?"

"No."

"Thank God! I don't think I could handle you sleeping with two of my ex-boyfriends."

* * * *

After leaving the salon, I stopped for a visit with Tristan, my shoe fetish co-conspirator. He ran up to me and we shared a few air kisses.

"Honey, I don't mean to sound crass but have you seen the inside of a gym lately?"

"Tristan, I'm pregnant! Not just fat for no reason!"

"Oooh! Okay, you get a free pass!" He smiled. "Come, sit! I have some cuties to show you!"

Every dainty size six and a half he brought out squeezed tighter than trailer trash spandex at the all-you-can-eat buffet. We tried a seven and a few fit but they pinched and poked at my feet as I tried my damndest to strut around the store in them.

"These won't work. Do you have anything more comfortable for me?"

"Um, honey, if you want comfort, there's an Easy Spirit down the street."

I gasped in horror.

Chapter 19

I barely slept the night before the photo shoot and a zit mysteriously appeared on my chin. Thank God for professional makeup artists. After my beautification process, I trotted to wardrobe in my new Easy Spirits—a pair of black leather boots from their exclusive collection. The vast selection rivaled my favorite boutiques but domineered in a major way. These affordable yet chic shoes with a bad rap made my feet feel as if they were walking on pillows.

The stylist led me to a rack of clothes and tried to find the most flattering outfit possible. The shoot would be mainly of my face but we tried to hide my baby bump anyway.

The photographer introduced himself and positioned me. I held up my book and flashed my fake cheesy grin as he snapped away.

"This is not working," Will the photographer said.

"I can stand different or do something else."

"No, it's your face and your body."

"Oh, sorry I don't jam my fingers down my throat like the anorexic models you're used to taking pictures of."

"You're misunderstanding me. You're gorgeous. You're just stiff. The only difference between you and a model is that they know how to be comfortable in front of the camera."

"Yeah, I'm sure that's the only difference." I laughed.

"Hey, do that again."

"What?"

"Laugh like that."

"I can't laugh on command."

"Okay. There's got to be something that can make you laugh. Picture me naked or in a pink Speedo." All he got out of me was half a smirk. "What if I do a little dance?"

He did some sort of leprechaun jig and got a small grin out of me. The camera snapped away.

"Hey Bob, come here," he yelled and a short chunky man walked over. "Do the thing."

The guy spun and did a Michael Jackson impression, moon walking and zombie-dancing all over the place. When he grabbed his balls and let out a high pitched, "Wooo!" I burst out laughing

"That's it right there," Will said and snapped away. When he finished, he called me over to look at the pictures on the screen. The first few looked completely lifeless and boring. But some of the others came out really good.

Will pointed to one of me laughing. "I like this one best. I can see the caption saying something like, 'What does Lexi Marshall find so amusing?'"

"Hmm...I like that! I'll have to tell my editor."

I gathered up my things and headed out of the studio. Will stopped me before I reached the door.

"Hey, I have this crazy idea. You wanna have dinner with me tonight?"

"Oh, wow," I said. The old Lexi would have definitely said yes to dinner with a super cute guy. This new Lexi didn't know what she should do with junior on board. But hey, it was just dinner. "Sure," I answered.

We exchanged numbers and he said he'd call later on in the day to confirm the details. I stopped at the deli and grabbed lunch for Marcus and me and surprised him at his office. His desk held a good six inches of paperwork with not one bare spot to set a coffee mug. I pulled the "baby wants to eat with daddy" card and convinced him to ignore it for fifteen minutes.

"I have a date tonight," I told him.

"Oh, really? I didn't think you would date while pregnant."

"Does it matter?"

"Do you think it's smart to bring someone new into our situation right now?"

"Marcus, just because I'm having your kid doesn't mean I am going to stop looking for my own companion. You have Kevin, I have nobody!"

"Okay, I get it! But I'm not real comfortable with some strange guy's penis coming near my child."

"Thanks for the visual but you don't have to worry. I promise."

Will called later that afternoon and we agreed to meet at Boingo's, a fun restaurant with brightly painted murals and cleverly named drinks. An eclectic mix of Mexican, Caribbean and Asian dishes lined the menu.

I found Will at the bar, his blond hair falling over one eye. How old was he? He looked mature, maybe late thirties, early forties. He sipped on a beer and flashed a gorgeous grin when he saw me. After a "hello" kiss on the cheek, he asked if I needed a drink. My thirst quencher of choice was a simple club soda.

We exchanged small pleasantries and he asked about my book.

"Do I get priority in the book signing line, since I did the pictures and all?"

"I'll have to clear it with my editor but I think I can pull some strings," I replied, flashing him my sexy smile.

We kept up our flirtatious banter until our table was ready. The hostess seated us under a faux palm tree with multi-colored twinkle lights wrapped around its trunk. She handed out the menus and asked if we needed anything from the bar. Will ordered another beer and I took a cranberry and Sprite.

I asked about his photography career. He described the exotic places he'd been and admitted to doing a large number of fashion model shoots.

"I'm sure you've dated them too," I added.

"I'd be lying if I said I didn't, but it gets old quick."

"Well, at least that's something. They may be beautiful, but us average girls have something on them. We're actually interesting!"

"Lexi, you are far from average," he said and put his hand on mine. His deep sapphire eyes burned into mine and I felt myself blush. He looked so damn hot. I didn't know if I'd be able to keep my word to Marcus.

The waitress interrupted our romantic moment by placing our meals on the table.

"This looks awesome," Will commented as he picked up his fork, ready to dig in.

"Yes, it does! I can't wait to try it. This mom and baby are starving!"

Will dropped his fork onto his plate making a loud clanging noise. The sound radiated through the bustling noise of the entire room like a whole box of silverware had been emptied onto his plate.

"Whoa, wait a minute. Are you pregnant?"

"Um, yeah."

"I didn't know that."

"How could you not? Didn't you notice my stomach at the studio or realize I didn't order any alcohol tonight?"

"I thought you didn't drink."

We ate our dinners practically in silence. Poor guy. He obviously had no clue he'd asked a woman and her unborn baby on a date. The check came and I offered to paying my share but he declined. We left the restaurant after that, no more drinks, no more flirting. I thanked him and told him it was nice to meet him. He reciprocated the sentiment after a quick hug but knew I would never hear from Will again. I decided right then and there to put a temporary hold on romantic ventures until after this kid popped out.

* * * *

The day I dreaded came—dress fitting day for Abby's wedding. I met her, Mom and a gaggle of giddy girls at the bridal shop. As soon as I walked in, Abby ran up to me and hugged me. I took my coat off and hung it up.

"Oh...My...God! Look at that adorable belly!" Abby screamed and immediately put her hands on me. This sudden invasion of personal space was the first time anyone beside my doctor had touched my stomach. Even Marcus resisted his urges to feel me up, though I knew how badly he wanted to.

I quickly stepped away, noticing a brief moment of shock in her eyes. The rest of the girls came over to ooh and ahh and Abby smiled with them as they asked all kinds of questions. Mom stood with tears in her eyes and I couldn't quite tell but they did appear to be happy tears.

"Okay, okay, stop this crap!" I demanded, maybe a bit harshly. I was not real comfortable with the attention being given to my swollen midsection.

The woman at the bridal shop walked over holding a pink satin form-fitted gown. I liked it aside from the hideous color, a style I would have loved to model with my old 34-24-34 perfect hourglass body. I didn't know how in the world it was going to work with my round baby body and I'd be much bigger before I actually wore it for the wedding.

The woman measured the girls, then came to me. She surveyed my body as she completely unrolled her measuring tape and asked, "Now, how many months pregnant will you be the day of the wedding?"

"Um, end of May, so about eight I guess."

She sighed and shook her head.

"What?"

"We'll have to order the dress a good deal bigger, then customize it to your body." She wrapped the tape around me in a few different spots. "A size fourteen should be large enough."

"Are you freaking kidding me? I normally wear a four! There's no way I need a dress that big!"

"I can order something smaller but if it comes in and it doesn't fit we'll have to order more fabric and there's no guarantee it will be here in time or match the exact dye of the dress fabric. It's your call."

"Fine," I answered through gritted teeth, completely miserable.

The woman rang up the dresses and each girl paid. When she came to mine, it rang up almost a hundred dollars more.

"Why is mine more?" I asked.

"Anything over a size twelve costs extra."

"Unbelievable," I said, handing over my credit card.

* * * *

I stopped at Smith & Roland later that afternoon to give Sheila the second half of Marisol in Love and found Amanda with her head on the table, sleeping.

"Amanda," I said and shook her. She slowly opened her eyes. "What are you doing?"

"Oh, um, just taking a little nap."

"Why? Are you okay?"

"I'm fine," she said, yawning. "I didn't get in till four AM last night. Had to be up at seven-thirty for classes."

"And why would you do that?" Late-night partying on a school night? Weird.

"Oh, you know how it is. You start with a drink or two and then a few more and end up, well... I don't have to give you all the steamy details," she said with a grin.

"Amanda, what are you doing?"

"I'm enjoying my college experience."

"You'll be enjoying yourself to a two-point-oh grade point average."

"Lexi, you sound like my mother."

Oh my God, I did! How could this have happened to me? I was Cool Lexi, never nagging, never criticizing, never reprimanding.

"And besides," she went on. "How can I write provocative sex scenes if I don't experience them for myself?"

She had me there. You can't write that stuff and make it believable unless you've actually contorted your body into the positions and felt the intense ripples of multiple orgasms. Oh, the nights of crazy sex I could write about! They would definitely not be suitable for a chick lit novel. I'd have to get into a whole different genre for those types of scenes.

We set to work outlining her big sex scene for her book. As Amanda detailed the night minute by minute I thought of my own sex life. If my calculations were correct, these couple months were the longest I'd ever gone without getting some. Do-it-yourself jobs didn't count. I craved a good orgasm like most women craved chocolate or coffee. And while both of those things rate pretty high on my "must have" list, I'd give them up completely to ensure my sexual happiness.

I read over Amanda's work and couldn't believe what my eyes were taking in. "Is this what you did last night?" I asked her.

"Yeah, pretty much. I embellished a little but it's mostly factual."

"Amanda, I don't know what to say. I'm in shock," I said, browsing page after page of whipped cream, melted wax and handcuffs.

"Oh, don't be. I've read worse in your novels."

"Just watch yourself, okay?"

* * * *

A few days later, Val called. I hadn't spoken to her in months. Since her demotion, we had no professional need for contact. I realized how much I missed my friend and almost screamed "yes" when she invited me to meet her for dinner.

"I got a new job. I'm leaving Smith and Roland," she said to me once we were seated at one of our favorite places.

"Val, that's great! Where are you going?"

"It's a small publishing house, but I'll be an editor again."

"I'll come with you!"

"No, you can't. Smith and Roland can give you so much that I can't. I won't be able to do photo shoots and book signings and the other marketing you're getting now. You're better off staying right where you are. Besides, you've got a little one on the way. You don't need any career hassles."

"Yeah, so you heard?"

"Even if I hadn't there's no hiding it."

"I know. It's ridiculous, isn't it? This thing keeps getting bigger and bigger. Some days I wake up and it looks like it's grown a few inches while I slept."

"Are you happy?" Val asked next.

"I don't know yet. I guess we'll have to wait and see."

"Well, from what I hear from my mom friends, you instantly fall in love with your baby when you see it."

"I hope so, cause right now all I feel is the heartburn and pain in my lower back."

I reached for my water glass and felt a sharp thump in my belly. It didn't hurt but it felt weird.

"Lexi, what's going on?" Val asked, noticing my astonished expression.

"I don't know. I felt a weird thump in my stomach."

"Apparently junior didn't like what you said. Haven't you felt the baby kick yet?"

"Not that I know of," I answered and felt the thump again.

I'd seen the baby in the ultrasound and heard its heartbeat but this made it much more real. This thing inside of me was alive and moving around and now I could actually feel it. As a tiny arm or foot or whatever thumped me again, a joy overcame me and I didn't quite know what to do with it.

My cellphone rang a familiar tune and I scrambled to answer it.

"Marcus, oh my God! You won't believe what just happened!"

"Hey," he said. "If my mother calls you, whatever you do, don't accept her invitation to lunch. Make up whatever story you want."

"Hel-lo! Don't you care what I just said?"

"Yes, sorry. What's going on?"

"I felt the baby kick!"

"Are you sure?"

"Pretty sure. What else can it be?"

"Wow! I'm sorry I missed it."

Val stood and gave me a silent little wave and mouthed for me to call her. I turned my attention back to my phone.

"So, why am I turning down lunch with your mother?"

"She's coming into the city and wants to get together. She mentioned inviting you too."

Even after the Wells' had moved to a ritzier neighborhood and our moms drifted apart, Marcus's mother still treated me like an extension of their family. I think she'd disapproved of some of my chosen teenage phases—the grunge phase and the unforgettable Madonna phase, complete with bustier, lace gloves and "Boy Toy" belt—but in the end I turned out a success and that's what mattered to her.

"And this is a problem because?" I asked and received silence. "Marcus, what's going on?"

"Okay, I haven't exactly told her she's going to be a grandmother."

"Marcus! We've only got four months till this kid crawls out of me! I can't believe you haven't told your parents yet!"

"I know! I know! I couldn't do it. They still haven't fully processed my exit from the closet. I couldn't hit them with another blow right away. You know how they are."

"Don't you think they deserve to know? The kid has their DNA running through it. I told my parents, for God's sake!"

"Okay, okay! You're right. I'll set up the lunch date, just you, me and her. We'll tell her then."

* * * *

Marcus and I met his mother at one of her favorite cafes for lunch. He begged me to wear the most concealing outfit I owned, but even a suit of armor couldn't hide the huge growth in my middle section. Nothing got past his mother and she'd know the second I took off my coat.

Marcus and I walked into the restaurant and I suddenly became nervous, a rarity for me. I felt like a kid who'd done something wrong and the principal had called their parents in. Mrs. Wells would take one look and start shooting me with questions, many of which were not my responsibility to answer. I decided to direct them all to Marcus. It was his fault for keeping her in the dark.

Marcus insisted on waiting in the lobby for his mother. He didn't want to piss her off by being seated without her.

A sleek black Towne Car pulled up in front of the restaurant and Mrs. Wells stepped out. The fur of her chinchilla coat fluttered in the wind as she approached the door of the café; she then waited for her driver to open it for her. She strutted to the coat check without even a glance in our direction.

Marcus informed the hostess that our party was ready to be seated and we followed her to a table. I walked behind Mrs. Wells, hiding my stomach. As she turned to sit, she looked right at my bump.

"Lexi, I had no idea you were pregnant. That's quite unexpected," she said as we sat. We gave our drink orders to the waitress, then she turned her attention back to me. "Marcus never mentioned you were with child. What an intriguing situation." Translation: What the hell are you thinking?

"How did your live-in lover handle the news? What is his name again?" she asked.

"Oh, well, Zak and I have ended our relationship." I looked at Marcus, hoping he would speak up.

"Surely he will be responsible and take care of his child."

"Ah, yes, the child will definitely be taken care of by its father." I shot Marcus another more evil look, ready to kick him under the table if I had to.

"Mother, you look lovely today. Did you have a facial this morning?"

"Marcus, you're buttering me," she said sternly. "Even as a child you always beat around the bush. You must get that from your father. Stop chewing your fingernails and say whatever dreadful thing it is you need to say."

"Um, this is pretty big," he started after putting his hand back in his lap. "I'm...the father of Lexi's baby. You're going to be a grandmother!"

"Marcus, it is very sweet of you, even chivalrous, to step in and take care of this baby but it's not your responsibility."

"Mother, it is my responsibility. The baby is mine, not Zak's. Lexi and I conceived this baby together. We didn't plan it but it happened and we're both happy about it."

A smile formed on her face, a genuine one, one I'd only seen a few times. Once on Christmas Eve a few years back after a few too many glasses of champagne. The other was at Marcus's graduation from law school.

"I always knew the two of you would end up together! How wonderful! When is the wedding? It can be small, yet beautiful. We'll plan quickly and you'll be united before the baby is born! We don't want him or her to be born a bastard, now do we?" she said with a hearty laugh, her dangling diamond earrings bobbing.

I looked at Marcus and knew her reaction pained him. He had to tell her yet again that he was gay.

"Lexi and I are not getting married."

"I suppose it can wait. We can hold off until the fall. Lexi, you'll have your figure back and a fitted gown will look stunning on you. You'll make such a gorgeous bride!"

"No," Marcus interjected. He looked her straight in the eyes, his own glazing over. "You're missing what I'm saying here. I'm still gay. I still love Kevin. The four of us will be a family— Lexi, Kevin, the baby and I."

Mrs. Wells looked down at her menu. "I thought this homosexual phase would have ended by now," she said under her breath, something most people would have kept as an inner thought.

"Mother, Kevin is wonderful and I'm in love. Doesn't that mean anything to you?"

"But you love Lexi. You've loved her for years."

"I do love her but not the way I love Kevin. We're perfect for each other, we're the same person. Why can't you accept it?"

I sat in my chair unable to move or breathe. My mom was odd and said things I didn't like but I had no problem telling her exactly where to go. Marcus couldn't do that. He always needed his mother's approval.

"Mother, I want you to meet him. I want you to meet the person who completes my world and makes me happy."

Mrs. Wells stared at her son, searching his face for a glimmer of recognition. How could she look into his eyes, see the child she raised, yet look at him like he was a stranger?

I learned many things from her that day, mainly how not to act as a mother.

"We'll see," she simply answered, turning her attention back to her menu. The waitress appeared and took our order and our awkward afternoon continued. Neither the topic of my pregnancy nor Marcus's relationship with Kevin came up again.

Chapter 20

After dressing in a bra and underwear, I stared into the mirror. It almost seemed comical that this huge protrusion of belly was actually connected to me, making me look like I could fall over at any moment for lack of improper bodily proportions. My face had become a bit chubby and dotted with tiny pimples here and there. My feet felt like they'd grown a few inches and none of my cute shoes came even close to fitting anymore. Nikes and ballet flats, from Easy Spirit, of course, were my only footwear options for the duration of this hostage situation.

Thumbing through the closet for a pair of black maternity pants, my gaze rested on my size four sexy low rise jeans, and my eyes teared up a bit. I turned away before letting my sadness grow, and pulled my maternity pants on, the huge belly patch stretching over my ever-growing bump. I couldn't really call it a bump anymore. It was clearly more of a mountain.

I slipped on a Kimono-styled maternity shirt and tried to do something with my crazy hair and skin. I'd dreaded this day more than any of the others I had to face lately: Abby's bridal shower. I was not an oohing and aahing type of gal and any social situation seemed to be an invitation for relatives and even a few strangers to come up to me cooing as they rubbed my stomach, yearning for just one little kick of my baby's foot.

Mom had planned a perfect afternoon tea for the event set in an atrium type room overflowing with flowers and trees and even some birds flying around. Tables were set with fancy floral-printed china and in the center sat a bowl of fresh flowers. Each arrangement included a miniature umbrella to keep with the shower theme.

"Alexandra, you shouldn't be carrying such a large gift in your condition!" Mom ran up to me, taking the present and setting it on the table with a million others. I didn't say a word to her. I didn't have the energy.

The second my coat came off, the oohs and aahs began. I plastered on my fakest grin as aunts and cousins who I rarely even spoke to crowded around, stroking me like some furry animal at the petting zoo. When my fondling limit had been reached, I excused myself to the bathroom. No one could deny a pregnant woman her trip to the toilet. I came out of the stall and found Aunt Matilda at the sink re-applying her bright red lipstick.

"I see you got yourself knocked up."

"Yep, it appears so." I couldn't wait for her next sarcastic remark. I always loved hearing what came out of her mouth.

"If I would've married that guy who asked, I mighta' birthed a brat or two."

"Really?" I recalled the man we'd heard stories about, the one who begged Aunt Matilda for years to marry him and eventually left her. Within a year, he had a wife and baby on the way.

"Yeah, it would have been nice to have some help around the house."

I laughed. Leave it to Aunt Matilda to want kids just for the free labor.

"Sometimes I wish I had one so I wasn't alone now."

I'd never once heard her mention being lonely. She always made it sound like being on her own was what she wanted and enjoyed. I walked out of the bathroom with a different opinion of Aunt Matilda. No longer was she my cool spinster aunt who didn't need anyone for anything. Now I saw a lonely woman who possibly regretted the decisions she'd made early in her life. If I remained single 'til the end, at least I'd have this kid to take care of me and spend time with me and love me. It had to. It didn't have a choice, right?

I rejoined the shower and made my way to the punch table, sighing as I reached for the ladle of the non-alcoholic punch.

"It's good to see you're not sucking down the wine punch. I'd hate to see your baby come out deformed."

Wendy stood next to me with an evil grin and sipped from her crystal punch cup. I ignored her and walked away. Maybe I'd calmed down a bit in my maternal state or maybe I was tired, but I didn't have the energy or desire to go toe to toe with her.

"I sure hope you've learned a thing or two about motherhood since you almost killed my child."

Okay, the gloves were off.

"You can't possibly believe I tried to kill your little brat!"

"Why did you cut his meat so big? Any person with even half a brain knows young children can't chew pieces of meat that big."

"It was an accident and if you would have gotten off your lazy ass and done it yourself there wouldn't have been a problem."

"You know Lexi, you're going to screw up your kid's life just like you've screwed up your own."

I wanted to hit her, scratch her eyeballs out and yank her frizzy hair, but I stayed calm.

"Well, one thing's for sure. If I parent my kid the exact opposite way you have yours, mine is sure to be polite and well-behaved. I may not have everything figured out or know right off the bat what the best thing is for my baby but I'm sure as hell going to give it the attention you don't give to yours. Instead of spoiling my kid I'll love it. Instead of leaving it with babysitters all the time so I can jaunt off on vacation alone, I'll spend quality time with him or her. Instead of ignoring my kid, I'll make sure they know every minute of every day that they are my number one priority."

I turned on my heel and walked away from her once again. She rambled on but I ignored it, taking my place at the head table. I watched Wendy stomp away and sit down next to her mother. Both of them scowled in my direction.

Abby welcomed her guests to the shower and after what seemed like a never-ending rambling of thank yous and introductions, lunch was served. I ate as many tiny sandwiches as the five bridesmaids combined and still felt hungry. At this rate it wouldn't be long 'til I reached the two-hundred-pound marker.

Abby started opening gifts and her giddy attendants leaped up to help. I didn't feel like moving, so when they offered me the job of writing down what gifts were from whom, I jumped on it.

I lounged in my chair with notepad and pen and kept reminding myself to stay conscious. I watched Abby open dozens of boxes filled with Wedgwood and Waterford and sheets consisting only of one hundred percent Egyptian cotton with a twelve hundred thread count. After an hour I longed for my own bed with its mere five hundred threads.

When the parade of name-brand gifts finally came to an end, I tried to make my getaway as Abby said her goodbyes to some of Daniel's family. Mom spotted me and foiled my great escape plan.

"Alexandra," she yelled as I retrieved my coat. "You can't go yet, dear. We haven't taken any pictures of you and Abigail and the other bridesmaids."

When I weighed a hundred and ten pounds and my flawless skin glimmered, I didn't mind posing for pictures. I reveled in it, actually. My current beached-whale look did not work for me and I didn't want it captured and treasured for years to come.

"Mom, I'm tired. Can I please go?"

"Honey, just a few. I promise it will only take a couple minutes."

I stood in a group with the other girls, trying to hide myself in the back and shot Mom my cheesy smile.

"Alexandra, come in the front next to Abigail. I can't see you and I want to make sure your cute little belly is in the picture."

If she had a clue at all she would have sensed the smoke coming out of my ears. As much as I wanted, I didn't blow up at her. I held my tongue and did as she asked, something new for me.

I finally escaped the family photo shoot and headed for home, thankful that Marcus and Kevin were out for the night. I took my Eternal CD and stuck it in the stereo, blasting it throughout the apartment. After exchanging dressy clothes for my comfiest pants, I sat in the baby's room, keeping the lights off as I stared out the window.

The baby seemed to like the music and went crazy doing flips and turns. An image of me, Rich and the baby flashed into my head. The three of us were dancing around the living room with the stereo cranked up loud. I wished so hard to be watching a vision from my future but knew this crazy daydream would never come true. I needed to erase Rich's face from my brain.

I felt a hand on my shoulder and for a brief moment thought Rich had come to me. When I whipped my head around, it was only Marcus standing there.

"Lex, what are you doing? You know this isn't good for you."

"I know. I can't help it." I began to cry.

"I'm getting rid of the CD. You can't keep doing this to yourself. I know you listen to it all the time and cry yourself to sleep."

"Marcus, I need it. I need something of him to hold onto."

Desperation tumbled from my lips as I melted into a puddle of misery. What had happened to me? I had only been this pathetic once in my life and vowed to never ever let a man do it to me again. But Rich wasn't any man. He was the man I loved.

"No, you need to forget about him and move on. Keeping the CD and hearing his voice constantly is just going to bring you more pain."

He was right. And reminding myself over and over that I couldn't have Rich was not good for me or the baby. I had to let him go, no matter how much I still wanted him.

Marcus tucked me into bed and the CD stopped, then with a snap! Marcus broke it in two. He knew me too well. I was not above searching through a trashcan filled with moldy leftovers to retrieve something I wanted. I cried myself to sleep knowing I'd never hear Rich's voice again.

* * * *

Marcus came with me for another prenatal exam. He jumped at any chance to hear the baby's heartbeat. I jumped at the chance for Marcus to take the day off from work and treat me to lunch. And lunch usually led to shopping. We'd make our way to some cute maternity store and Marcus would buy me new clothes. He loved spoiling me and I loved taking full advantage of it.

As the doctor measured my ever-growing uterus, she asked if we'd signed up for any child birthing classes.

"Uh...no," I answered. "Are we supposed to?"

"I feel it's very beneficial for the parents. There is a General Child Birth class and many others including a Baby Basics class and a Breast-feeding class. Have you chosen how you will feed your baby yet?"

"Wow. No, I haven't. I guess I have a lot to think about."

The doctor handed us a few sheets of paper listing the classes we could take. "Sign up for as many as you like."

Marcus and I read over the list as we sat for lunch. They offered a class for everything.

"Baby Massage looks interesting. And so does Teach Your Baby to Read." His eyes scanned up and down the page. "But I think we should definitely take the Childbirth Class and Baby Basics."

"What is Baby Basics?"

"It sounds like an Idiots Guide to Baby Raising. It's perfect for us!"

"Ha ha." I laughed sarcastically but he was right. I couldn't remember if I'd ever held a baby in my life and if I had, it surely wasn't a newborn. "What is the childbirth one about?"

"It prepares the parents for the birth and teaches breathing techniques and massage to help the mother during labor and delivery. It says here that they promote a natural birth without the use of drugs."

"I'm giving a huge emphatic no on that class!"

"Why? The drugs are not healthy for the baby."

"Marcus, you can't possibly ask me to push this gigantic baby out a hole the size of a nickel and expect me to do it drug-free. You are insane. And besides, what makes you the expert on healthy babies?"

"Well, Kevin mentioned his sister Jeannette went au naturale for her deliveries and she did just fine. One was even a water birth."

"If the drugs weren't safe, they wouldn't use them. And I don't want to hear what other super women did. This woman does not have crazy powers and will have drugs. End of discussion."

"Okay, truce. Your vagina, your decision. Now what about the breast-feeding thing? Jeanette insists it's a total bonding experience with the baby."

"Okay, I'm gonna slap you if you mention Jeanette again. I haven't given any thought to the whole kid-sucking-on-my-tit-thing. I don't know if I can handle it."

"Lexi, it's the best food for the baby. It's a very natural thing to do."

"What is up with all this natural shit? It's the twenty-first century. I'm taking advantage of all the technology out there. Sign me up for Epidurals for Beginners and Formula Making One-oh-One."

Chapter 21

I hadn't seen Sheila since I dropped off the finished copy of Marisol in Love. She left me a voice mail asking me to stop in her office the next time I was in the building. I arrived early the next afternoon and knocked on her door.

"What?" she bellowed.

I peeked my head in. "It's me. You said you wanted to see me."

"Yes," she said, looking up from her computer. "Jesus, you're a house!"

"Um, yeah, thanks for noticing."

"Is that kid gonna pop out any second?"

"No," I said, trying to remain calm. "I still have three months."

"Are they sure there's only one in there?"

"Yes. Don't we have more important things to talk about?"

"I read Marisol in Love and its okay. I made some notes," she said and handed them to me. "The beginning was great, hearts and flowers and tons of the crap most women love to read. The end got messy and confusing and boring. Fix up the beginning so it's not so perfect. It needs more conflict. And change the ending too. Make me believe they are meant to be."

How could I write a story about star-crossed lovers who would move heaven and earth to be together? I didn't know how that felt.

I found Amanda sitting in the conference room, feet up on the table, lounging back with her cellphone. Her smile stretched from one gold-hooped ear to the other. She giggled and twirled her hair with her finger, totally flirting with someone on the other end.

"Okay, I gotta go," she said when she saw me. "I'll see you tonight, okay?" She hung up the phone and tossed her head back and sighed. "What am I going to do?"

"What's up?" I asked.

"That was Chris—total hottie! I made plans to see him tonight but I kinda already have something going on with Mike."

"What happened to Rob?"

"Oh, he's so last week." She went on to give me all the explicit details about Chris and Mike and a bunch of other guys. She seemed to be dating half the male student body at NYU, if you could even call it dating.

"You're getting a little out of hand here, don't you think?"

"I'm doing what you told me—living my life and having a great time doing it. And besides, it's not like I'm sleeping with all of them."

"How many are you sleeping with?"

"Just a couple. Well, maybe one more after tonight if things go good with Chris!"

"And these guys don't mind that you're having sex with other guys?"

"Oh, they don't know. I'm so bad!"

"Why don't you attach a ticket dispenser to your hip so the guys can take a number and wait for the use of your snatch?" I barked at her.

Amanda's mouth fell open and she stared at me, tears welling in her eyes. She ran off before they trickled down her cheeks.

What had I done? I didn't mean to upset her, but she needed to realize how her sex-capades made her look. I had told her to go out and live her life but that didn't mean she should sleep around. Did I somehow give this poor impressionable girl the wrong idea? Was it my fault she was having sex with all these different guys? I couldn't help but blame myself.

My own college experience was a blur of drunken party nights, most of which I couldn't even remember. The "Walk of Shame" moments stood out most—waking next to some guy I hardly recognized then making that embarrassing stroll home. How on earth did I make it without a sexually transmitted disease or two? I didn't want that for Amanda.

I walked out of the conference room and tried to find her. My pregnant body didn't allow me much speed, but I sprinted as fast as I could. Nothing. I called her cellphone and each time it rang, then went to voice mail.

The next few weeks I didn't see Amanda at all. She stopped coming to the office for our mentoring sessions and didn't return any of my phone calls. I left her one last voice mail begging her to call me but I understood if she didn't want to. I wished her happiness and success in life and made sure she knew I was always here if she needed me. There was nothing else I could do, and it saddened me to lose another friend.

* * * *

After a morning of tedious work and a well-deserved afternoon of shopping and a facial, I walked into the apartment and Marcus and Kevin stopped me the second I stepped through the threshold.

"Wait! We have a surprise for you!" they yelled and covered my eyes, leading me around the apartment. When Marcus pulled his hands away, my mouth fell open. The baby's room walls were now a delicate shade of yellow with vertical stripes a shade or two darker. The crib, armoire and changing table all sat in their perfect positions. I looked around the room, instantly envisioning a stack of diapers on the changing table and tiny shirts folded and sitting inside the armoire. On the wall above the crib, in perfect script read the words, "Other things may change us but we start and end with family."

"Oh my God! Did you do this all today?"

"The shop called to let us know the furniture came in and could be delivered whenever we wanted. Kevin and I started painting the second you walked out the door this morning."

I hugged them both and thanked them, truly touched by their hard work. I sat in my chair and envisioned the future: me sitting with my perfect baby and rocking him to sleep. Marcus and Kevin were there, ready and willing to do anything I needed. They were so cute together, cuddling the baby, looks of love being exchanged between them. The only thing missing was someone for me to share it with.

* * * *

Mom called and invited me to the house for dinner. I found it to be a little odd but odd was Mom's middle name. She told me to bring Marcus too.

"Well, what about Kevin?" I asked.

"Oh, sure, honey! The more the merrier!"

As we rode out to my parent's house on Saturday I got a weird feeling. Most times I felt a smidgen of dread whenever I attended a get-together with my family, but this felt different.

We walked in the door and were greeted with an exuberant, "Surprise!" Dozens of beaming faces stood before us while a banner across the wall informed us we had walked into a Baby Shower. Pink and blue balloons filled every corner and twisted streamers criss-crossed the room. Basically it looked like a party store had thrown up inside and I'd been shoved head first into my worst nightmare. I put on my fake happy smile and greeted the million pairs of open arms all waiting to pet me and talk baby talk to my stomach.

Mom appeared in the foyer, hugged me, then bestowed upon me a pin with blinking lights that read "Mom-to-Be." As if the belly wasn't enough, I needed a neon sign to highlight it even more.

For the next hour, I obligatorily listened to story after story of nitty-gritty birthing details. If I had to hear one more tale of the dreaded episiotomy, the artichoke spinach dip and chicken salad croissant I'd eaten were going to make a quite a stain on Mom's cream carpet. I excused myself to the bathroom for a few seconds to re-grasp some of my sanity.

The most amusing part of the shower was introducing Marcus as the father of my child and Kevin as his boyfriend. Was it wrong to relish other people's confusion? If I had to sit there and listen to gory stories and let people invade my personal space, at least I could have this one small guilty pleasure. The looks on the faces of my relatives and my mother's friends were priceless. I wished I had a camera to catch them all. It would have been a fun collage for the wall.

The gift opening portion of the program started and I sat front and center with all eyes on me. I felt like a carnival attraction— everyone sat quiet, waiting for me to do my trick. In this instance they were waiting for the present to be opened so they could coo at its cuteness. Boxes overflowed with pastel colored pajamas and bibs, bottles and rattles.

"Oh my God! Look how tiny it is!" I heard from one of the onlookers as I pulled out another footed outfit. I didn't think it looked tiny at all. The tag read "Size: Newborn" but it was way bigger than the things that went into my vagina, including my Big Boy UltraVibe 5000. It put even the fattest cucumber to shame. If this mint green, teddy-bear covered outfit was the size my kid was going to be when it came out, they better give me a double dose of the drugs.

I managed to get a few things I needed: one of those vibrating chair things, a baby monitor and a high chair. Mom and Abby brought their gift in last. The biggest box of the night had me wondering what could possibly be inside.

I peeled back the shiny duck print wrapping paper to unveil a stroller and baby carrier combo. I examined the picture on the box and it was actually a chic stroller, or as chic as a stroller can come, I suppose. It had everything: cup holder for my lattes, cellphone holder and an MP3 player. The whole thing was a sophisticated black, no frilly lace or animal prints at all. I was truly touched, knowing Mom and Abby actually took my personality and lifestyle into consideration when picking it out. I got up and hugged them both and really meant it. In my cheerful mood I even agreed to participate in a shower game. They looked like they were going to burst with joy.

I said my goodbyes while Dad loaded up his gas guzzling SUV with all my baby treasures. The party wasn't so bad after all. Now that motherhood was barely two months away, I needed to get used to family crap and parties and stuff.

Marcus and Kevin took the rest of the night to put together all the new things. I watched as one read directions while the other put tab A into slot B. They smiled and cheered in celebration when they finished construction on baby gadget number one. Kevin began rubbing Marcus's back, then kissed him gently, one of those I'm-not-trying-to-get-in-your-pants-I-just-love-you kisses. I remembered those kisses and missed them a lot.

I thought of Zak and the entire last year we were together. I couldn't remember one intimate moment. Then the memories of Rich came rushing in. Every moment with him was intimate and special. Granted, we never made it out of the honeymoon phase, but if I had to guess, it would have been like that for the rest of our lives.

I heard the call of my whirlpool tub beckoning me and my aching body to come and relax for a bit. After running the water and throwing in a little bubble bath, I lowered my huge self into the tub and closed my eyes as I leaned back on my inflated bath pillow. The image of Rich's face popped into my head once again. Marcus could break his CD and order me to get over him but he couldn't erase the picture of his face from my brain.

It had been ages since I'd had sex and my body told me it needed something, anything, even if it was my own hands. I couldn't recall a section in my pregnancy book about masturbation. If regular sex with a penis practically jabbing the kid in the head was okay, I couldn't see any reason why pleasuring yourself wasn't. I had no other options and the more I sat and thought of the image of Rich's face front and center in my brain, the hornier I got.

I imagined Rich's arms around me, squeezing me tight, him thrusting into me. I recalled a kinky night where I'd tied his hands to the bed with my Hermes scarf and had my way with him. Next a softer, more romantic vision entered my thoughts. Rich kissed nearly every inch of my body before making love to me, his eyes only on mine, a Tantric sort of love-making. The last vision flashed to a bubble bath we took together. His tight abs and sexy tattoos were on display and he made sure I came twice before he worried about himself.

In the solitude of a different bathroom I brought myself to orgasm picturing Rich's face when we'd get off together. But instead of feeling relaxed and euphoric, I felt alone and cold. Rich wasn't there to hold me afterward and whisper into my ear how amazing and beautiful I was.

I dressed and went straight to bed, and once again cried myself to sleep. I never used to be this way. Could I blame it all on pregnancy hormones or for the first time in my life was I truly heart broken? I had thought Joe shattered my heart all those years ago. But after one night of crying until my eyes no longer held tears, I'd super glued my heart back together and got on with my life, vowing to never let a man damage me that way again. Why couldn't I do that now?

* * * *

A bizarre dream interrupted my peaceful slumber.

Marcus, Kevin and I arrived at the hospital on circus day. All the nurses and doctors wore clown costumes and bright red noses. A bearded lady sat me in a wheel chair with enough balloons tied to it to lift me into outer space, then pushed me to a delivery room decorated in a rainbow of colors. A man stood in the corner doing a knife-and-fire-eating act as a popcorn machine pop-pop-popped, then exploded, sending the fluffy puffs into the air and all over the floor. I moved into the bed as excitement continued around me. Who knew labor would be so much fun?

A monkey came running in and jumped on my bed. He cranked his little music box and the tune That's What Friends are For began playing. I found it to be completely odd until I snapped out of my dream, realizing my cellphone was ringing.

The clock read 3:26 AM.

"Hello?" I answered already knowing it was Amanda.

"Lexi," I heard on the other end. Through sobs she continued, "Please help me."

"Where are you?" I demanded and found myself in protective mode. She gave me the address and I wrote it down. "I'll be there as soon as I can, okay? It's going to be all right."

I kept her on the phone and listened to her cry, pushing any and all horrible thoughts from my brain as I concentrated on dressing myself as quickly as possible. I then crept out of the apartment. If Marcus or Kevin knew where I was going, they'd have a shit fit.

"Are you sure that's where you want to go?" the cab driver asked when I gave him my destination.

"Yes. Now. Go!"

I turned my attention back to Amanda and tried to calm her down. She spoke but I couldn't understand any of her words. They kept coming out in hyperventilated sobs.

The cab pulled up in front of the building and I told him to wait for me. The neighborhood reminded me of a scene from a cop drama I'd watched the night before. An eerie mist fell on the garbage ridden street as low-lifes in dirty ragged clothes walked with liquor bottles concealed in brown paper bags. An argument broke out on the stoop of the brownstone next door, piercing the still night with a, "Fuck you, bitch!"

What appeared to be a transvestite prostitute asked if I wanted some lovin'. I ignored him or her and continued up the steps where the sounds of stoner music murmured from inside. The door opened and a few kids stumbled out. I dashed inside and was instantly surrounded by a cloud of smoke and the strong scent of weed. My eyes scanned the dimly-lit room, finding it hard to see anything at all. The only light source was a seventies style floor lamp with five red light bulbs in it. Someone was huddled in the corner and instead of finding Amanda, I found a kid shooting up heroine.

With my phone still to my ear I moved to the quietness of the kitchen where one lonely party guest poured a shot of something and asked if I wanted one. I ignored him and talked to Amanda, still holding on the line. She'd calmed down and led me to a locked bathroom door. After verifying who I was, she let me in and I immediately wrapped my coat around her half-naked body. I didn't ask where her shirt was or why one of her bra straps was broken.

I walked Amanda out of the house through a maze of people and into the pouring rain on the street. I hurried her into the waiting cab and told the driver to go. We rode in silence while periodic flashes of light revealed her tear streaked face and fat lip.

As soon as we got to the apartment, I started a bath and helped her undress. In her catatonic state she stayed quiet and wouldn't look up at me. My mind could only imagine what she'd gone through that night. Was it all my fault? Had Karma done enough to me personally and now sought her revenge on the people I cared about? How could I live with myself if Amanda's life was being screwed because of me?

I helped her into the bathtub and threw all her clothes in the garbage can. They were moist and filthy and smelled like a mix of smoke and beer. I assumed she'd never want to look at them again.

Upon returning to the bathroom, I found her sobbing in the tub. Even with the straggled hair hanging in her face, a deep purple bruise on her cheek shone through. What the hell do you do in a situation like this? I knelt on the floor next to her and gently poured water over her head. Like caring for a child, I washed her hair and lathered up a washcloth, cleaning as much of her as I could, then drained the tub.

After toweling her off and helping her into some soft pajamas, I laid her in my bed and pulled the covers up to her chin. I crawled in next to her and cradled her in my arms as she cried herself to sleep.

Chapter 22

Daylight brought many questions to my mind. What was Amanda doing in such a rough neighborhood at such a disgusting house? Was she drunk or on something stronger? Did someone hurt her or—God forbid—rape her? I wondered if I should call the police or get her to a hospital. I left Amanda sound asleep in the bed and found Marcus sipping his coffee and reading the paper in the kitchen.

"Good Morning!" he said cheerfully.

"Not for me," I answered and explained what happened barely five hours earlier.

After listening to a lecture on how stupid I was for not waking him so he could go instead, I asked, "What do I do?"

"Talk to her and find out what happened."

"Marcus, you didn't see her last night. I don't know if she'll be ready to talk now or ever. I wish I knew how to make this all better."

"You'll find a way."

I let Amanda sleep a couple more hours, checking on her every half hour or so. Marcus made us some French toast. Last thing I needed was a food disaster, so cooking lessons would wait 'til another day. I arranged a plate for Amanda on a bed tray with some orange juice and strawberries and took it into the bedroom. After setting the tray on the dresser, I sat on the edge of the bed and smoothed the hair out of her face. The bruise had turned a purple-green shade.

"How are you feeling?" I asked after she opened her eyes.

"I'm okay."

"I brought you some breakfast. You need to eat something."

She quietly sat up and let me put the tray across her lap. I gave her some space and time to eat and took the opportunity to pull my hair back and change out of my pajamas. When she finished, I moved the tray and sat on the bed next to her.

"Do you want to talk about it?"

She shook her head.

"Okay. We'll talk when you're ready but I need to ask you something now and I need you to answer me truthfully. Did someone rape you?"

She shook her head "no" again and I felt somewhat relieved. A rape may not have occurred but something awful had happened and my gut told me I wasn't far off. I left her alone, telling her she could stay as long as she liked, and walked back to the living room where Marcus and Kevin sat folding laundry together.

"What are we going to do?" I sighed as I plopped down on the chair.

"I know, poor kid. I'm sure she went through hell last night."

"How are we going to deal with our own kid? I'll be a nervous wreck every time he or she leaves my sight. And it never ends, does it? You worry about them till the day you die, wondering if they're happy, if they're healthy, if they have enough money..."

"She's totally in mom mode," Kevin said, nudging Marcus.

"Completely. Isn't it adorable?"

"You two are ridiculous," I said, but they were right. I was turning into a mom and my kid wasn't even breathing air yet.

Marcus and Kevin went on with their Sunday afternoon, taking in an exhibit at the art museum. I had planned to go with them but I couldn't leave Amanda. While she slept, it gave me the perfect opportunity to play with all the new baby things we'd acquired as shower gifts. I turned on the bouncing, vibrating chair thingy and all the books were right. That thing was awesome! How nice would it be to crawl into it right about now and take a nap?

We'd also received a CD player for the crib and some classical baby music. I attached it to the side of the crib and pressed Play. It sounded nice—a calming symphony of cellos, violins and harps. But would Baby Marshall like it?

All of a sudden an extremely important question popped in my head. What the heck were we going to name this kid? I'd given not even one glance at a "thousand and one" baby name book. And would it be a Marshall or a Wells, or a Marshall-

Wells, or even Wells-Marshall? Where was Marcus when I had these life-altering questions?

I hadn't even begun to think of a first name for this kid. Such a huge decision. I didn't want my kid made fun of for a choice I made before they could add their input. He or she would be stuck with whatever I picked for the rest of their life or at least until they were old enough to legally change it on their own.

Taking a seat back on the floor, I sorted through the pile of baby clothes. The mound varied with shades of cream, green and yellow, seeing we didn't know what genitalia we were dealing with yet. I held up one of the pajama type outfits and cradled it in my arms, imagining my baby's little head in the crook of my arm, its feet kicking around in the air.

"Wow, the room looks really great." Amanda stood there looking much better than when I'd last laid eyes on her. The pair of baby pajamas remained in my arms as she sat on the floor next to me. She looked right into my eyes. "If you care for this baby even a tenth of the way you cared for me last night, he or she is going to be very lucky."

Amanda relayed the story of her night. I tried to keep my face as still as possible. I didn't want to appear shocked, even through the part where she had unprotected sex with that Chris guy or when they went to the party afterward and got high snorting cocaine. I kept my facial expression as unfazed as possible when she told me how she and Chris went to an empty bedroom and started to get into it again only to have the door open and a couple more guys come in, friends of Chris's. They each took their turn with her and she allowed them. She finally had enough and said "no" when one guy turned her over and tried to have anal sex with her. He wasn't all too thrilled and hit her across the face.

"Then Chris said," Amanda went on, "'come on, guys. This bitch ain't worth the hassle. She's just a dirty little whore. There's clean pussy down the hall.' Lexi, I never felt so disgusting in my whole life." She began to cry.

I put my arms around her. "Those guys are assholes and they're wrong."

"No, they're not. I have been a total whore lately. I don't even know why."

"I don't ever want to hear you talk like that about yourself. You are a beautiful, wonderful and brilliant woman and you deserve respect. What they did to you was wrong and demoralizing."

"But I let them do it. I gave them my permission."

"It doesn't matter. They took advantage of you."

"I don't know how everything spun out of control. I'm sorry I acted the way I did toward you. Lexi you're my best friend and I hate myself for running out on you. You were only trying to point out my stupid behavior."

"It's all over now." I hugged her again.

"I don't know what I would have done if you hadn't answered your phone."

"You don't have to worry about that. I am always here when you call."

* * * *

Marcus signed us up for birthing classes against my wishes and the first one started the following week. I agreed to go but in no way consented to a med-free delivery. We joined ten other huge pregnant couples with our pillows in tow. The instructor introduced herself and listed off her credentials.

"I take a no nonsense approach to labor and delivery. I don't believe in sugar coating anything. Labor is exactly how it sounds—hard work. You have to put in one hundred and ten percent effort to achieve your goal."

She wheeled in a large screen TV with a DVD player and pressed Play. We immediately heard the hee-hee-who-who breathing of a woman in labor. Her coach stood at her side holding her hand and cheering her on. The camera panned to her lower region and I made a mental note to get a wax the week before my due date. If there was going to be a room full of people staring at my crotch, I at least wanted it to look tidy and presentable.

The nurses ordered her to push and the woman did as she was told, grunting and roaring like a Tyrannosaurus Rex. Her vagina opened wide enough for a freight train to pass through.

As she pushed some more, what appeared to be a head came charging out of her covered in a gooey, red slime. I glanced around the room at every man's face, each with a look of horror as they watched the events unfold before their eyes. Their facial expressions told me they were having second thoughts about this wonderful thing called childbirth. I know I certainly was.

Every woman in the room had a tear in their eye watching the miracle of life take place. Marcus had the same look as the women. He squeezed my hand. "Isn't it amazing?"

"Uh, yeah, amazing all right. I'm amazed that woman isn't screaming obscenities."

"You're not going to do that, are you?" he asked, his face now showing fear.

"Don't worry. I won't embarrass you."

"People, please keep quiet," the Delivery Drill Sergeant yelled at us. "This is important. Pay attention."

After one last push, the doctor pulled the baby's shoulders and rest of its body out. The wiggling goo-covered human was placed on Mom's stomach while Proud Papa gleefully cut the umbilical cord. The mom smiled down at her baby and I thought the video was over. No such luck. It continued with a detailed account of the placenta delivery and the doctor stitching up where the mom's vagina had torn.

A torn vagina. Is that what I had to look forward to? Good thing I was already doomed to be single forever. No man who wasn't already chained to me for life would ever want to come within ten yards of my stretched out, torn up, worn out vagina ever again. Might as well close it off with a sign reading "Condemned."

The Drill Sergeant lectured about breathing techniques and the proper times to use hee-hee-who-who versus hee-hee-whooooooooooooo. I tuned her out. The only thing I really needed to know was when the epidural would be available.

"And for all you weaklings out there," she started, "here is how an epidural works." She brought out a huge needle and demonstrated on a dummy where it went.

"Marcus, they're going to put a needle in my spine?"

"Yeah, I read how they do it. It's actually a catheter and it's placed into the epidural space of the spine through two of your vertebrae and it sends a continuous stream of the medication."

"Wow, a hole through my vertebrae and into my spine. That's pretty terrifying."

"If you're scared you don't have to do it."

"Thousands of women do it every day. I'll take my chances."

* * * *

Marcus and I walked home past the bookstore where I'd be doing the book signing. A two foot by three foot poster of my face was brilliantly displayed in the shop window. Sheila had gone with the one of me laughing and my suggestion for a caption, "What does Lexi Marshall find so amusing?" The bottom of the poster read, "Find out May 5th when Lexi signs her new book, Marisol Takes Manhattan." I liked the poster and I actually looked pretty good. Not bad for a preggo.

Sheila hoped the posters would generate a buzz, selling copies of the book when it hit shelves a month before the book signing and of course even more sales when I actually met with my fans. I was excited for that part. It would be nice to put faces with the women I inspired and the ones who took comfort in my pages.

Chapter 23

Abby called to let me know the bridesmaids dresses had arrived at the bridal shop and she'd made an appointment for me and the rest of the girls for the fitting. She liked doing things all together. I wanted to back out at the last minute, claiming pregnancy fatigue, but figured I should just get it over with. Why delay the inevitable?

I sat in a room with the five other girls. They sported their cute shoes, trendy clothes and stick thin figures while I sat there bloated, wearing the same outfit I'd worn only three days earlier, with parts of my ass cheeks hanging off the tiny chair. Not only had this baby staked claim to my stomach, it made my ass gigantic too. Even during my first year of college when I gained the dreaded Freshman Fifteen, my ass never got this big.

The same snobby wedding dress coordinator wheeled out a rack filled with pukey pink satin dresses. They were seriously the color of Pepto Bismol, but Abby squealed with glee over them. After the size zero and two dresses were handed out, the coordinator dragged a pink tent off the rack and handed it to me. The other girls had already disrobed and slipped into the form-fitted dresses, each wearing hers like a glove.

Having no desire to show off my stretch marks to these anorexic girls, I took my tent to another fitting room, removed the twenty-ton dress from the bag and stepped into what felt like miles of fabric. One hand cinched the side of the dress so it wouldn't fall down and the other lifted up the hem so I wouldn't trip on it. They could probably make an entire dress out of the extra material.

"This thing is friggin' huge," I said as I returned to the main room, glaring at the dress coordinator.

"You'll only get bigger before the wedding and we need to make sure we'll have enough fabric. In my experience, pregnant women always gain more weight then they plan," she said rather smugly.

She turned me around and pinned some of the fabric in place. I could hear her mumbling under her breath but couldn't quite make out her words.

"Do you have some sort of problem with me?" I asked her.

"No, not you specifically. Pregnant women make so much more work for us."

"I'm not exactly pleased with this awkward body either but that's the way it is. It's your job to fit bridesmaids for dresses and I am a bridesmaid. I also happen to be pregnant, so deal with it and at least try to be somewhat professional."

"Well," she huffed. "This is all I can do for now. You'll have to come back a week before the wedding. You'll only continue to get bigger and I won't do alterations on this just to re-do them later."

"Fine." I hobbled back to the dressing room. When I came out fully dressed in my own clothes, I handed the dress over to her without putting it back on the hanger or neatly into the dress bag. I wanted to get out of there as soon as I could.

Walking out onto the street, the cold air rushed my hot face. The refreshing whoosh relieved my tension as I breathed it in deeply, then exhaled. This uptight, so-in-need-of-a-triple-orgasm snob wasn't going to get to me. She could kiss my dimpled ass. I treated myself to a decadent chocolate chocolate-chip muffin and headed toward the apartment, deciding to gain as much weight in this pregnancy as I wanted. The gym would be waiting when I was ready to work it off. For now, I'd enjoy the calories and maybe gain a couple extra pounds to piss off Ms. High and Mighty a little more.

I continued walking with a guilty smirk on my face, thinking of a hilarious prank to play on the dress bitch. What would she do if my water suddenly broke while she was doing my final fitting? The imagined look on her face actually made me chuckle out loud.

On the path ahead of me stood Rich with his arms wrapped around a tall blonde. Unsure of what to do, I froze. I didn't want him to see me and certainly did not want to interrupt their embrace on the sidewalk. Feeling quite stalker-like, I ducked off to the side and watched them.

They pulled away, both of them smiling ear to ear. Her pretty face with its high cheekbones looked young, definitely more

Rich's age. Her long hair shimmered in the early spring sun and her eyes seemed to sparkle as they looked up into his.

She stepped into a cab and he waved goodbye, still flashing his most cheesy grin. I knew that grin. It only appeared when he was truly and completely at bliss. I'd seen it myself after making love with him and a billion other times when we were together. It meant he was happy and this woman was the reason.

I'd always thought seeing Rich with another woman would destroy me, sending me into another never-ending pit of self-loathing and pity. Surprisingly though, it didn't. Seeing him happy gave me a warm feeling inside. If our breakup meant he'd found someone perfect for him, who made him smile that true smile all the time, then it was all meant to be. I finally knew how to love someone, fully and completely. Rich had found his bliss and it didn't matter that it wasn't with me.

I watched him walk off down the street and would no longer cry myself to sleep picturing his face or masturbate to the memories of us making love. Our time had passed and I was on my way to being over him. A part of me would always love Rich, but now I would think of him and fill with nostalgia. The ache of him leaving was gone.

* * * *

Marcus often worked late, leaving Kevin and I on our own for dinner. The two of us had become pretty close over the few months we'd been living together. I could see why Marcus loved him so much. He was a good man and did his best to take care of me when Marcus wasn't around.

We sat eating our penne pasta with wild mushroom sauce—his specialty.

"I was thinking of having a little party. What do you think?" I asked him.

"Sure. What kind of party?"

"Oh, I don't know. Nothing big, a simple gathering of my friends. Sort of a last hurrah before the baby is born."

"Sounds like a good idea. Who would you invite?"

"My friend list is rather on the short side these days but Amanda and Val definitely. I guess Brenda and Rachel too. Maybe even my editor Sheila. You can invite Jeanette and Jeff and some of your and Marcus's friends."

I ran the idea past Marcus the next day

"Sounds like a great idea, but Brenda, really?"

"Yes. Do you have a problem with it?"

"No, not at all. If you want a home-wrecking, boyfriend-screwing slut at your party, then I'm all for it!" He flashed me his mischievous smile, the one that surely made Kevin's heart melt and protruding appendage stand tall.

"I'm over it now. Must be the hormones. I'm more forgiving than I used to be."

"Well, should we invite Zak then?" he asked sarcastically.

"Let's not push it."

I made a few phone calls inviting guests to our soiree. Rachel squealed with joy when she answered my call and told me how ecstatic the reconciliation with Brenda made her. They wouldn't miss the party for anything.

I planned out what food to order and what wine to buy. It saddened me to stay stone sober for the whole thing. I missed my drunken nights with friends but needed to face facts that my carefree days would soon be long gone.

Amanda arrived at the party first, toting a box wrapped in baby paper with a yellow bow on top.

"What's this for?" I asked.

"It's for you and the baby. You know, like a baby shower gift."

"Oh, you didn't need to do that. This party isn't a request for gifts!"

"I know. But I couldn't come empty-handed!"

After ripping the paper and lifting the lid, I found some strange-looking blanket sort of thing sitting inside.

"It's a swaddling blanket. My sister swore by it when her baby was first born."

"Oh," I said, completely clueless. I looked over the picture on the package. The description explained how babies love the feeling of being tightly wrapped, reminding them of the womb. "Thanks. I'm sure the baby will love it."

As the other guests arrived, they brought more presents for us. I felt guilty. The party wasn't a way for us to get more stuff.

"As soon as I found out you were pregnant I just had to go out shopping for you! I love babies!" Rachel said with enough enthusiasm to light up Manhattan.

Even Brenda brought a present. I pulled a little black t-shirt out of a gift bag. It read "My Mom Rocks." It was a total Brenda gift and I loved it.

I relaxed and caught up with my girlfriends. Marcus played the proud papa and waited on me hand and foot, which I adored. I talked and laughed and enjoyed every minute of the night. I felt like my old self, with the exception of my big belly and having to visit the bathroom every ten minutes.

* * * *

Marcus, Kevin and I attended the Baby Basics Class together. I looked around the room as it slowly began filling with pregnant ladies and dads-to-be. No sign of Delivery Drill Sergeant. Relief filled me when a petite woman in pink and blue puppy dog scrubs welcomed us to class. She made her way around and introduced herself to each couple individually. Our threesome was sort of awkward to explain.

"I see we have mom here and who are these dashing gentlemen?" she asked.

"This is Marcus, the dad, and Kevin, dad number two," I answered.

"Wonderful!" she said, not one glimmer of judgment. "Welcome to the class. I hope it is informative for you."

She took her place in the front of the room and we all took seats. She handed out a few sheets of paper with basic baby info on them and began a lesson on baby care, pointing to a diagram of a baby up on the wall. As she discussed the clipping of fingernails and cleaning out of stuffed up noses, my heart began beating faster and my head spun.

"Lex, you okay?" Marcus asked me.

I shook my head up and down but my mind raced with questions. How do you clip baby nails? I could barely do my own. And cleaning every nook and cranny on his or her body? What if I missed a spot? Was my kid doomed to be the dirty baby with a drippy nose and crusty crevices?

Next she covered diaper changing and brought out a box of babies. Of course they were fake babies, but very life-like fake babies. She handed one to each couple and also a diaper, explaining the proper techniques for cleaning a boy and a girl as well as how to properly attach the diaper.

"And remember class, your real baby will be kicking and probably screaming the whole time you are doing this. But no need to fret, you'll have it down to a science in no time at all!"

She seemed quite confident in me. I didn't have nearly a tenth of that confidence in myself.

Chapter 24

Book signing day finally arrived and I bought myself a whole new outfit for the occasion, trying to look as stylish as possible. It almost seemed frivolous to spend such an exorbitant amount on clothes I'd barely wear for another month. But Marcus treated me, so it was his hard earned money, not mine, and I got over that feeling quite quickly.

I arrived bright and early at the Book Nook Book Shop, the cutest place in the area, and thumbed through the latest best sellers. I'd always loved this store, finding myself in here many times before my first book was published, browsing shelf upon shelf of flashy covers, wishing and dreaming of the day mine would be among them.

The bookstore owner led me to a table in the back of the store covered with stacks of my new book and a bunch of colored pens to write with. I took my seat in a big fancy desk chair. Its comfy leather molded perfectly to my sore pregnant body.

The posters for the book signing listed a starting time of ten AM, but by nine forty-five a dozen fans stood in line to talk to me. I felt like such a celebrity!

As the line grew and grew, I stared down it in amazement. I'd never realized how many fans I had. I'd received royalty checks for my books, but couldn't possibly compare those figures to actual in-the-flesh faces.

My readers seemed genuinely happy to meet me. Most of them asked questions about my books that I was happy to answer, and I found it really fun to share my inspirations with them and the real life people my characters were based on. I posed for pictures with some of my fans while others just wanted my Jane Hancock on the inside of their book.

One reader thanked me for the portrayal of Marisol in the new book. She could identify with her, as she had done the same thing a few years earlier when she moved to Manhattan to chase a dream. To her, Marisol wasn't some fictitious character. She was a real person, a friend. For the first time in my career, I truly felt like my stories did more than entertain someone for a few hours. My readers felt connected to Marisol and my story. Giving them someone to identify with, even a fake person, felt incredibly inspiring. Marisol was a lot like me too. And that meant my readers were identifying with me. I started to feel a real kinship with the women I wrote for. Knowing there were people out there just like me was quite comforting.

The line died down by one o'clock. The bookshop owner came over and told me we could call it a day. The signing should have ended at noon, so I thought it a great success to continue as long as I did.

My stomach rumbled loudly as I cleaned up, but someone asked, "Do you have time to sign one more?"

"Sure!" As I looked up, two gorgeous eyes stared back at me. They could only belong to one person.

"For you, anything!" I said to Rich. I took the book from him and signed it, "The best in life to you always, Lexi Marshall," and handed it back to him.

"I read it cover to cover in like two days," he said. "It's really good."

"Thanks. I meant what I said in the acknowledgment. You were a huge part of it and I'll always be thankful."

He smiled and started to walk away, but turned back around. "Do you want to get some lunch?" he asked.

I thought for a second. I couldn't go back to misery and depression, a pitiful woman incapable of getting over her ex. But looking at him now, I didn't feel depressed. I saw an old friend.

"Absolutely! Let me get my things," I said as I stood up.

"Wow, look at you!" he said.

I'd momentarily forgotten he hadn't seen me in my enlarged state.

"Uh, yeah. It's kind of out there isn't it?"

"You look great," he replied, smiling.

I gave him a simple "thanks" for the sincere compliment, buttoned up my coat as much as I could around my big belly, and followed Rich out the door.

"So, how are things going?" he asked once we hit the street.

"Good. I moved in with Marcus and Kevin. The baby's room is all ready. The book sales are going great. I really can't complain about anything. How about you?"

"Same shit, different day. Still working for Uncle Walt. I'm almost finished with school though and I can't wait. Just a couple more exams."

"Wow, that's great. Any plans after that?" I felt like my mother and her prying ways. "I'm sorry. It's none of my business. You don't have to answer."

"No, it's okay. I sent resumes to a few places, looking to get in with a production company. I might have to start at the bottom, but that's the way it works, I guess. I might be keeping my job at the Luxury Inn a little longer than I planned."

We arrived at the deli and ordered some sandwiches, keeping up the small talk while we ate. Rich asked about Amanda, and my sister too. I asked how his friends were.

The conversation lulled and Rich looked uneasy and nervous. Was he thinking about his girlfriend? Our lunch meeting had gone on long enough.

"I should get going." I stood and grabbed for my coat.

"Yeah, me too."

"Thanks for the conversation. I'm glad to see you're doing so well."

He nodded his head, almost looking sad. I said my goodbye and walked out into the sun.

"Lexi, wait."

Why'd he chase after me? He had a girlfriend, a new start. We'd done lunch and that was enough.

"I can't leave it like this. Can we go somewhere to talk, someplace private?"

I agreed, unsure if private was such a good idea. Marcus would yell at me for it later.

Rich and I walked to the park. With only a few people here and there, it was as close to private as I was going to get. We found a quiet bench to sit on. I sat speechless, waiting for him to say whatever he needed to.

"I don't even know where to start," he said, fidgeting with his hands. "I've missed you so much."

Against my better judgment, I felt the need to be honest with him. "I missed you more than I ever thought possible and it took me a long time to accept that you couldn't love me the way I needed you to."

"I'm sorry for the way I handled everything. I wish I could go back and change it."

"No. You reacted truthfully. I can't fault you for that. You needed to do what was best for you."

"I did love you," he said, then looked right into my eyes. "I still love you."

My heart fluttered with hope and it took every ounce of courage within me to squash it dead.

"Love isn't always enough. I know that now. I need someone who can handle this crazy family arrangement with Marcus and Kevin. I need someone who wants to stick around and be there for me and my baby."

"I hate myself for leaving you. Can't I try to be the man you need?"

"It would be selfish of me to ask you to change your life to suit what I need." I couldn't believe those words came out of my mouth.

"You're not asking, I'm offering."

"Rich, please don't make this so hard on me." I tried to go on without breaking into a million tears. "You are not ready for this kind of life."

"How can you tell me what I'm ready for? I love you and I want to make this work. I've been miserable without you!"

"Miserable? I saw you a few weeks ago with a redhead on the street. You held her and looked happier than I'd ever seen you look before and it made me happy! That's what I want for you."

"Redhead?" he asked himself, searching his brain. "Oh, Stacey. She's my younger sister."

"Your sister?"

"Yeah, she's got some modeling thing going in the city. I hadn't seen her in years. She finally got out of the trailer park."

"Oh, so you're obviously not dating her then."

"I haven't been with anyone since we broke up."

We sat quiet while birds chirped around us and the sun glistened through the budded trees. A hot dog cart clamored past, its scent drifting into my nostrils.

"Lexi, please let me have another chance to show you how much I love you and how dedicated I am to a relationship with you."

"That's the problem," I said. "It's not just me anymore. Soon I'll be a mom and nothing will ever be the same. I'm a package deal now. I need someone who can handle the responsibility.

Can you honestly tell me you're ready to be an instant step-dad?"

"I don't know."

"That's not good enough."

I stood and said a final goodbye. Rich looked as miserable as I felt, his expression bringing back the painful memories of our breakup. I walked away before he could say anything else, praying not to collapse into the puddle of sorrow that I felt like. This was for the best, even if both of our hearts were breaking once again.

* * * *

A few days later, I vegged on my couch taking in some daytime entertainment. My toes were swollen like fat little sausages and hurt like hell. I popped a couple chalky antacids to combat the heartburn caused by a glass of water while the burrito I'd eaten for lunch hours earlier had settled in my stomach just fine.

I dozed off only to be jolted awake by the intercom buzzer. Having no desire to leave my cozy couch cocoon, I ignored it. But the relentless visitor kept pressing the button every three-point-five seconds.

"Delivery for Lexi Marshall," I heard when I finally got my lazy ass to the buzzer.

"Okay, come on up."

I searched my brain and couldn't remember ordering anything online. And we'd received all the items Marcus and Kevin bought at the baby shop. But then again, I had an affliction I labeled "pregnancy brain." My baby was leeching all of my brain cells. It's like calcium. Doctors recommend that pregnant women take a supplement because if they don't the baby will take all the calcium and the mom's bones will become deficient. In the case of brain cells, there is no supplement. Sometimes I couldn't remember what I'd done barely five minutes earlier. In this sick world where pregnant women were given all sorts of bodily ailments, regular flatulence wasn't enough. They needed brain farts as well.

The doorbell rang and I opened it to find a burly man standing there with a vase full of yellow roses. He shoved the huge heavy glass into my hands, then expected me to sign his notebook. I set the arrangement down on the coffee table while he impatiently waited for my signature.

Once the door was closed, I stared at the beautiful arrangement sitting before me. Who would have sent them to me? The roses smelled like Smarties candies and it radiated into the entire room. I reached for the enclosure card, recognizing the handwriting immediately.

Lexi, if the only way to have you in my life is by friendship, then I'll do it. I can't go the rest of my life without seeing your face. Please accept these as a gift of pure friendship, nothing more.

Always, Rich.

Would a platonic relationship with Rich work? I didn't have a clue. But could I go the rest of my life never seeing his face, either? I grabbed my cellphone and dialed his number.

"Hey, I got the roses. Thank you."

"Oh, do you like them?"

"Of course, they're gorgeous. You really didn't have to do that."

"I had to tell you how I feel. Can we do this—the friendship thing?"

"I didn't know what to tell you when I dialed your number. I'm still not sure it's the best thing for either of us, but I think we should try."

"I'm so happy to hear you say that," he said with a relieved sigh. "Just hearing your voice is comforting."

"I know what you mean."

Chapter 25

When the day came for the final dress fitting for Abby's wedding, I felt completely awful. For me, a two-hour stretch of sleep was considered a huge success and walking anywhere had become a daunting task. After arriving at the dress shop, I squashed my huge feet into the tiny dyed-to-match shoes just like the ugly stepsisters did in Cinderella. They were on and that's all that mattered. My toes could fall off from lack of circulation for all I cared.

The woman at the boutique pinned the dress around me without saying a word. She remembered our last conversation and obviously knew better than to start up another argument with a pregnant woman. A small victory for preggo bridesmaids everywhere.

"Come back on Wednesday and I'll have the dress finished. If there are more adjustments that need to be made, we'll still have a couple days."

"Thank you. I appreciate your professionalism and tact this time."

She half smiled at me before I walked out of the shop.

I met up with Amanda, our last meeting before she went home to Ohio for the summer. Our usual Friday shopping fest and Happy Hour had been replaced with brainstorming sessions and coffee at a quiet cafe. She didn't say it but I knew she was still dealing with the party incident.

"I met someone," Amanda said as we sipped our lattes.

"Oh, really?" I asked with raised eyebrows.

"He's a Journalism major. We paired up for a project in one of our classes. His name is Glenn."

"Hmm, sounds interesting. Obviously you have a lot in common, career wise, right?"

"Yeah. And he's sweet, from a small town like I am. We spent a lot of time together working on the project."

"Anything romantic happen?" I asked, curious to how fast she was moving with this guy.

"No, nothing at all. Just a few flirtatious conversations. I know he's interested but I want to take it slow. I feel like I can be myself with him and it's okay."

Amanda had traveled miles since the day we met. This once shy and unsure girl had sat on a huge mountain of insecurities. I had helped bring out what she felt inside and built up her confidence. Some of that confidence had gotten a little out of hand but she'd found a happy medium. She now knew what she wanted out of life and I was proud to have a part in it all.

I sat there and lost myself in my thoughts. If I could help Amanda become a mature woman, maybe my kid stood a chance after all. I might not be able to make him the perfect pancake or sew up a stellar dinosaur costume for the school play, but I could do more. I could teach him to be confident.

"I also decided to stay here for the summer," she said next. "Aunt Sheila gave me a paying job and said I could stay with her. I won't be making much but at least I can see where this thing goes with Glenn. He stays in the city for the summer too."

"So, you really like him?" I asked.

"Yeah, I think so. It will be nice to spend time with him and not worry about the project, when things are due and all that crap. We can relax."

Amanda and I went our separate ways. I told her to keep in touch and not be a stranger over the summer. She said I'd better call her when the baby was born so she could be his first visitor.

* * * *

For my thirty-three week prenatal appointment, the doctor did the same old thing—she measured my belly and listened for the baby's heart beat. I expected to be on my merry way in ten minutes max.

"Okay, Lexi, I don't have a pediatrician written down in your file. Who have you chosen?"

"Pediatrician? I don't need to pick one now, do I?"

"You need to have one before the baby is born. The doctor will examine the baby in the hospital and you'll be taking him or her for their first check-up a week after they're born."

"Oh. How the heck do I choose a pediatrician?"

"I can give you a list to look over. Give them a call and do a few interviews. Find someone you're comfortable with."

I called Marcus immediately after I left the doctor's office.

"Oh my God! Did you know we need to pick a pediatrician, like, now?"

"No, I didn't realize that," Marcus answered quietly.

"You have to come home. We need to do this right now!"

"Lexi, I can't leave work today. That's why I couldn't come with you to your appointment, remember? I have responsibilities here."

"You have a responsibility to me and this baby. I can't believe you're being like this!"

"We'll discuss pediatricians when I come home tonight, okay?"

I felt my face become hot. "Don't worry. I'll do it myself!" I hung up on him.

I shook off Marcus's insensitivity and sat looking at the unending list of doctors. How the heck do you pick a doctor from a photocopied list? There weren't even stars next to some of the names, noting which ones were better than the others. I didn't have any mom friends to seek advice from and Marcus obviously had more important things to do at the moment.

I took out a black marker, ready to narrow down the list. First to be eliminated were all the names I couldn't pronounce. It would be nice if I could at least say their name correctly when I called to make an appointment with them. Next I eliminated all male doctors. I knew it was absurd to eliminate all males from my list in the rare chance one could be a pedophile but in this day and age you can't be too careful.

On the list remained ten female pediatricians. I did not have a desire to meet with and interview that many doctors, so I crossed off three that were too far away from the apartment and two more whose names I just didn't like.

I began calling the offices of the remaining five to set up the interviews. Right off the bat the first two were not accepting new patients. I talked with the receptionists at each of the last three, setting up appointments throughout the next week.

When Marcus walked in the door after work, I certainly gave him the cold shoulder. I looked right through him when he came over and put a hand to my stomach.

"How's baby been this afternoon?"

"Oh, now you care about his well-being?" I said, pulling away from him.

"Lex, come on. You called me this afternoon at the worst possible time."

"There shouldn't be a worst possible time to call you, Marcus! You should be available for me and the baby all the time!"

"It's been a long day and I'm tired. I refuse to argue with you," he said, then walked to his bedroom to change out of his suit and tie.

I went to the kitchen and noisily opened the drawer holding the take-out menus. Marcus and I always ordered something when Kevin worked late.

"Where's the list?" Marcus asked when he returned.

"It's taken care of. I looked at it, narrowed them down and made appointments. You can go with me or not. I don't really care." I concentrated on the menu in my hands. My eyes began to tingle as the listing of sandwiches on the Happy Hoagies menu started to blur.

"Lex, come here," Marcus said and led me to the couch in the living room. "What's going on? Why are you being so weird today?"

The tears burst out as I tried to speak. "Why don't you care about us?"

He immediately wrapped both arms around me and rubbed my back. "You know there is nothing farther from the truth. I love you and I love the baby."

"I know," I answered back through sobs. How did I go from angry and cold to blubbering sap in a mere ten seconds flat? This roller coaster of emotion known as pregnancy sucked big time and after months of being strapped into it, I was definitely ready to get off.

"I had a rough day and you called right in the middle of chaos at the office. Normally I would have been able to drop everything for you."

I calmed down and showed him the list. He said we would go with whatever pediatrician I felt most comfortable with and promised to attend each and every interview, asking all the important questions I was sure to forget.

* * * *

Marcus and I visited with Doctor Simon first. We walked into an inviting office filled with neat wooden toys and little chairs for the young patients to sit on. The walls were decorated with murals of butterflies and animals and children running after them. I felt as if I'd jumped into a children's picture book, surrounded by cheeriness and joy. It was exactly what a children's doctor's office should look like.

The nurse showed us around the office, pointing out the separate well child waiting room and sick child waiting room, the coffee station for parents. Next she showed us the examination rooms, each having a different theme for the decor. I especially liked the Charlotte's Web room.

The tour ended at Dr. Simon's office. A petite woman with shoulder length curls sat behind a huge cherry wood desk that made her look even smaller. Her wide smile almost looked out of proportion for her small body. She stood and greeted us as we walked in.

"Hello! You must be Lexi Marshall. I read your latest book in only a week's worth of lunch breaks! It's making its way through the office as we speak!"

I loved her already.

"Thank you," I said, stretching my hand out to shake hers. "And this is Marcus Wells, the baby's father."

We sat and Marcus jumped right into asking his pertinent questions: office hours, after hours care, blah, blah, blah. That stuff was important, but my concerns lay in how gentle she'd be and if she'd care for my baby just like her own.

I loved how she listened like Marcus's ramblings were the most important things on Earth. And when she spoke, her sweet voice answered each and every one of his questions with complete confidence. I watched the way her cheeks puffed out when she smiled and she kept her hands neatly folded on her desk. They looked like soft hands.

"Okay, Marcus, don't you think you've interrogated her enough?" I asked and gave a little giggle. "Sorry, he's a lawyer. He can't help himself."

"No, it's good to ask these questions. Then there are no surprises down the road. Is there anything else you want to know?"

"Nope," I said, cutting Marcus off from asking yet another question. "I think we know all we need to know. Sign us up!"

"Lex, hold on. Don't you want to meet with the other doctors before making a decision?"

"No. I like Doctor Simon. I don't need to meet anyone else."

"Okay, as long as you're sure."

"Absolutely!" I said out loud as my inner monologue sang, "Oh yes! I love this doctor!" I'd made millions of decisions throughout my lifetime, but for some reason this decision seemed so monumental and I felt quite excited about it. I was doing something right for my baby.

"Let's celebrate!" I said to Marcus once we'd left the office.

"What are we celebrating?"

"My first parenting decision, of course!"

"Same old Lexi," he said, shaking his head. "Any excuse to celebrate! Where do you want to go?"

"Ooh, let's hit that new expensive ice cream shop! I've been craving some hot fudge!"

"Anything you want, Mommy."

Looking to his face, it suddenly becoming morphed and distorted as my eyes glazed with tears. My lips turned up in an unfightable smile.

"What?" Marcus asked.

"You called me mommy."

"Yeah, and?"

"I'm really going to be a mommy aren't I?"

"Yep, there's no turning back now! Since when have you become the sensitive type?"

"I don't know," I said, drying my eyes. "It's so not me."

Chapter 26

I picked up my dress for Abby's wedding and to my amazement it fit perfectly. I didn't look too bad in it either, standing at the mirror alone. Once the other bridesmaids were in the picture, I'd be Shamu in pink satin.

Only three days remained before the wedding and the fatigue of pregnancy made it hard to do everything. On a normal day I could barely make it to eight before passing out on the couch. How would I attend every pre-wedding function without snoozing where I stood? The next few days would include the bridesmaid's luncheon and bachelorette party, the rehearsal and rehearsal dinner. Add in manicure, pedicure, facial, and massage appointments. I didn't even want to think about the actual wedding day, sitting through makeup application and an excruciating up-do. I hated having my hair done up. Most stylists had zero patience for naturally curly hair. A fancy hair do always left me with a headache.

For my one last night of relaxation before the wedding drama took over, I pulled on my favorite flannel maternity pajamas, popped some popcorn and snuggled on the couch in a cashmere blanket to watch Gone with the Wind on the classic movie channel. But before Scarlet even made it to the barbecue, Marcus and Kevin came bursting through the door in the middle of an argument. I watched them verbally duke it out, not even sure what the problem was. They both noticed me at the same time and paused their shouting match. Only the sound of Scarlet O'Hara's voice surrounded us as she chanted a flirtatious "fiddle dee dee" and charmed her beaux.

"Do what you want," Kevin said and stormed off.

Marcus's shoulders slumped as he shuffled off in the opposite direction leaving me with my jaw in my lap. I'd never witnessed them in anything more serious than a playful spat which I guessed to be the start of foreplay.

"Sorry, Lex," Marcus apologized when he came back into the living room, a glass of wine in his hand. "We didn't realize you were here."

"Is everything okay?"

"Yes, it's fine. Kevin is being ridiculous."

"Why? Talk to me."

Marcus sat and immediately put his hand to my stomach like he did every day when he came home from work. It seemed to be his way of refreshing himself after a long hectic day. I felt the baby kick his hand as if he knew his daddy needed a pick-me-up.

"So what happened?" I asked.

"Kevin mentioned that big party his company is throwing. I completely forgot it's this Saturday. He's pissed I forgot and went ahead and told you I'd be your date to the wedding."

"Well, yeah, I'd be pissed too."

"I know. He told me about it during a huge case a few months ago. My stress level was through the roof and I don't remember much of anything from that time."

"You know what you have to do, right?"

"Yeah, I know. I'll make it up to Kevin somehow."

"No, you idiot! Go to the party! There is no way I'm holding you to some pity date for my little sister's wedding! You'll be bored out of your mind. Please, go fix it with Kevin. He's mad because he loves you and he wants to show you off."

"Lex, I can't let you go to the wedding alone. Who's gonna help you all night and spin you around the dance floor?"

"Trust me, there isn't going to be any spinning! And I'm sure there will be plenty of people willing to fetch me things."

He leaned down to my belly, rubbing it again. "Your mom is the best but I'm sure you know that already."

* * * *

Twenty-four hours later I squeezed my bloated self into the hippest maternity outfit I could find—not an easy thing to do— and hoped that mounds of sparkly, chunky jewelry detracted from my gargantuan stomach. The reason was a night on the town with six skinny bitches in sexy little numbers and I needed to at least try to fit in. I didn't want to go to begin with, but Abby insisted the Maid of Honor had to be present at the bachelorette party. I made her no promises, agreeing only to dinner and I'd see where it went from there.

The girls had deemed a Hummer limo the perfect transportation for the night, complete with hot pink cheetah print leather seats, mirrored ceiling and fully stocked bar. I sat with my fake smile sipping on my sparkling cider, watching the clock tick in slow motion.

As Abby and the bridesmaids got drunker and drunker, I felt less and less like one of the girls, and more like their chaperone for the night, pulling them away from nasty looking guys and saying "no" when they wanted to order up yet another round of Blowjob shots.

I'd only seen my sister drunk twice before this. Abby's twenty-first birthday celebration ended with her hands and knees on the floor of a bar bathroom. We'd used the remaining contents of the soap dispenser to clean her up that night. The second time was her college graduation. After she'd had several shots of Tequila Rose, I recognized the same glazed look in her eyes and knew everything she consumed would be coming back out.

As we drove, I noticed the sign for the Luxury Hotel and Suites and asked the limo driver to pull over. He and I helped the six drunken girls into the lobby and plopped them down on the couches. A friendly face smirked at me over the front desk.

"Wild night?" Rich asked.

"Yeah, I guess you could say that. Abby's bachelorette party."

"Oh, I see."

"You got a couple rooms for them? My mother will freak if I send them home like this."

He smiled and handed me three room keys. Rich and I got the girls settled in the rooms, leaving the bathroom lights on for a guide. At some point during the night they'd all be leaning over the porcelain, praying to the man upstairs for their heaving to end.

I hobbled my way back to the lobby. Yes, I had that pregnancy waddle thing going on. I'd noticed it a few days earlier, arriving just in time for my big embarrassing walk down the aisle.

"Thanks again," I said to Rich, his bright blue eyes twinkling. "I'm beat, so I'm gonna grab a cab. Have a good night, okay?"

"Yeah, thanks. Hey, give me a call. Maybe we can do dinner or something before you have the baby."

"Yeah, I'd like that."

I smiled and turned on my heel. As I shuffled toward the door, an idea jumped into my brain.

"Hey," I said before turning back around. "The wedding is Saturday. Marcus was supposed to go with me but something came up and now he can't. I dread telling my Nazi-bride sister she has to pay a hundred and fifty dollars for a person who isn't coming. Do you maybe wanna take Marcus's place and be my date? If you can't it's not a big deal."

"Yeah, it'll be fun," he answered.

"Great!" I said with a goofy grin. "I'll call you with the details."

* * * *

Friday began with a whirlwind of spa and beauty treatments. Abby and the other girls battled dry heaves and headaches while I laughed at their expense and fully enjoyed my pampering.

We sat for lunch at two o'clock. Abby noticed the clock and turned an even paler shade of white. "In twenty-four hours I'll be walking down the aisle."

"I know, it's exciting, right?" one of her bridesmaids managed in a perky tone.

"I don't know. What if I'm not ready? What if Daniel's not ready? Oh my God! What am I going to do?"

"What are you saying, Abby?" I asked. The poor thing. I had never seen her unsure about anything in her life.

"What if this is a mistake? What if we do this and end up hating each other?"

"Then I guess you get a divorce and start all over again."

"Divorce!" she shrieked and broke down sobbing right at the table.

Might not have been the most appropriate thing to say to a worried bride the day before her wedding.

Abby had imagined this day since she was eight years old and picked up her first issue of Modern Bride Magazine at the super market. While other girls played dress-up with feather boas and shiny jewelry, Abby dressed in a white veil and walked down a pretend aisle in the living room of our house. She'd waited so long for this and I wasn't going to let her fall apart now.

"Abby, come on. You've been with Daniel for how long now, five years? You've been living together. There's no surprise there. What could possibly change? Daniel is a great guy and you'll make a great wife. You're perfect for each other. It's a marriage made in heaven."

"Really?" Maybe Abby didn't have life all figured out the way I thought she did. Maybe fear and frustration filled her just like the rest of us.

"Yes! You know I'm right."

"Daniel is great, isn't he?" She smiled and wiped away her tears.

Was this what sisters were supposed to do for one another? Help each other through the hard stuff, support them when they think they can't do something? We'd never had that kind of relationship before. It was new and different, but I kinda liked it.

* * * *

By the time we met at the church for rehearsal, the bride-to-be and her five bridesmaids looked refreshed and ready for anything. You never would have known the mess they were barely a few hours earlier. Abby beamed as she practiced her big walk down the aisle.

I stood at Abby's left side while Pastor John went over the ceremony. He barely even acknowledged my existence and simply referred to me as the Maid of Honor. Apparently he was way over me.

The organist practiced her jubilant exit music as Abby and Daniel joined hands and floated down the aisle. I then locked arms with the ogre-esque best man. Apparently all families have a kid who could have been adopted. Daniel's brother stood over six feet tall and equaled probably two of him. His brother's hairy arms and sagging jeans made him the total opposite of the preppy, stick-like Daniel and the rest of the groomsmen. I took much comfort in my monstrous escort—his large stomach almost matched the size of mine.

Daniel's parents hosted the rehearsal dinner, an elegant affair that surely mirrored what Abby had planned for the wedding reception. I expected nothing but the highest level of sophistication for this shindig.

A few toasts were offered up to the Bride and Groom, one from Dad and another from Daniel's father. Pastor John gave a never-ending blessing for the meal and I tried my hardest not to faint from starvation.

The evening continued and dinner guests happily mingled around the room, talking and laughing. I sat at the table alone, watching everyone. Abby came and sat next to me, setting a package on the table wrapped in silver paper with a sparkly ribbon tied around it.

"What's this?" I asked.

"Your Maid of Honor gift."

"Oh, I didn't realize the job entitled me to a present," I said, smiling.

"Yes, and I had the toughest time ever finding the perfect thing."

I slowly tore the paper and lifted the lid of the box. The face of a gorgeous silver watch stared back at me, sparkly with diamonds and sapphires encircling it. My breathing almost stopped.

"Abby, I don't know what to say."

I looked up and she smiled. "Thank you is sufficient."

"Well, then, thank you!" I hugged her and pulled the dainty watch out of its box.

"There's an inscription on the back," Abby stated and I flipped it over to read it.

my sister, my friend

the one I look up to

My eyes welled with tears. Abby looked up to me? Growing up, we never found anything we could both relate to. We simply had nothing in common. But maybe that was my easy excuse. I couldn't possibly offer her anything she would find useful, so why try? I had never been what a big sister should be.

"So, I take it you like it?" she asked. I looked up to see tears in her eyes too. We sat there, a pair of sappy sisters, finally coming to a place in our lives where we acted the way sisters should.

Chapter 27

The morning of the wedding at my parents' house was a chaotic mess of hair stylists, makeup artists and Abby weeping every five minutes. She no longer had the pre-wedding jitters but instead became overly sentimental about everything. The makeup artist looked like she wanted to scream when she re-did Abby's makeup for the third time.

Dad and Andy came downstairs dressed to the nines in their sleek black tuxes. I hadn't seen Andy in anything other than athletic wind pants and a baseball cap in years. He'd even shaved and taken his blond locks to a barber for the occasion. My twin could be handsome when he put some effort into it.

I hobbled up to my room once my hair and make-up were in check. Staring up at my dress hanging on the back of the door, I wondered how the hell I'd get into it and zip it up all on my own. As if by some weird mother-daughter vibe thing, Mom knocked on the door to ask if I needed any help. I gladly opened the door and accepted it. She held the dress as I stepped into it then zipped it up for me.

"I know it's Abby's day, but she has a bunch of gals to help her dress. I thought my services would be needed elsewhere."

I felt my eyes tear up and turned to hug my mom. "Thank you."

When we pulled apart, I looked into her eyes. They looked familiar. Why hadn't I ever noticed it before? They were brown like mine. I'd always thought Abby and Andy got their blond hair and blue eyes from Mom. They were perfect copies of her. After all this time, constantly feeling like an outsider in every sense of the word, I finally felt like part of the family, like I did belong there.

Squeals of excitement echoed from downstairs and we found Abby weeping yet again as she read the enclosure card that came with two-dozen red roses that had just been delivered. Her groom-to-be was waiting for her.

We posed for pictures with floral bouquets in various shades of pink. Only the most unique flowers would suffice: miniature calla lilies, sweet pea, orchids and French tulips. Regular tulips were so passé. Abby chose to make my cluster of blooms larger so I stood out as her honor attendant. I assured her it wasn't necessary—I'd stick out plenty. The bigger bouquet worked to my advantage though, more flowers to hide my huge belly.

The Marshall Family posed for a group shot, something we hadn't done in years.

"Lexi, can you move a hair to the left?" the photographer directed.

"Yeah, move it, fat ass!" Andy whispered to me with a huge grin on his face.

"Fuck you, dick wad!" I whispered back. smiling just as big. This was our equivalent to saying "I love you."

The photographer asked the rest to move away and snapped a few pictures of Abby and I. He then asked to take a few artistic shots of Abby with her hands on my stomach.

"Oh, Lexi, we don't have to do that."

"No, it's okay. I want to."

She looked at me and tears welled once again.

"No, don't do that! Monique will kill you if she has to fix your face again!"

Abby smiled as she put her hands to my stomach. I felt a little thump right where her hand rested and Abby quickly pulled away.

"Oh my God!"

"Aunt Abby, your niece or nephew is saying hello."

She slowly placed her hand back in the same spot and the baby kicked her again. Abby started to laugh and cry at the same time. As she talked to my baby, tears rolled down her face and I felt my own come trickling down too. I caught mom's expression out of the corner of my eye. Her eyes lit up at the scene before her.

The makeup artist fixed our makeup yet again and we piled into the limousines and headed over to the church. Dad and Abby stayed tucked inside the car while the rest of us went inside. Most of the guests were already seated. I caught a glimpse of Rich as he hurried in to find a seat. He mouthed a quick "hi" to me with his classic grin.

Dad and Abby walked into the vestibule of the church as Pachabel's Canon in D started the procession of bridesmaids and groomsmen down the aisle. Dad hugged and kissed us both and I took my place in line. I began my walk down the aisle alone as the doors behind me closed, hiding Abby before her grand entrance took place.

A real smile shone on my face as I glided down the aisle, for what I thought would be an awfully embarrassing stroll became an honored promenade. I winked at Rich, who'd found a seat next to Aunt Matilda. I saw Mom dab her eyes as Daniel's best man met me three-quarters of the way and escorted me the remainder.

The soft music ended and the tinkling of a bell rang out to inform the guests they should stand. The church sat impossibly quiet. Not a single cough or sneeze should dare interrupt this moment. We anxiously waited for Abby to appear at the end of the aisle.

Never in my life had I dreamed of doing the whole big wedding thing. I'd always envisioned a quickie Justice of the Peace ceremony followed by a gathering of my closest friends at a super chic restaurant. But that moment, those few brief seconds when everyone is waiting for you, your arrival. All eyes waiting to see you, to awe at regal beauty. This made me long for the whole matrimonial shebang.

The doors opened and the sun shone in brightly behind Abby and Dad, framing them. Wagner's Wedding March played as they made their journey down the aisle. I watched my sister walk the way she'd dreamed of since she was a little girl. She embodied all things Abby—sweetness, sincerity, modesty and beauty. I looked over to Daniel, his eyes glazed over, a smile reaching from one ear to the other.

The ceremony began with Pastor John welcoming Abby and Daniel and their guests. The bride and groom stared at each other, almost oblivious to everything else around them. They were the only two people on earth that mattered.

Abby handed me her bouquet for the exchanging of vows and rings. They promised to love each other till the day they died and to care for each other no matter what stumbled into their paths.

Would I ever find a complete love like that?

Pastor John exclaimed a joyous, "You may now kiss the bride!" and cheers and clapping erupted from every corner of the church.

"Let me be the first to proudly introduce, Mr. and Mrs. Daniel Sneed!"

I handed Abby her bouquet before she and Daniel began their walk up the aisle as husband and wife.

"Thank you, Lexi," she said to me, and I knew it was for more than just handing her the flowers.

* * * *

After posing for pictures in church and at the botanical gardens, we arrived at the reception. It did not disappoint one bit and the affair shouted "Abby" from every angle. Soft violin music played as guests entered the room and candlelight from the tables gave off a warm glow. I posed with Abby, Andy, Mom and Dad so an uncle I couldn't quite remember the name of could snap a picture. As we parted to mingle, I felt a hand on my back.

"There's the most gorgeous bridesmaid on the planet!"

I turned and found Rich standing before me. "Oh, stop! Not with this huge stomach!"

"No, Lexi, you are completely beautiful. You're glowing. Those stick thin girls have nothing on your curves!"

"Well, okay, if you put it that way," I replied, smiling.

* * * *

Dinner concluded and the mandatory dances started. Abby and Daniel swayed their way through a soft and sultry rendition of The Way You Look Tonight performed by the band Abby'd chosen for the event. Ogre, whose name was actually Timothy, and I laughed through most of the wedding party dance as our bellies made for a very awkward dance hold.

When my Maid of Honor duties were finally completed, I found Rich walking away from the bar carrying two drinks.

"Hey, you interested in taking me for a whirl around the dance floor?" I asked.

"Absolutely! First let me deliver this vodka tonic to Aunt Matilda."

I watched as he deposited the drink in her hands. She raised her glass to me and nodded. Rich took my hand and led me to the edge of the dance floor. I thought my belly would be in the way but somehow we managed and his embrace felt comfortable. I breathed in his cologne and looked up at him.

"Thanks for coming," I said.

"There's nowhere else I'd rather be right now."

We continued our slow movements and I felt myself slip into a soft swirling tornado of me and Rich, just us and the music, my body in his arms. I felt things I knew I shouldn't have as his hands caressed my back, my mind wandering to erotic places. Then I felt something that I knew I really shouldn't be feeling.

"Oh, my God!" I said and stopped swaying.

"What's wrong?"

"Um, well, I think my water just broke."

Chapter 28

A dumbfounded "What?" was Rich's first reaction.

"Um, yeah, it's kinda trickling down my leg and I think it's pooling on the dance floor."

We headed toward the exit as the slow music switched to an up-tempo swing number. Why had my water had broken a whole month early? A shriek then echoed behind us. Aunt Darla and Uncle Sal were flat on their asses. They must have slipped on my puddle.

Rich reached for his cellphone and called a cab. He told them a woman was in labor and asked if they could hurry. The car arrived shortly after the call and Rich helped me into it, as what I'd thought were Braxton Hicks contractions all day became stronger and closer together. This had to be real labor.

"Thank you," I said as he climbed in, "but you don't have to come. Go home." Another stronger contraction brought a grimace to my face. "I'll be okay, really."

"No, I'm coming with you. I won't leave you now."

The cab drove on and Rich held me tight. I squeezed his hand with each contraction, praying we'd get to the hospital in warp speed. No such luck. A car accident caused a back-up of traffic and we were almost at a stand-still.

Rich called the doctor for me and then called ahead to the hospital. They'd be ready and waiting for us. He called Marcus, getting his voicemail every time. He tried Kevin's cell too, but the party was probably too loud for them to hear their phones ringing.

As traffic crawled on, the pain became unbearable. My insides felt like they were being ripped apart, thrown on the floor and stomped on with metal football cleats. I could handle normal pain—a cut, a headache or a stubbed toe. This pain was different. This would have brought me to my knees if I wasn't already sitting. I wanted to curl into the fetal position and sob out obscenities. Rich held my hand and told me it would be okay, but I couldn't imagine that it would be.

"You know how to deliver a baby, right?" I asked him, trying to make a joke.

His reaction was complete panic. "Sir." He banged on the plexiglass partition between us and the driver. "We need to get to the hospital now!"

We made it past the pileup and within minutes arrived at the ER entrance to St. Mark's hospital. Rich helped me out of the car and my dress resembled a rag that had been left out in the rain. I tried to walk but each step stopped me dead in my tracks with my legs almost buckling under me. A nurse rushed out with a wheel chair and wheeled me in, Rich jogging right beside me.

We rushed through Admissions, then sped into an exam room. The nurse gave me a hospital gown to change into. I stood from my wheel chair, trying to steady myself on the exam table as another strong contraction wrenched my body.

"Dad," the nurse said, "you'll have to give Mom some help getting out of that dress."

Without flinching or correcting her, he unzipped my dress and dropped it to the floor. Complete and utter embarrassment flooded me. I hated for him to see me huge and pregnant and naked. I in no way resembled the sexy woman he remembered.

I looked up at him as tears streamed down my flushed cheeks. "Thank you," I managed to get out. "You don't have..." I started again, but another contraction interrupted my words.

"Lexi, I'm not leaving you."

He helped me out of my underwear and bra and into the hospital gown and waited with me as waves of pain relentlessly surged at my body, each one taking my breath away. I tried to remember the breathing techniques but they were a completely forgotten memory.

My OBGYN came in for a look. It felt like she shoved her whole arm up inside me.

"Wow!" she said. "You're already at eight and a half centimeters. I wouldn't be surprised if this baby was here within the hour!"

Only an hour to go. The pain continued, but I found some relief in knowing it would all end soon.

"Okay," I said. "Can I have my epidural now?"

"I'm sorry Lexi, it's too late. The baby's head will be crowning before the anesthesiologist even gets here."

"What? You're fucking kidding me, right?" I said through panicked sobs.

"I'm sorry. Your labor has progressed very quickly. There just isn't time."

"No! Please! Do something! I can't push this kid out without any drugs!"

Rich squeezed my hand and smoothed my hair. "Yes, you can. You can do this. I know you can."

Tears streamed down my cheeks as I cried out through another painful contraction. The nurses came to escort me to a delivery room, helping me off the exam table and back into the wheel chair. As we rolled down the hall, Rich's cellphone rang in his pocket and he received multiple dirty looks from hospital staff. He ignored them and answered anyway.

"Marcus, Thank God! Lexi's in labor. You need to get here right away," he said. "The baby's gonna be here in about an hour."

The nurses settled us in a homey delivery room complete with lacey curtains and oak cabinets. It reminded me of my parents' bedroom. I flashed back to a memory from high school, having sex with my boyfriend on their bed—the ultimate defiance.

Another wave of crushing pain exploded in my abdomen and jolted me back to reality. My doctor's face re-appeared in the doorway and she performed another exam of my cervix.

"Lexi, you're almost there! It's almost time to push!"

I started to panic once again. How could I do this? More than just the pain of childbirth ran through my mind. I wasn't ready to be a mom. I hadn't finished reading the stack of parenting books Marcus bought me. I still had a dozen Bringing Home Baby episodes saved on my DVR. I didn't know how to wash baby clothes or even how the infant carrier thingy worked. What should I do when he cried? How much would I feed him? I was supposed to have more time to prepare myself!

"Let me go check on another patient. When I come back, we should be able to start."

The nurses walked around the room getting things ready, bringing out the instruments they'd need for the baby and putting everything in its place.

My cellphone in my purse rang out and I motioned for Rich to hand it to me. It was my mother's ring tone.

"Alexandra, where are you? Why did you leave your sister's wedding?"

"It only took you an hour and a half to notice I was gone?" Another contraction took over my body.

"I can't believe this!" she scolded. "You're the Maid of Honor! You have a responsibility to your sister! You missed the cake cutting and the bouquet toss. And you didn't even say good bye!"

"Mother, I'm in fucking labor for God's sake! Can you shut up for one minute?"

"Oh...dear. You're having the baby? Now?"

"Yes!" I screamed as another contraction attacked me like an Ultimate Fighting champion.

"Oh, heavens! My little girl is having a baby!" She wept through the phone. "We'll be there as soon as we can."

Knowing they'd be on their way comforted me. I wasn't sure why, but it did. I hung up with her as my doctor walked back in. She took another look down below.

"You're ten centimeters dilated. It's time."

My heart thumped wildly as sweat covered my body. This was it. No way out. No turning back. Rich stood next to me and looked so calm. How could he be calm? I was a friggin' mess!

A nurse came over and began to tell me how to lie and what to do with my legs. The voice sounded oddly familiar. I turned to find Delivery Drill Sergeant looking back at me.

"Oh, no. Not you!"

"Lexi, you need to relax," she said calmly and with a hint of care and concern. This couldn't be the same woman. "All right, let's get these legs up. With the next contraction we're going to count to ten and you're going to bear down and push."

"No, I can't!" I sobbed.

"You can and you will. Now take a deep breath."

The contraction started and I drew in the deepest breath I could. Delivery Drill Sergeant counted and Rich's hand grasped my leg. I tried my hardest to push.

"With all that piss and vinegar inside you, I know you can push better than that."

I barely got to rest five seconds before another contraction came.

"Come on, give me all you got! Don't wimp out on me!" Drill Sergeant yelled and started another count of ten.

I looked over at Rich and he smiled. "Are you gonna let her talk to you like that? Show her what you're made of."

I pushed again and felt a burn in my vagina like flames were shooting out if it instead of a kid.

"There you go, Lexi! I can see the baby's head!" my doctor yelled out. "Come on, another push and the head will be out!"

A head. My baby's head was almost out! I found a strange courage and used it for all it was worth. I gathered it up, took my next deep breath, and with everything inside me I concentrated it into a push.

"There we are! The head is out!"

Two people entered the room. Marcus and Kevin appeared at my side, decked out in their chic tuxedos. They quickly removed their coats and Delivery Drill Sergeant joined Rich on my other side.

"I'm so sorry we couldn't get here sooner." Marcus had tears in his eyes and kissed my sweaty forehead.

"Okay guys, we need to help Lexi with one more push! Deep breath now!" Drill Sergeant began her counting.

I pushed as hard as I could, crushing Marcus's hand with my left and Rich's with my right. My eyes squeezed shut and I gritted my teeth. Anything I could do to make the push count for more.

The pressure in my crotch disappeared and I heard the doctor yell, "It's a boy!"

I laid my head back on the pillow to catch my breath. As I stared at the ceiling, my chest heaving up and down, I wondered why I didn't hear a baby's cry. Everything was silent.

I tried to sit up to see him, to find out what was going on. Was my baby okay? Was he alive? My heart stopped beating.

I sat up enough to see him lying on the delivery table in front of the doctor. She hastily cleaned his nose and mouth, getting the crap out so he could breathe. His motionless little arms and legs suddenly flailed around and he let out a loud cry.

Tears of joy streamed down my face. Janice, the Delivery Drill Sergeant, laid him on my chest as he wailed. I cradled his tiny body, his eyes tightly closed as his arms and legs stretched out and pulled in again.

"I think he may be hungry," the nurse suggested and without even the tiniest hesitation, I pulled out my breast. I didn't know what I was doing but that's what he needed and it was no longer about me or my hang-ups.

He latched onto my nipple like a champ and was instantly content. He curled his tiny fingers around mine and I fell deeply, madly in love.

"You're a natural," Janice said to me and looked down at my baby boy. "He's doing great."

She clamped off his umbilical cord and brought a blanket to wrap around him. After only a minute, he was done eating and I reluctantly let go so he could be washed, weighed and measured. The doc continued with cleaning me up. I didn't even want to know what my lower region looked like.

Marcus and Kevin went over to the baby, intently watching the nurse as she went through her routine of measurements. Rich stayed at my side.

"I must look a mess," I said to him as I pushed soaked stray hairs from my face and wiped my cheeks.

"No, not at all."

"You really don't have to stay, you know."

"If you don't want me here, I'll leave, but there's nowhere else on Earth I'd rather be right now."

I smiled at him as Marcus walked over with our baby boy, cradling him in his arms. Just his head stuck out of his burrito-like wrap job covered with a tiny blue cap. I'd seen Marcus happy but this was miles beyond that. This was euphoria. He kissed the baby's nose and handed him to Kevin.

After giving Kevin the standard two-point-five minutes of cuddling time, I succumbed to my separation anxiety and playfully demanded they give me my baby back. I stared into his angelic face and he opened his eyes, deep brown eyes just like mine. I could see myself in them. Could he see me? Could he see himself in my watery eyes?

"Any thoughts on a name?" Marcus asked.

"Um, actually, yeah. I do. What do you think of Preston?"

"I love it. I think it's perfect."

"Well, that settles it then," I said and turned to my perfect little man. "Welcome to the world, Preston Marshall Wells."

Chapter 29

The nurses finished their jobs and left. My doctor sewed up where my vagina had torn and told me she'd check on me in the morning. Marcus and Kevin left to make the obligatory phone calls and Rich and I were left alone in the room with Baby Preston.

"Thank you for everything you did," I said to him. "I don't know what I would have done without you tonight."

"You would have done just fine. There's nothing you can't do, Lexi. I knew that the moment I met you. I knew you were a woman who never let anything get in her way."

I smiled at him and he smiled back. "Do you want to hold him?"

Rich nodded and reached for my baby, completely at ease. He stood and rocked his body back and forth ever so slightly.

"Wow, you're great at the whole baby thing!"

"Yeah, when both your older sisters have a few kids before the age of eighteen, you learn to hold a baby real quick."

Rich sat in a chair next to the bed gazing into my sweet baby's face and talked to him. A range of emotions ran through my body, the main one being love. Love for my baby and love for Rich.

Preston started to wiggle and cry. Rich handed him back to me and I instinctively fed him again. I didn't care that Rich was there. Surprisingly, I felt completely at ease with the whole breastfeeding thing.

Looking down at my baby's face, I couldn't believe he was mine. This sweet angel had been given to me and I had no clue what I could have possibly done right with my life to deserve him, this tiny bundle of good karma.

Rich took my hand and kissed it tenderly. I looked into his eyes and knew he had something to say, something important.

"Lexi, I love you. That's all there is to it. I watched you today, literally pushing past your fears, and witnessed the strong woman you are. I love you more now than ever. I want to be by your side and be a part of your life, if you'll let me."

I knew what I wanted to say, what my heart wanted me to say, but the brain had its opinions and hesitations too.

Rich could sense it. "I told you I wasn't sure if I was ready to be an instant dad. But I look at him now and watch the way you are with him and I know I am ready. He is a part of you and I couldn't possibly love him any less than I love you. I can't for one second imagine walking out this door and not being a part of both your lives."

Tears flowed down my cheeks as I stared up into Rich's glossy eyes. Was I dreaming?

"Please say something?" he begged.

I squeezed his hand tight. "I love you too."

He leaned over and kissed me. Our lips touched and reconnected us after months apart, months I spent trying to erase him from my heart. I'd thought I succeeded, but he never was gone. Maybe my heart knew he'd be back, when the time was right for him. When the time was right for both of us.

Preston fell asleep nursing, so I fixed my gown and tucked everything back in. I held his body close to me, smelling him, nuzzling his tiny nose with mine. Rich lay asleep in an extremely uncomfortable looking chair. I watched him breathe and found an extreme peace in my life.

I looked to my baby's face once again, then noticed a woman out of the corner of my eye. It was me, my reflection, Karma, smiling at me from the doorway. I thought back to the day she first came into my life and screwed it up. One horrific day that started a downward spiral of misery. Thinking about it now and knowing all the good that came from those bad things, I couldn't go on hating her. Although Karma took my life and everything that mattered to me and threw it up in the air, where I landed was much more of a heaven than the deepest fiery hell. There were times I'd thought I would never be happy again, but all along Karma had been my friend. She knew what was best for me. I had her to thank for the good in my life. I knew what my purpose was. I knew where I belonged. It was with Rich and my baby—

our baby. I had in front of me a life filled with promise. I had it all.

New book ideas began popping into my head. They were stories of women, moms, dealing with day-to-day life, love, headaches, the ups and downs of making it work and finding the path to eternal bliss. Maybe I could invent my own genre of fiction: Having-It-All-Lit.

What is life without love and laughter? If you ask Stephanie Haefner, she will say, "A whole lot of nothing!"

Combining a love story with comedy is what a good book is all about for Stephanie. She is always on the lookout for the next story that will have her aching from laughter one minute and her heart fluttering the next. She hopes to convey those same emotions for her readers.

As the mom of two amazing little people, Stephanie finds it hard to imagine life without some comic relief. When the house is a war zone, the kids have tied each other up, and the hubby is asking where dinner is, what else is there to do but laugh? Well, a toddler-esque fist-swinging tantrum is an option too...but who is that really helping?

And a world without love, passion, romance... If that ever happens, better stick her in a mental institution.